Arthur Thomas Quiller-Couch

The golden Pomp

A Procession of English Lyrics from Surrey to Shirley

Arthur Thomas Quiller-Couch

The golden Pomp
A Procession of English Lyrics from Surrey to Shirley

ISBN/EAN: 9783744772600

Printed in Europe, USA, Canada, Australia, Japan

Cover: Foto ©Andreas Hilbeck / pixelio.de

More available books at **www.hansebooks.com**

THE GOLDEN POMP

A PROCESSION OF ENGLISH LYRICS

FROM SURREY TO SHIRLEY

ARRANGED BY

A. T. QUILLER COUCH

'*Aurea pompa venit.*'
OVID

METHUEN AND CO.: LONDON
J. B. LIPPINCOTT COMPANY
PHILADELPHIA
1895

TO

ARTHUR J. BUTLER

PREFACE

A word must be said upon the scope of this book, and another upon its arrangement.

It is a book of Lyrics: and after comparing several definitions, I take the Lyric to be a short poem—essentially melodious in rhythm and structure—treating summarily of a single thought, feeling, or situation. This circumscription includes the Sonnet, and excludes the Ballad and the Ode, in which the treatment is sustained and progressive rather than summary. The line is notoriously hard to draw; but in practice we find it moderately easy to discern a Lyric such as 'Crabbed Age and Youth,' or 'Come Sleep, O Sleep!' from an Ode (even though it be not a true Pindaric) such as Spenser's 'Epithalamion,' or a Ballad such as Drayton's 'Agincourt.'

The epoch of Italian influence upon English song—of that influence which first made itself felt in the verses of Surrey and Wyatt, and was not fairly quenched by the influence of France until the Restoration—falls naturally into two parts; two great creative days with no night between,—for the twilight in which Shirley sang was already trembling with the dawn of Milton. The lyrics in this volume are flowers of the first and incomparably brighter of these two creative days; and at the risk of failing to *follow it quite to its close I have stopped short with those poets—with Herrick and Herbert and Shirley—who were born before Elizabeth died. Again the rule may seem a rude one, and it was no sooner made than broken to include Crashaw; but again in practice it will be found (I hope) beyond expectation just.*

Now as for the arrangement, the reader may or may not make head and tail of it. And certainly had my purpose been scholastic I had missed my opportunity in not forming up the poets in their birthday order, for in this case the birthday order happens to be full of instructiveness. Day does not move towards night more steadily or by more regular stages than the English lyric passed from

' The soote season that bud and bloom forth brings ' . . .

through

' Roses, their sharp spines being gone,
Not royal in their smells alone,
But in their hue ' ; . . .

and on to

' The glories of our blood and state
Are shadows, not substantial things.'

My aim, however, was not to instruct, but merely to please, and to this end I laid down two rules at the beginning. The first—with a reservation presently to be noted —was to choose only the best lyrics of the period; to gather my flowers with a single eye to

' Beauty making beautiful old rhyme ' ;

and to make no effort to distinguish this anthology from others by including verses for their rarity rather than their worth. My second rule was to arrange this garland, as far as I could, so that each flower should do its best by its neighbours, either as a foil or by reflection of its colour in thought and style. With this object a piece has here and there been included which on its own merits had fallen below the general standard. An instance occurs on page 256, where Herrick's 'Born was I to be Old' follows the two famous and more exalted anacreontics of Shakespeare and Fletcher. As a foil to these it exemplifies that earthliness of Herrick which is the defect of his fine quality of concreteness. But he is amply vindicated on other pages. I find, on revising the proofs, that some few flowers have dropped out of their proper places. But on the whole I trust that a fairly continuous chain of thought and feeling has been woven from the beginning, which treats of morning, and youth, and spring—

> *' Flower of the season, season of the flowers,*
> *Son of the sun, sweet spring,'*

to Raleigh's noble conclusion of the whole matter.

In saying that no single piece has been selected for its rarity, I should be sorry to seem for a moment to pretend to any unusual acquaintance with the byways of Elizabethan poetry; for indeed I have done little more than exercise a right of choice in gardens prepared by such distinguished Elizabethan scholars as Mr. A. H. Bullen and Doctors Hannah and Grosart. My debt to Mr. Bullen's volumes of ' Lyrics from the Elizabethan Song-Books,' apparent to the initiated on every third or fourth page, is acknowledged from time to time in the Notes: to acknowledge it everywhere was impossible. To Dr. Grosart I am particularly obliged, who, on hearing that this anthology was contemplated, wrote and placed the stores of his Elizabethan learning at my disposal. His offer reached me when the great part of the book stood already in print; and the advantage taken of it has been therefore all too slight: but the goodwill that prompted it—the goodwill of a veteran scholar towards a trifling recruit—is pleasant to record and remember.

A. T. QUILLER-COUCH.

THE HAVEN, FOWEY,
 Oct. 18*th*, 1894.

THE GOLDEN POMP

THE GOLDEN POMP

I

Hark, hark! the lark at heaven's gate sings,
　And Phœbus 'gins arise,
His steeds to water at those springs
　On chaliced flowers that lies;
And winking Mary-buds begin
　To ope their golden eyes:
With everything that pretty bin,
　My lady sweet, arise:
　　Arise, arise.

Shakespeare.

II

MATIN-SONG

Pack clouds, away, and welcome, day!
　With night we banish sorrow.
Sweet air, blow soft; mount, lark, aloft
　To give my Love good-morrow!

A

Wings from the wind to please her mind,
  Notes from the lark I 'll borrow :
Bird, prune thy wing, nightingale, sing,
  To give my Love good-morrow ;
    To give my Love good-morrow
    Notes from them both I 'll borrow.

Wake from thy nest, robin red-breast,
  Sing birds in every furrow,
And from each bill let music shrill
  Give my fair Love good-morrow !
Blackbird and thrush in every bush,
  Stare,[1] linnet, and cocksparrow,
You pretty elves, amongst yourselves
  Sing my fair Love good-morrow :
    To give my Love good-morrow,
    Sing, birds, in every furrow.

T. Heywood.

III

WHILST IT IS PRIME

Fresh Spring, the herald of love's mighty king,
  In whose cote-armour richly are display'd
All sorts of flowers the which on earth do spring
  In goodly colours gloriously array'd,—

Go to my Love, where she is careless laid
  Yet in her Winter's bower not well awake :
Tell her the joyous time will not be stay'd
  Unless she do him by the fore-lock take :

[1] Starling.

Bid her therefore herself soon ready make
  To wait on Love amongst his lovely crew :
Where every one that misseth then her make,[1]
  Shall be by him amerced with penance due.

Make haste therefore, sweet Love, whilst it is prime,
For none can call again the passèd time.

E. Spenser.

IV

THE INVOCATION

PHŒBUS, arise !
  And paint the sable skies
With azure, white, and red ;
Rouse Memnon's mother from her Tithon's bed,
That she thy carriere may with roses spread ;
The nightingales thy coming each-where sing ;
Make an eternal spring !
Give life to this dark world which lieth dead ;
Spread forth thy golden hair
In larger locks than thou wast wont before,
And Emperor-like decore
With diadem of pearl thy temples fair :
Chase hence the ugly night
Which serves but to make dear thy glorious light.

This is that happy morn
That day, long wishèd day
Of all my life so dark
(If cruel stars have not my ruin sworn

[1] Mate.

And fates not hope betray),
Which, only white, deserves
A diamond for ever should it mark :
This is the morn should bring into this grove
My Love, to hear and recompense my love.
Fair King, who all preserves,
But show thy blushing beams,
And thou two sweeter eyes
Shalt see than those which by Penéus' streams
Did once thy heart surprise :
Nay, suns, which shine as clear
As thou when two thou did to Rome appear.
Now, Flora, deck thyself in fairest guise :
If that ye winds would hear
A voice surpassing far Amphion's lyre,
Your stormy chiding stay ;
Let zephyr only breathe
And with her tresses play,
Kissing sometimes these purple ports of death.

The winds all silent are ;
And Phœbus in his chair
Ensaffroning sea and air
Makes vanish every star :
Night like a drunkard reels
Beyond the hills to shun his flaming wheels :
The fields with flowers are deck'd in every hue,
The clouds with orient gold spangle their blue :
Here is the place—
And nothing wanting is, save She, alas !
Drummond of Hawthornden.

v

THE LOVE-CALL

PHYLLIDA. Corydon, arise, my Corydon !
    Titan shineth clear.
CORYDON. Who is it that calleth Corydon ?
    Who is it that I hear ?
PHYL. Phyllida, thy true love, calleth thee,
    Arise then, arise then,
      Arise and keep thy flock with me !
COR. Phyllida, my true love, is it she ?
    I come then, I come then,
      I come and keep my flock with thee.

PHYL. Here are cherries ripe for my Corydon ;
    Eat them for my sake.
COR. Here's my oaten pipe, my lovely one,
    Sport for thee to make.
PHYL. Here are threads, my true love, fine as
      silk,
    To knit thee, to knit thee,
      A pair of stockings white as milk.
COR. Here are reeds, my true love, fine and neat,
    To make thee, to make thee,
      A bonnet to withstand the heat.

PHYL. I will gather flowers, my Corydon,
    To set in thy cap.
COR. I will gather pears, my lovely one,
    To put in thy lap.

PHYL. I will buy my true love garters gay
   For Sundays, for Sundays,
    To wear about his legs so tall.
COR. I will buy my true love yellow say,[1]
   For Sundays, for Sundays,
    To wear about her middle small.

PHYL. When my Corydon sits on a hill
   Making melody—
COR. When my lovely one goes to her wheel,
   Singing cheerily—
PHYL. Sure methinks my true love doth excel
   For sweetness, for sweetness,
    Our Pan, that old Arcadian knight.
COR. And methinks my true love bears the
   bell
   For clearness, for clearness,
    Beyond the nymphs that be so bright.

PHYL. Had my Corydon, my Corydon,
   Been, alack ! her swain—
COR. Had my lovely one, my lovely one,
   Been in Ida plain—
PHYL. Cynthia Endymion had refused,
   Preferring, preferring
    My Corydon to play withal.
COR. The Queen of Love had been excused
   Bequeathing, bequeathing
    My Phyllida the golden ball.

[1] *Soie*, silk.

Phyl. Yonder comes my mother, Corydon,
　　　　Whither shall I fly?
Cor. Under yonder beech, my lovely one,
　　　　While she passeth by.
Phyl. Say to her thy true love was not here:
　　　　Remember, remember,
　　　　　　To-morrow is another day.
Cor. Doubt me not, my true love, do not fear;
　　　　Farewell then, farewell then!
　　　　　　Heaven keep our loves alway!

Anon.

VI

CORINNA'S MAYING

Get up, get up for shame! The blooming morn
Upon her wings presents the god unshorn.
　　See how Aurora throws her fair
　　Fresh-quilted colours through the air:
　　Get up, sweet slug-a-bed, and see
　　The dew-bespangled herb and tree!
Each flower has wept and bow'd toward the east,
Above an hour since, yet you not drest;
　　Nay! not so much as out of bed?
　　When all the birds have matins said,
　　And sung their thankful hymns, 'tis sin,
　　Nay, profanation, to keep in,
Whenas a thousand virgins on this day
Spring, sooner than the lark, to fetch in May.

Rise, and put on your foliage, and be seen
To come forth, like the spring-time, fresh and
      green,
      And sweet as Flora. Take no care
      For jewels for your gown or hair:
      Fear not; the leaves will strew
      Gems in abundance upon you:
Besides, the childhood of the day has kept,
Against you come, some Orient pearls unwept.
      Come, and receive them while the light
      Hangs on the dew-locks of the night,
      And Titan on the eastern hill
      Retires himself, or else stands still
Till you come forth! Wash, dress, be brief in
      praying:
Few beads are best when once we go a-Maying.

Come, my Corinna, come; and coming, mark
How each field turns a street, each street a park,
      Made green and trimm'd with trees! see how
      Devotion gives each house a bough
      Or branch! each porch, each door, ere this,
      An ark, a tabernacle is,
Made up of white-thorn neatly interwove,
As if here were those cooler shades of love.
      Can such delights be in the street
      And open fields, and we not see't?
      Come, we'll abroad: and let's obey
      The proclamation made for May,
And sin no more, as we have done, by staying,
But, my Corinna, come, let's go a-Maying.

There's not a budding boy or girl this day
But is got up and gone to bring in May.
    A deal of youth, ere this, is come
    Back, and with white-thorn laden home.
    Some have despatch'd their cakes and cream,
    Before that we have left to dream :
And some have wept and woo'd, and plighted troth,
And chose their priest, ere we can cast off sloth :
    Many a green-gown[1] has been given,
    Many a kiss, both odd and even :
    Many a glance, too, has been sent
    From out the eye, love's firmament :
Many a jest told of the keys betraying
This night, and locks pick'd : yet we're not a-
    Maying.

Come, let us go, while we are in our prime,
And take the harmless folly of the time !
    We shall grow old apace, and die
    Before we know our liberty.
    Our life is short, and our days run
    As fast away as does the sun.
And, as a vapour or a drop of rain,
Once lost, can ne'er be found again,
    So when or you or I are made
    A fable, song, or fleeting shade,
    All love, all liking, all delight
    Lies drown'd with us in endless night.
Then, while time serves, and we are but decaying,
Come, my Corinna, come, let's go a-Maying.
                                    R. Herrick.

[1] Tumble on the grass.

VII

THE MERRY MONTH OF MAY

Is not thilke the merry month of May,
When love-lads masken in fresh array?
How falls it, then, we no merrier been,
Ylike as others, girt in gaudy green?
Our blanket liveries been all too sad
For thilke same season, when all is yclad
With pleasaunce; the ground with grass, the woods
With green leaves, the bushes with blossoming buds.
Young folk now flocken in every where
To gather May buskets[1] and smelling brere;
And home they hasten the postes to dight,
And all the kirk-pillars ere day-light,
With hawthorne buds and sweet eglantine,
And garlands of roses and sops-in-wine.

Spenser.

VIII

O, THE month of May, the merry month of May,
    So frolic, so gay, and so green, so green, so green!
O, and then did I unto my true love say,
    Sweet Peg, thou shalt be my Summer's Queen.

Now the nightingale, the pretty nightingale,
    The sweetest singer in all the forest choir,
Entreats thee, sweet Peggy, to hear thy true love's
        tale:
    Lo, yonder she sitteth, her breast against a brier.

[1] Small bushes.

But O, I spy the cuckoo, the cuckoo, the cuckoo!
    See where she sitteth; come away, my joy:
Come away, I prithee, I do not like the cuckoo
    Should sing where my Peggy and I kiss and toy.

O, the month of May, the merry month of May,
    So frolic, so gay, and so green, so green, so green!
O, and then did I unto my true love say,
    Sweet Peg, thou shalt be my Summer's Queen.
                                        T. Dekker.

IX

MY FAIR A-FIELD

SEE where my Love a-maying goes
    With sweet dame Flora sporting!
She most alone with nightingales
    In woods delights consorting.

Turn again, my dearest!
    The pleasant'st air's in meadows;
Else by the river let us breathe,
    And kiss amongst the willows.
                                        Anon.

X

UPON JULIA'S HAIR FILL'D WITH DEW

DEW sat on Julia's hair,
    And spangled too,
Like leaves that laden are
    With trembling dew:

Or glitter'd to my sight
  As when the beams
Have their reflected light
  Danced by the streams.

Herrick.

XI

SWEET-AND-TWENTY

O Mistress mine, where are you roaming?
O, stay and hear; your true love 's coming,
  That can sing both high and low:
Trip no further, pretty sweeting;
Journeys end in lovers meeting,
  Every wise man's son doth know.

What is love? 'tis not hereafter;
Present mirth hath present laughter;
  What 's to come is still unsure:
In delay there lies no plenty;
Then come kiss me, sweet-and-twenty,
  Youth 's a stuff will not endure.

Shakespeare.

XII

LOVE'S EMBLEMS

Now the lusty spring is seen;
  Golden yellow, gaudy blue,
  Daintily invite the view:
Everywhere on every green

Roses blushing as they blow,
  And enticing men to pull,
Lilies whiter than the snow,
  Woodbines of sweet honey full :
    All love's emblems, and all cry,
    ' Ladies, if not plucked, we die.'

Yet the lusty spring hath stay'd ;
  Blushing red and purest white
  Daintily to love invite
Every woman, every maid :
Cherries kissing as they grow,
  And inviting men to taste,
Apples even ripe below,
  Winding gently to the waist :
    All love's emblems, and all cry,
    ' Ladies, if not plucked, we die.'
J. Fletcher.

XIII

THE IMPATIENT MAID

WHEN as the rye reach'd to the chin,
And chop cherry, chop cherry ripe within,
Strawberries swimming in the cream,
And schoolboys playing in the stream ;
Then O, then O, then O, my true love said,
'Til that time come again
She could not live a maid !
Geo. Peele.

XIV

IT WAS A LOVER AND HIS LASS

It was a lover and his lass,
　With a hey, and a ho, and a hey nonino,
That o'er the green corn-field did pass,
　In the spring time, the only pretty ring time,
When birds do sing, hey ding a ding, ding;
Sweet lovers love the spring.

Between the acres of the rye,
　With a hey, and a ho, and a hey nonino,
These pretty country folks would lie,
　In the spring time, the only pretty ring time,
When birds do sing, hey ding a ding, ding;
Sweet lovers love the spring.

This carol they began that hour,
　With a hey, and a ho, and a hey nonino,
How that life was but a flower
　In the spring time, the only pretty ring time,
When birds do sing, hey ding a ding, ding;
Sweet lovers love the spring.

And, therefore, take the present time
　With a hey, and a ho, and a hey nonino,
For love is crownèd with the prime
　In the spring time, the only pretty ring time,
When birds do sing, hey ding a ding, ding;
Sweet lovers love the spring.

Shakespeare.

XV

TO THE VIRGINS, TO MAKE MUCH
OF TIME

Gather ye rosebuds while ye may,
  Old Time is still a-flying:
And this same flower that smiles to-day
  To-morrow will be dying.

The glorious lamp of heaven, the sun,
  The higher he's a-getting,
The sooner will his race be run,
  And nearer he's to setting.

That age is best which is the first,
  When youth and blood are warmer;
But being spent, the worse, and worst
  Times still succeed the former.

Then be not coy, but use your time,
  And while ye may, go marry:
For having lost but once your prime
  You may for ever tarry.

Herrick.

XVI

LOSS IN DELAY

Shun delays, they breed remorse;
Take thy time while time is lent thee;
  Creeping snails have weakest force,
Fly their fault, lest thou repent thee.
    Good is best when soonest wrought,
    Linger'd labours come to nought.

Hoist up sail while gale doth last,
Tide and wind stay no man's pleasure ;
Seek not time when time is past,
Sober speed is wisdom's leisure.
After-wits are dearly bought,
Let thy fore-wit guide thy thought.

Time wears all his locks before
Take thy hold upon his forehead ;
When he flies he turns no more,
And behind his scalp is nakèd.
Works adjourn'd have many stays,
Long demurs breed new delays.

R. Southwell.

XVII

CARPE DIEM

Love in thy youth, fair Maid, be wise ;
Old Time will make thee colder,
And though each morning new arise
Yet we each day grow older.
Thou as heaven art fair and young,
Thine eyes like twin stars shining ;
But ere another day be sprung
All these will be declining.
Then winter comes with all his fears,
And all thy sweets shall borrow ;
Too late then wilt thou shower thy tears,
And I too late shall sorrow.

Anon.

XVIII

CRABBED AGE AND YOUTH

Crabbed Age and Youth
Cannot live together:
Youth is full of pleasance,
Age is full of care;
Youth like summer morn,
Age like winter weather;
Youth like summer brave,
Age like winter bare.
Youth is full of sport,
Age's breath is short;
Youth is nimble, Age is lame;
Youth is hot and bold,
Age is weak and cold;
Youth is wild, and Age is tame.
Age, I do abhor thee;
Youth, I do adore thee;
O, my Love, my Love is young!
Age, I do defy thee:
O, sweet shepherd, hie thee!
For methinks thou stay'st too long.

Shakespeare.

XIX

TO BE MERRY

Let's now take our time
While we're in our prime,
And old, old age, is afar off:

B

For the evil, evil days
Will come on apace,
Before we can be aware of.

Herrick.

XX

VIVAMUS

Come, my *Celia*, let us prove,
While wecan, the sports of Love ;
Time will not be ours for ever,
He at length our good will sever.

Spend not then his gifts in vain :
Suns that set may rise again ;
But if once we lose this light,
'Tis with us perpetual night.

Why should we defer our joys?
Fame and rumour are but toys.
Cannot we delude the eyes
Of a few poor household spies?

Or his easier eyes beguile,
So removèd by our wile?
'Tis no sin Love's fruit to steal,
But the sweet theft to reveal :
    To be taken, to be seen,
    These have crimes accounted been.

B. Jonson.

XXI

TIME AND LOVE

1

WHEN I have seen by Time's fell hand defaced
The rich proud cost of outworn buried age ;
When sometime-lofty towers I see down-razed,
And brass eternal slave to mortal rage ;

When I have seen the hungry ocean gain
Advantage on the kingdom of the shore,
And the firm soil win of the watery main,
Increasing store with loss and loss with store ;

When I have seen such interchange of state,
Or state itself confounded to decay,—
Ruin hath taught me thus to ruminate—
That Time will come and take my Love away.

This thought is as a death, which cannot choose
But weep to have that which it fears to lose.

XXII

2

SINCE brass, nor stone, nor earth, nor boundless sea,
But sad mortality o'ersways their power,
How with this rage shall beauty hold a plea,
Whose action is no stronger than a flower?

O, how shall summer's honey breath hold out
Against the wreckful siege of battering days,
When rocks impregnable are not so stout,
Nor gates of steel so strong, but time decays?

O fearful meditation! Where, alack!
Shall Time's best jewel from Time's chest lie hid?
Or what strong hand can hold his swift foot back?
Or who his spoil of beauty can forbid?

O none, unless this miracle have might,
That in black ink my love may still shine bright.

Shakespeare.

XXIII

SECOND THOUGHTS

1

BEAUTY, sweet Love, is like the morning dew,
Whose short refresh upon the tender green
Cheers for a time, but till the sun doth show,
And straight 'tis gone as it had never been.

Soon doth it fade that makes the fairest flourish,
Short is the glory of the blushing rose;
The hue which thou so carefully dost nourish,
Yet which at length thou must be forced to lose.

When thou, surcharged with burthen of thy years,
Shalt bend thy wrinkles homeward to the earth;
And that, in Beauty's Lease expired, appears
The Date of Age, the Calends of our Death—

But ah, no more!—this must not be foretold,
For women grieve to think they must be old.

XXIV

2

I MUST not grieve my Love, whose eyes would read
Lines of delight, whereon her youth might smile;
Flowers have time before they come to seed,
And she is young, and now must sport the while.

And sport, Sweet Maid, in season of these years,
And learn to gather flowers before they wither;
And where the sweetest blossom first appears,
Let Love and Youth conduct thy pleasures thither.

Lighten forth smiles to clear the clouded air,
And calm the tempest which my sighs do raise;
Pity and smiles do best become the fair;
Pity and smiles must only yield the praise.

Make me to say when all my griefs are gone,
Happy the heart that sighed for such a one.

S. Daniel.

XXV

WHEN DAFFODILS BEGIN TO PEER

WHEN daffodils begin to peer,
   With heigh! the doxy over the dale,
Why, then comes in the sweet o' the year;
   For the red blood reigns in the winter's pale.

The white sheet bleaching on the hedge,
　With heigh ! the sweet birds, O, how they sing !
Doth set my pugging[1] tooth on edge ;
　For a quart of ale is a dish for a king.

The lark that tirra-lirra chants,
　With heigh ! with heigh ! the thrush and the jay,
Are summer songs for me and my aunts,
　While we lie tumbling in the hay.

Shakespeare.

XXVI

CUCKOO

When daisies pied and violets blue,
　And lady-smocks all silver-white,
And cuckoo-buds of yellow hue
　Do paint the meadows with delight,
The cuckoo then, on every tree,
Mocks married men ; for thus sings he,
　　　　Cuckoo ;
Cuckoo, cuckoo : O word of fear,
Unpleasing to the married ear !

When shepherds pipe on oaten straws,
　And merry larks are ploughmen's clocks,
When turtles tread, and rooks, and daws,
　And maidens bleach their summer smocks,
The cuckoo then, on every tree,
Mocks married men ; for thus sings he,
　　　　Cuckoo ;
Cuckoo, cuckoo : O word of fear,
Unpleasing to the married ear.

Shakespeare.

[1] Thievish.

XXVII

THE ousel-cock, so black of hue,
    With orange-tawny bill,
The throstle with his note so true,
    The wren with little quill;
The finch, the sparrow, and the lark,
    The plain-song cuckoo gray,
Whose note full many a man doth mark,
    And dares not answer nay.

Shakespeare.

XXVIII

SPRING

SPRING, the sweet Spring, is the year's pleasant king;
Then blooms each thing, then maids dance in a ring,
Cold doth not sting, the pretty birds do sing—
    Cuckoo, jug-jug, pu-we, to-witta-woo!

The palm and may make country houses gay,
Lambs frisk and play, the shepherds pipe all day,
And we hear aye birds tune this merry lay—
    Cuckoo, jug-jug, pu-we, to-witta-woo!

The fields breathe sweet, the daisies kiss our feet,
Young lovers meet, old wives a-sunning sit,
In every street these tunes our ears do greet—
    Cuckoo, jug-jug, pu-we, to-witta-woo!
        Spring, the sweet Spring!

T. Nashe.

XXIX

PIPING PEACE

You virgins that did late despair
  To keep your wealth from cruel men,
Tie up in silk your careless hair:
  Soft peace is come again.

Now lovers' eyes may gently shoot
  A flame that will not kill;
The drum was angry, but the lute
  Shall whisper what you will.

Sing Io, Io! for his sake
  That hath restored your drooping heads;
With choice of sweetest flowers make
  A garden where he treads;

Whilst we whole groves of laurel bring,
  A petty triumph for his brow,
Who is the Master of our spring
  And all the bloom we owe.[1]

James Shirley.

XXX

A ROUND

SHAKE off your heavy trance!
  And leap into a dance
Such as no mortals use to tread;
  Fit only for Apollo
To play to, for the moon to lead,
  And all the stars to follow!

Francis Beaumont.

[1] Own.

XXXI

ANOTHER

Hey, nonny no!
Men are fools that wish to die!
Is't not fine to dance and sing
When the bells of death do ring?
Is't not fine to swim in wine,
And turn upon the toe,
And sing hey, nonny no!
When the winds blow and the seas flow?
Hey, nonny no!

Anon.

XXXII

ANOTHER

On a fair morning, as I came by the way,
Met I with a merry maid in the merry month of May;
When a sweet love sings his lovely lay
And every bird upon the bush bechirps it so gay:
With a heave and ho! with a heave and ho!
Thy wife shall be thy master, I trow.
Sing care away, care away, let the world go!
Hey, lustily all in a row, all in a row,
Sing care away, care away, let the world go!

Anon.

XXXIII

ANOTHER

Now that the Spring hath fill'd our veins
   With kind and active fire,
And made green liv'ries for the plains,
   And every grove a quire:

Sing we a song of merry glee,
  And Bacchus fill the bowl.
1. Then here's to thee; 2. And thou to me
  And every thirsty soul.

Nor Care nor Sorrow e'er paid debt,
  Nor never shall do mine;
I have no cradle going yet,
  Not I, by this good wine.

No wife at home to send for me,
  No hogs are in my ground,
No suit in law to pay a fee,
  —Then round, old Jocky, round!

All.

Shear sheep that have them, cry we still,
But see that no man 'scape
  To drink of the sherry
  That makes us so merry
And plump as the lusty grape.

Wm. Browne.

XXXIV

TO LIVE MERRILY AND TO TRUST TO GOOD VERSES

Now is the time for mirth,
  Nor cheek or tongue be dumb;
For, with the flowery earth,
  The golden pomp is come.

The golden pomp is come ;
   For now each tree does wear,
Made of her pap and gum,
   Rich beads of amber here :

Now reigns the rose, and now
   Th' Arabian dew besmears
My uncontrollèd brow
   And my retorted hairs.

Homer, this health to thee !
   —In sack of such a kind
That it would make thee see
   Though thou wert ne'er so blind.

Next, Virgil I 'll call forth
   To pledge this second health
In wine, whose each cup 's worth
   An Indian commonwealth.

A goblet next I 'll drink
   To Ovid, and suppose,
Made he the pledge, he 'd think
   The world had all one nose.

Then this immensive cup
   Of aromatic wine,
Catullus, I 'll quaff up
   To that terse muse of thine.

Wild am I now with heat:
 O Bacchus, cool thy rays!
Or frantic I shall eat
 Thy thyrse and bite the bays.

Round, round the roof does run,
 And being ravish'd thus,
Come, I will drink a tun
 To my Propertius.

Now to Tibullus, next,
 This flood I 'll drink to thee:
But stay, I see a text
 That this presents to me :—

Behold, Tibullus lies
 Here burnt, whose small return
Of ashes scarce suffice
 To fill a little urn.

Trust to good verses then :
 They only will aspire
When pyramids, as men,
 Are lost i' th' funeral fire.

And when all bodies meet
 In Lethe to be drown'd,
Then only numbers sweet
 With endless life are crown'd.

       Herrick.

XXXV

MAN'S MEDLEY

HARK how the birds do sing,
    And woods do ring:
All creatures have their joy, and man hath his.
    Yet if we rightly measure,
      Man's joy and pleasure
Rather hereafter than in present is.

    To this life things of sense
      Make their pretence;
In th' other angels have a right by birth:
    Man ties them both alone,
      And makes them one
With th' one hand touching heaven, with t' other
  earth.

    In soul he mounts and flies,
      In flesh he dies;
He wears a stuff whose thread is coarse and round,
    But trimm'd with curious lace,
      And should take place
After [1] the trimming, not the stuff and ground.

    Not that he may not here
      Taste of the cheer:
But as birds drink and straight lift up their head,
    So must he sip and think
      Of better drink
He may attain to after he is dead.

1 According to.

> But as his joys are double,
> So is his trouble;
> He hath two winters, other things but one:
> Both frosts and thoughts do nip
> And bite his lip;
> And he of all things fears two deaths alone.
>
> Yet ev'n the greatest griefs
> May be reliefs,
> Could he but take them right and in their ways.
> Happy is he whose heart
> Hath found the art
> To turn his double pains to double praise.

Geo. Herbert.

XXXVI

VIRTUE

> Sweet day, so cool, so calm, so bright!
> The bridal of the earth and sky,—
> The dew shall weep thy fall to-night;
> For thou must die.
>
> Sweet rose, whose hue, angry and brave,
> Bids the rash gazer wipe his eye,
> Thy root is ever in its grave,
> And thou must die.
>
> Sweet spring, full of sweet days and roses,
> A box where sweets compacted lie,
> My music shows ye have your closes,
> And all must die.

Only a sweet and virtuous soul,
Like season'd timber, never gives;
But though the whole world turn to coal,
    Then chiefly lives.

Geo. Herbert.

XXXVII

THE MESSAGE

Ye little birds that sit and sing
    Amidst the shady valleys,
And see how Phillis sweetly walks
    Within her garden-alleys;
Go pretty birds about her bower;
Sing pretty birds, she may not lower;
Ah me! methinks I see her frown!
    Ye pretty wantons warble.

Go tell her through your chirping bills,
    As you by me are bidden,
To her is only known my love
    Which from the world is hidden.
Go pretty birds and tell her so,
See that your notes strain not too low,
For still methinks I see her frown;
    Ye pretty wantons warble.

Go tune your voices' harmony
    And sing, I am her lover;
Strain loud and sweet, that every note
    With sweet content may move her:

And she that hath the sweetest voice,
Tell her I will not change my choice;
Yet still methinks I see her frown!
   Ye pretty wantons warble.

O fly! make haste! see, see, she falls
   Into a pretty slumber!
Sing round about her rosy bed
   That waking she may wonder:
Say to her, 'tis her lover true
That sendeth love to you, to you;
And when you hear her kind reply,
   Return with pleasant warblings.
T. Heywood.

XXXVIII

TO THE WESTERN WIND

Sweet western wind, whose luck it is,
   Made rival with the air,
To give Perenna's lips a kiss,
   And fan her wanton hair:

Bring me but one, I'll promise thee,
   Instead of common showers,
Thy wings shall be embalm'd by me,
   And all beset with flowers.
Herrick.

XXXIX

PHYLLIDA AND CORYDON

In the merry month of May,
In a morn by break of day,
Forth I walk'd by the wood-side
Whenas May was in his pride:
There I spyed all alone
Phyllida and Corydon.
Much ado there was, God wot!
He would love and she would not.
She said, never man was true;
He said, none was false to you.
He said, he had loved her long;
She said, Love should have no wrong.
Corydon would kiss her then;
She said, maids must kiss no men
Till they did for good and all;
Then she made the shepherd call
All the heavens to witness truth
Never loved a truer youth.
Thus with many a pretty oath,
Yea and nay, and faith and troth,
Such as silly shepherds use
When they will not Love abuse,
Love, which long had been deluded,
Was with kisses sweet concluded;
And Phyllida, with garlands gay,
Was made the Lady of the May.

N. Breton.

c

XL

THE BLOSSOM

On a day—alack the day!—
Love, whose month was ever May,
Spied a blossom passing fair
Playing in the wanton air:
Through the velvet leaves the wind,
All unseen, 'gan passage find;
That the lover, sick to death,
Wish'd himself the heaven's breath.
' Air,' quoth he, ' thy cheeks may blow;
Air, would I might triumph so!
But, alas, my hand hath sworn
Ne'er to pluck thee from thy thorn:
Vow, alack, for youth unmeet;
Youth so apt to pluck a sweet.
Do not call it sin in me,
That I am forsworn for thee;
Thou for whom Jove would swear
Juno but an Ethiope were;
And deny himself for Jove,
Turning mortal for thy love.

Shakespeare.

XLI

THE FAIRY LIFE

1

Over hill, over dale,
  Thorough bush, thorough brier,
Over park, over pale,
  Thorough flood, thorough fire,

I do wander everywhere,
Swifter than the moon's sphere;
And I serve the fairy queen,
To dew her orbs upon the green:
The cowslips tall her pensioners be;
In their gold coats spots you see;
Those be rubies, fairy favours,
In those freckles live their savours:
I must go seek some dew-drops here,
And hang a pearl in every cowslip's ear.

Shakespeare.

XLII

2

You spotted snakes, with double tongue,
  Thorny hedgehogs, be not seen;
Newts and blind-worms, do no wrong;
  Come not near our fairy queen.

    Philomel, with melody
    Sing in our sweet lullaby;
  Lulla, lulla, lullaby; lulla, lulla, lullaby:
      Never harm,
      Nor spell nor charm,
    Come our lovely lady nigh;
    So, good night, with lullaby.

Weaving spiders, come not here;
  Hence, you long-legg'd spinners, hence!
Beetles black, approach not near;
  Worm, nor snail, do no offence.

Philomel, with melody
Sing in our sweet lullaby;
Lulla, lulla, lullaby; lulla, lulla, lullaby:
    Never harm,
    Nor spell nor charm,
Come our lovely lady nigh;
So, good night, with lullaby.

Shakespeare.

XLIII

3

PUCK *sings*:

Now the hungry lion roars,
    And the wolf behowls the moon;
Whilst the heavy ploughman snores,
    All with weary task fordone.
Now the wasted brands do glow,
    Whilst the scritch-owl, scritching loud,
Puts the wretch that lies in woe
    In remembrance of a shroud.
Now it is the time of night,
    That the graves, all gaping wide,
Every one lets forth his sprite,
    In the churchway paths to glide:
And we fairies, that do run
    By the triple Hecate's team,
From the presence of the sun,
    Following darkness like a dream,

Now are frolic; not a mouse
Shall disturb this hallow'd house:
I am sent with broom before
To sweep the dust behind the door.

Shakespeare.

XLIV

4

COME unto these yellow sands,
   And then take hands:
Courtsied when you have, and kiss'd,
   The wild waves whist,
Foot it featly here and there;
And, sweet sprites, the burthen bear.
     Hark, hark!
      Bow, wow,
     The watch-dogs bark:
      Bow, wow.
     Hark, hark! I hear
The strain of strutting chanticleer
Cry, Cock-a-diddle-dow!

Shakespeare.

XLV

5

WHERE the bee sucks, there suck I;
In a cowslip's bell I lie:
There I couch when owls do cry.
On the bat's back I do fly
After summer merrily:
   Merrily, merrily, shall I live now,
   Under the blossom that hangs on the bough.

Shakespeare.

XLVI

THE FAIRY QUEEN PROSERPINA

Hark, all you ladies that do sleep !
  The fairy-queen Proserpina
Bids you awake and pity them that weep.
  You may do in the dark
    What the day doth forbid ;
  Fear not the dogs that bark,
    Night will have all hid.

But if you let your lovers moan,
  The fairy-queen Proserpina
Will send abroad her fairies every one,
  That shall pinch black and blue
    Your white hands and fair arms
  That did not kindly rue
    Your paramours' harms.

In myrtle arbours on the downs
  The fairy-queen Proserpina,
This night by moonshine leading merry rounds,
  Holds a watch with sweet Love,
    Down the dale, up the hill ;
  No plaints or groans may move
    Their holy vigil.

All you that will hold watch with Love,
  The fairy-queen Proserpina
Will make you fairer than Dione's dove :

Roses red, lilies white,
  And the clear damask hue,
Shall on your cheeks alight:
  Love will adorn you.

All you that love or loved before,
  The fairy-queen Proserpina
Bids you increase that loving humour more:
  They that have not fed
    On delight amorous
  She vows that they shall lead
    Apes in Avernus.

T. Campion.

XLVII

LOVE'S HARVESTERS

ALL ye that lovely lovers be
  Pray you for me:
Lo here we come a-sowing, a-sowing,
And sow sweet fruits of love;
In your sweet hearts well may it prove!

Lo here we come a-reaping, a-reaping,
To reap our harvest fruit!
And thus we pass the year so long,
And never be we mute.

Geo. Peele.

XLVIII

THE PASSIONATE SHEPHERD TO HIS LOVE

Come live with me and be my Love,
And we will all the pleasures prove
That hills and valleys, dales and fields,
Or woods or steepy mountain yields.

And we will sit upon the rocks,
And see the shepherds feed their flocks
By shallow rivers to whose falls
Melodious birds sing madrigals.

And I will make thee beds of roses
And a thousand fragrant posies;
A cap of flowers, and a kirtle
Embroider'd all with leaves of myrtle.

A gown made of the finest wool
Which from our pretty lambs we pull;
Fair-linèd slippers for the cold,
With buckles of the purest gold.

A belt of straw and ivy-buds
With coral clasps and amber studs:
And if these pleasures may thee move,
Come live with me and be my Love.

The shepherd swains shall dance and sing
For thy delight each May morning:
If these delights thy mind may move,
Then live with me and be my Love.

C. Marlowe.

XLIX

HER REPLY

IF all the world and love were young,
And truth in every shepherd's tongue,
These pretty pleasures might me move
To live with thee and be thy Love.

But Time drives flocks from field to fold;
Where rivers rage and rocks grow cold;
And Philomel becometh dumb,
The rest complains of cares to come.

The flowers do fade, the wanton fields
To wayward winter reckoning yields:
A honey tongue, a heart of gall,
Is fancy's spring but sorrow's fall.

Thy gowns, thy shoes, thy beds of roses,
Thy cap, thy kirtle, and thy posies,
Soon break, soon wither—soon forgotten,
In folly ripe, in reason rotten.

Thy belt of straw and ivy-buds,
Thy coral clasps and amber studs,—
All these in me no means can move
To come to thee and be thy Love.

But could youth last, and love still breed,
Had joys no date, nor age no need,
Then those delights my mind might move
To live with thee and be thy Love.

Sir W. Raleigh.

L

UNDER THE GREENWOOD TREE

AMIENS *sings*:

UNDER the greenwood tree,
Who loves to lie with me,
And turn his merry note
Unto the sweet bird's throat,
Come hither, come hither, come hither:
Here shall he see
No enemy
But winter and rough weather.

Who doth ambition shun,
And loves to live i' the sun,
Seeking the food he eats,
And pleased with what he gets,
Come hither, come hither, come hither;
Here shall he see
No enemy
But winter and rough weather.

JAQUES *replies*:

If it do come to pass
That any man turn ass,
Leaving his wealth and ease
A stubborn will to please,
Ducdame, ducdame, ducdame:
Here shall he see
Gross fools as he,
An if he will come to me.

Shakespeare.

LI

AMIENS' SONG

Blow, blow, thou winter wind,
Thou art not so unkind
  As man's ingratitude;
Thy tooth is not so keen,
Because thou art not seen,
  Although thy breath be rude.
Heigh ho ! sing, heigh ho! unto the green holly:
Most friendship is feigning, most loving mere folly:
  Then heigh ho, the holly :
  This life is most jolly.

Freeze, freeze, thou bitter sky,
That dost not bite so nigh
  As benefits forgot:
Though thou the waters warp,
Thy sting is not so sharp
  As friend remember'd not.
Heigh ho! sing, heigh ho ! unto the green holly :
Most friendship is feigning, most loving mere folly:
  Then heigh ho, the holly !
  This life is most jolly.

                              Shakespeare.

LII

SPRING'S WELCOME

WHAT bird so sings, yet so does wail?
O 'tis the ravish'd nightingale.
Jug, jug, jug, jug, tereu! she cries,
And still her woes at midnight rise.
Brave prick-song!   Who is 't now we hear?
None but the lark so shrill and clear;
Now at heaven's gate she claps her wings,
The morn not waking till she sings.
Hark, hark, with what a pretty throat
Poor robin redbreast tunes his note;
Hark how the jolly cuckoos sing
Cuckoo! to welcome in the spring!
Cuckoo! to welcome in the spring!

J. Lyly.

LIII

ON A BANK AS I SAT A-FISHING

THIS day Dame Nature seem'd in love;
The lusty sap began to move;
Fresh juice did stir th' embracing vines,
And birds had drawn their valentines;
The jealous trout that low did lie
Rose at the well-dissembled fly;
There stood my friend, with patient skill
Attending of his trembling quill.

Already were the eaves possess'd
With the swift pilgrim's daubèd nest ;
The groves already did rejoice
In Philomel's triumphing voice ;
The showers were short, the weather mild,
The morning fresh, the evening smiled ;
Joan takes her neat-rubb'd pail, and now
She trips to milk the sand-red cow ;
Where for some sturdy football swain
Joan strokes a syllabub or twain ;
The fields and gardens were beset
With tulip, crocus, violet ;
And now, though late the modest rose
Did more than half a blush disclose,
Thus all look'd gay and full of cheer
To welcome the new-liveried year.
Sir H. Wotton.

LIV

THE HAPPY COUNTRYMAN

WHO can live in heart so glad
As the merry country lad ?
Who upon a fair green balk
May at pleasure sit and walk,
And amid the azure skies
See the morning sun arise,—
While he hears in every spring
How the birds do chirp and sing :
Or before the hounds in cry
See the hare go stealing by :

Or along the shallow brook,
Angling with a baited hook,
See the fishes leap and play
In a blessèd sunny day:
Or to hear the partridge call,
Till she have her covey all:
Or to see the subtle fox,
How the villain plies the box;
After feeding on his prey,
How he closely sneaks away,
Through the hedge and down the furrow
Till he gets into his burrow:
Then the bee to gather honey,
And the little black-haired coney,
On a bank for sunny place,
With her forefeet wash her face:
Are not these, with thousands moe
Than the courts of kings do know,
The true pleasing spirit's sights
That may breed true love's delights?
But with all this happiness,
To behold that Shepherdess,
To whose eyes all shepherds yield
All the fairest of the field,
—Fair Aglaia, in whose face
Lives the shepherds' highest grace:
For whose sake I say and swear,
By the passions that I bear,
Had I got a kingly grace,
I would leave my kingly place

And in heart be truly glad
To become a country lad;
Hard to lie, and go full bare,
And to feed on hungry fare,
So I might but live to be
Where I might but sit to see
Once a day, or all day long,
The sweet subject of my song:
In Aglaia's only eyes
All my worldly Paradise.

N. Breton.

LV

SWEET CONTENT

1

Sweet are the thoughts that savour of content;
   The quiet mind is richer than a crown;
Sweet are the nights in careless slumber spent;
   The poor estate scorns fortune's angry frown:
Such sweet content, such minds, such sleep, such
      bliss,
Beggars enjoy, when princes oft do miss.

The homely house that harbours quiet rest,
   The cottage that affords nor pride nor care,
The mean that 'grees with country music best,
   The sweet consort of mirth and modest fare,[1]
Obscurèd life sets down a type of bliss:
A mind content both crown and kingdom is.

R. Greene.

[1] Orig. 'Music's fare.'   'Modest fare' is Mr. W. J. Linton's
conjecture.

LVI

2

Art thou poor, yet hast thou golden slumbers?
    O sweet content!
Art thou rich, yet is thy mind perplex'd?
    O punishment!
Dost thou laugh to see how fools are vex'd
To add to golden numbers golden numbers?
    O sweet content!   O sweet, O sweet content!
Work apace, apace, apace, apace;
Honest labour bears a lovely face;
Then hey nonny nonny—hey nonny nonny!

Can'st drink the waters of the crispèd spring?
    O sweet content!
Swim'st thou in wealth, yet sink'st in thine own tears?
    O punishment!
Then he that patiently want's burden bears,
No burden bears, but is a king, a king!
    O sweet content!   O sweet, O sweet content!
Work apace, apace, apace, apace;
Honest labour bears a lovely face;
Then hey nonny nonny—hey nonny nonny!

T. Dekker.

LVII

THE COUNTRY'S RECREATIONS

Quivering fears, heart-tearing cares,
Anxious sighs, untimely tears,
    Fly, fly to courts!
    Fly to fond worldlings' sports

Where strain'd sardonic smiles are glozing still,
And grief is forced to laugh against her will;
    Where mirth's but mummery,
    And sorrows only real be!

Fly from our country pastimes, fly,
Sad troop of human misery!
    Come, serene looks,
    Clear as the crystal brooks,
Or the pure azured heaven, that smiles to see
The rich attendance of our poverty!
    Peace, and a secure mind,
    Which all men seek, we only find.

Abusèd mortals! did you know
Where joy, heart's ease, and comforts grow,
    You'd scorn proud towers,
    And seek them in these bowers
Where winds sometimes our woods perhaps may
      shake,
But blustering care could never tempest make,
    Nor murmurs e'er come nigh us,
    Saving of fountains that glide by us.

Here's no fantastic mask, nor dance
But of our kids that frisk and prance:
    Nor wars are seen
    Unless upon the green
Two harmless lambs are butting one another—
Which done, both bleating run, each to his mother;
    And wounds are never found,
    Save what the ploughshare gives the ground.

D

Here are no false entrapping baits
To hasten too-too hasty Fates;
    Unless it be
    The fond credulity
Of silly fish, which worldling-like still look
Upon the bait, but never on the hook:
    Nor envy, unless among
    The birds, for prize of their sweet song.

Go, let the diving negro seek
For gems hid in some forlorn creek;
    We all pearls scorn
    Save what the dewy morn
Congeals upon each little spire of grass,
Which careless shepherds beat down as they pass;
    And gold ne'er here appears
    Save what the yellow Ceres bears.

Blest silent groves!   O may ye be
For ever mirth's best nursery!
    May pure contents
    For ever pitch their tents
Upon these downs, these meads, these rocks, these
      mountains,
And peace still slumber by these purling fountains;
    Which we may every year
    Find when we come a-fishing here!

Anon.

LVIII

THE SHEPHERD'S WIFE'S SONG

Ah, what is Love? It is a pretty thing,
As sweet unto a shepherd as a king;
    And sweeter too;
For kings have cares that wait upon a crown,
And cares can make the sweetest love to frown:
    Ah then, ah then,
If country loves such sweet desires do gain,
What lady would not love a shepherd swain?

His flocks are folded, he comes home at night,
As merry as a king in his delight;
    And merrier too;
For kings bethink then what the state require,
Where shepherds careless carol by the fire:
    Ah then, ah then,
If country loves such sweet desires do gain,
What lady would not love a shepherd swain?

He kisseth first, then sits as blithe to eat
His cream and curds as doth the king his meat;
    And blither too;
For kings have often fears when they do sup,
Where shepherds dread no poison in their cup:
    Ah then, ah then,
If country loves such sweet desires do gain,
What lady would not love a shepherd swain?

To bed he goes, as wanton then, I ween,
As is a king in dalliance with a queen;
    More wanton too;
For kings have many griefs affects to move,
Where shepherds have no greater grief than love:
    Ah then, ah then,
If country loves such sweet desires do gain,
What lady would not love a shepherd swain?

Upon his couch of straw he sleeps as sound
As doth a king upon his beds of down;
    More sounder too;
For cares cause kings full oft their sleep to spill,
Where weary shepherds lie and snort their fill:
    Ah then, ah then,
If country loves such sweet desires do gain,
What lady would not love a shepherd swain?

Thus with his wife he spends the year, as blithe
As doth the king at every tide or sithe;[1]
    And blither too;
For kings have wars and broils to take in hand,
Where shepherds laugh and love upon the land:
    Ah then, ah then,
If country loves such sweet desires do gain,
What lady would not love a shepherd swain?

R. Greene.

---

[1] Time.

LIX

COUNTRY NIGHTS

The damask meadows and the crawling streams
   Sweeten and make soft thy dreams:
The purling springs, groves, birds, and well-weaved
      bowers,
   With fields enamellèd with flowers,
Present thee shapes, while phantasy discloses
   Millions of lilies mixt with roses.
Then dream thou hearest the lamb with many a
      bleat
   Woo'd to come suck the milky teat;
Whilst Faunus in the vision vows to keep
   From ravenous wolf the woolly sheep;
With thousand such enchanting dreams, which meet
   To make sleep not so sound as sweet.
Nor can these figures so thy rest endear
   As not to up when chanticleer
Speaks the last watch, but with the dawn dost rise
   To work, but first to sacrifice:
Making thy peace with Heaven for some late fault,
   With holy meat and crackling salt.

Herrick.

LX

   Heigho! chill go to plough no more!
      Sit down and take thy rest;
   Of golden groats I have full store
      To flaunt it with the best.

But I love and I love, and who thinks you?
The finest lass that ever you knew:
Which makes me sing when I should cry
Heigho! for love I die.

Anon.

LXI

THE SHEPHERD'S LASS

My Love is neither young nor old,
Nor fiery-hot nor frozen-cold,
But fresh and fair as springing-briar
Blooming the fruit of love's desire:
Not snowy-white nor rosy-red,
But fair enough for shepherd's bed;
And such a love was never seen
On hill or dale or country green.

Anon.

LXII

A WELCOME

Welcome, welcome! do I sing,
Far more welcome than the spring;
He that parteth from you never,
Shall enjoy a spring for ever.

He that to the voice is near
    Breaking from your iv'ry pale,
Need not walk abroad to hear
    The delightful nightingale.
                Welcome, welcome . . .

He that looks still on your eyes,
    Though the winter have begun
To benumb our arteries,
    Shall not want the summer's sun.
                        Welcome, welcome . . .

He that still may see your cheeks,
    Where all rareness still reposes,
Is a fool if e'er he seeks
    Other lilies, other roses.
                        Welcome, welcome . . .

He to whom your soft lip yields,
    And perceives your breath in kissing,
All the odours of the fields
    Never, never shall be missing.
                        Welcome, welcome . . .

He that question would anew
    What fair Eden was of old,
Let him rightly study you,
    And a brief of that behold.
                        Welcome, welcome . . .
                            Wm. Browne.

LXIII

DAMELUS' SONG OF HIS DIAPHENIA

Diaphenia like the daffadowndilly,
White as the sun, fair as the lily,
    Heigh ho, how I do love thee!
I do love thee as my lambs
Are belovèd of their dams—
    How blest were I if thou wouldst prove me!

Diaphenia like the spreading roses,
That in thy sweets all sweets encloses,
  Fair sweet, how I do love thee !
I do love thee as each flower
Loves the sun's life-giving power,
  For death, thy breath to life might move me.

Diaphenia, like to all things blessèd
When all thy praises are expressèd,
  Dear joy, how I do love thee !
As the birds do love the spring,
Or the bees their careful king :
  Then in requite, sweet virgin, love me !

H. Constable.

LXIV

SAMELA

Like to Diana in her summer weed,
Girt with a crimson robe of brightest dye,
    Goes fair Samela.
Whiter than be the flocks that straggling feed
When wash'd by Arethusa fount they lie,
    Is fair Samela.
As fair Aurora in her morning grey,
Deck'd with the ruddy glister of her love
    Is fair Samela ;
Like lovely Thetis on a calmèd day
Whenas her brightness Neptune's fancies move,
    Shines fair Samela.

Her tresses gold, her eyes like glassy streams,
Her teeth are pearl, the breasts are ivory
  Of fair Samela.
Her cheeks like rose and lily yield forth gleams;
Her brows bright arches framed of ebony:
  Thus fair Samela
Passeth fair Venus in her bravest hue,
And Juno in the show of majesty:
  For she's Samela.
Pallas in wit,—all three, if you will view,
For beauty, wit, and matchless dignity,
  Yield to Samela.

        R. Greene.

LXV

A DITTY

IN PRAISE OF ELIZA, QUEEN OF THE SHEPHERDS

SEE where she sits upon the grassy green,
  O seemly sight!
Yclad in scarlet, like a maiden Queen,
  And ermines white:
Upon her head a crimson coronet
With Damask roses and Daffadillies set:
  Bay leaves between,
  And Primroses green,
Embellish the sweet Violet.

Tell me, have ye beheld her angelic face
  Like Phœbe fair?
Her heavenly haviour, her princely grace,
  Can ye well compare?

The Red rose medled [1] with the White yfere,[2]
In either cheek depeinten lively cheer:
        Her modest eye,
        Her majesty,
Where have you seen the like but there?

I saw Calliope speed her to the place
        Where my goddess shines;
And after her the other Muses trace
        With their violines.
Bin they not bay-branches which they do bear
All for Eliza in her hand to wear?
        So sweetly they play,
        And sing all the way,
That it a heaven is to hear.

Lo, how finely the Graces can it foot
        To the instrument:
They dancen deftly, and singen soot [3]
        In their merriment.
Wants not a fourth Grace to make the dance even?
Let that room to my Lady be given.
        She shall be a Grace,
        To fill the fourth place,
And reign with the rest in heaven.

Bring hither the Pink and purple Columbine,
        With Gillyflowers;
Bring Coronations,[4] and Sops-in-wine
        Worn of Paramours:

---

[1] Mixed.   [2] Together.   [3] Sweet.   [4] Carnations.

Strow me the ground with Daffadowndillies,
And Cowslips and Kingcups and loved Lilies :
    The pretty Paunce [1]
    And the Chevisaunce [2]
Shall match with the fair Flower-delice. [3]
Spenser.

LXVI

SIRENA

Near to the silver *Trent*
    Sirena dwelleth ;
She to whom Nature lent
    All that excelleth ;
By which the Muses late
    And the neat Graces
Have for their greater state
    Taken their places ;
Twisting an anadem
    Wherewith to crown her,
As it belonged to them
    Most to renown her.
        On thy bank,
        In a rank,
        Let thy swans sing her,
      And with their music
        Along let them bring her.

Tagus and *Pactolus*
    Are to thee debtor,
Nor for their gold to us
    Are they the better:

[1] Pansy.   [2] Wall-flower.   [3] Iris.

Henceforth of all the rest
　　Be thou the River
Which, as the daintiest,
　　Puts them down ever.
For as my precious one
　　O'er thee doth travel,
She to pearl paragon
　　Turneth thy gravel.
　　　　　　　On thy bank . . .

Our mournful Philomel,
　　That rarest tuner,
Henceforth in April
　　Shall wake the sooner,
And to her shall complain
　　From the thick cover,
Redoubling every strain
　　Over and over:
For when my Love too long
　　Her chamber keepeth,
As though it suffer'd wrong,
　　The Morning weepeth.
　　　　　　　On thy bank . . .

Oft have I seen the Sun,
　　To do her honour,
Fix himself at his noon
　　To look upon her;
And hath gilt every grove,
　　Every hill near her,
With his flames from above
　　Striving to cheer her:

And when she from his sight
  Hath herself turnèd,
He, as it had been night,
  In clouds hath mournèd.
       On thy bank . . .

The verdant meads are seen,
  When she doth view them,
In fresh and gallant green
  Straight to renew them;
And every little grass
  Broad itself spreadeth,
Proud that this bonny lass
  Upon it treadeth:
Nor flower is so sweet
  In this large cincture,
But it upon her feet
  Leaveth some tincture.
       On thy bank . . .

The fishes in the flood,
  When she doth angle,
For the hook strive a-good
  Them to entangle;
And leaping on the land,
  From the clear water,
Their scales upon the sand
  Lavishly scatter;
—Therewith to pave the mould
  Whereon she passes,
So herself to behold
  As in her glasses.
       On thy bank . . .

When she looks out by night,
  The stars stand gazing,
Like comets to our sight
  Feartully blazing;
As wond'ring at her eyes
  With their much brightness,
Which so amaze the skies,
  Dimming their lightness.
The raging tempests are calm
  When she speaketh,
Such most delightsome balm
  From her lips breaketh.
          On thy bank . . .

In all our *Brittany*
  There 's not a fairer,
Nor can you fit any
  Should you compare her.
Angels her eye-lids keep,
  All hearts surprising;
Which look whilst she doth sleep
  Like the sun's rising:
She alone of her kind
  Knoweth true measure,
And her unmatchèd mind
  Is heaven's treasure.
          On thy bank . . .

Fair *Dove* and *Derwent* clear,
  Boast ye your beauties,
To *Trent* your mistress here
  Yet pay your duties:

My Love was higher born
  Tow'rds the full fountains,
Yet she doth moorland scorn
  And the *Peak* mountains;
Nor would she none should dream
  Where she abideth,
Humble as is the stream
  Which by her slideth.
        On thy bank . . .

Yet my poor rustic Muse
  Nothing can move her,
Nor the means I can use
  Though her true lover:
Many a long winter's night
  Have I waked for her,
Yet this my piteous plight
  Nothing can stir her.
All thy sands, silver *Trent,*
  Down to the *Humber,*
The sighs that I have spent
  Never can number.
     On thy bank,
     In a rank,
     Let thy swans sing her,
    And with their music
     Along let them bring her.
          M. Drayton.

LXVII

PERIGOT AND WILLY'S ROUNDELAY

Perigot. It fell upon a holy eve,
  Willy.　　(Hey ho, holiday !)
   Per. When holy fathers wont to shrive,
  Will.　　(Now 'ginneth this roundelay),
   Per. Sitting upon a hill so high,
  Will.　　(Hey ho, the high hill !)
   Per. The while my flock did feed thereby,
  Will.　　　The while the shepherd's self did spill ;

   Per. I saw the bouncing Bellibone,
  Will.　　(Hey ho, Bonnibell !)
   Per. Tripping over the dale alone ;
  Will.　　(She can trip it very well :)
   Per. Well deckèd in a frock of gray,
  Will.　　(Hey ho, gray is greet ![1])
   Per. And in a kirtle of green say ;[2]
  Will.　　(The green is for maidens meet.)

   Per. A chaplet on her head she wore,
  Will.　　(Hey ho, the chaplet !)
   Per. Of sweet violets therein was store,
  Will.　　—She sweeter than the violet.
   Per. My sheep did leave their wonted food,
  Will.　　(Hey ho, silly sheep !)
   Per. And gazed on her as they were wood,[3]
  Will.　　—Wood as he that did them keep.

---

[1] Weeping.　　[2] *Soie*, silk.　　[3] Wild, distraught.

PER. As the bonny lass pass'd by,
WILL.   (Hey ho, bonny lass !)
PER. She roved at me with glancing eye,
WILL.   As clear as the crystal glass :
PER. All as the sunny beam so bright,
WILL.   (Hey ho, the sunbeam !)
PER. Glanceth from Phœbus' face forth-right,
WILL.   So love into my heart did stream.

PER. The glance into my heart did glide,
WILL.   (Hey ho, the glider !)
PER. Therewith my soul was sharply gride ;[1]
WILL.   Such wounds soon waxen wider.
PER. Hasting to wraunch the arrow out,
WILL.   (Hey ho, Perigot !)
PER. I left the head in my heart-root.
WILL.   It was a desperate shot.

PER. There it rankleth aye more and more,
WILL.   (Hey ho, the arrow !)
PER. Nor can I find salve for my sore :
WILL.   (Love is a cureless sorrow.)
PER. And if for graceless grief I die—
WILL.   (Hey ho, graceless grief !)
PER. Witness, she slew me with her eye.
WILL.   Let thy folly be the prief.[2]

PER. And you that saw it, simple sheep—
WILL.   (Hey ho, the fair flock !)
PER. For prief thereof my death shall weep
WILL.   And moan with many a mock.

[1] Pierced.   [2] Proof.

E

Per. So learn'd I love on a holy eve—
Will.   (Hey-ho, holy day !)
Per. That ever since my heart did grieve :
Will.   Now endeth our roundelay.

Spenser.

LXVIII

A ROUNDELAY

BETWEEN TWO SHEPHERDS

Tell me, thou skilful shepherd swain,
    Who's yonder in the valley set ?
O, it is she, whose sweets do stain
    The lily, rose, the violet !

Why doth the sun against his kind
    Stay his bright chariot in the skies ?
He pauseth, almost stricken blind
    With gazing on her heavenly eyes.

Why do thy flocks forbear their food,
    Which sometime was their chief delight ?
Because they need no other good
    That live in presence of her sight.

How come these flowers to flourish still,
    Not with'ring with sharp Winter's breath ?
She hath robb'd Nature of her skill,
    And comforts all things with her breath.

Why slide these brooks so slow away,
  As swift as the wild roe that were?
O, muse not, shepherd, that they stay,
  When they her heavenly voice do hear.

From whence come all these goodly swains,
  And lovely girls attired in green?
From gathering garlands on the plains,
  To crown our fair the Shepherds' Queen.

The sun that lights this world below,
  Flocks, flowers, and brooks will witness bear;
These nymphs and shepherds all do know
  That it is she is only fair.

M. Drayton.

LXIX

FAIR AND FAIR

ŒNONE. Fair and fair, and twice so fair,
          As fair as any may be;
        The fairest shepherd on our green,
          A love for any lady.
  PARIS. Fair and fair, and twice so fair,
          As fair as any may be;
        Thy love is fair for thee alone,
          And for no other lady.
ŒNONE. My love is fair, my love is gay,
          As fresh as bin the flowers in May,
        And of my love my roundelay
        My merry, merry, merry roundelay,

Concludes with Cupid's curse,—

'They that do change old love for new,
Pray gods they change for worse!'
AMBO SIMUL. They that do change old love for new,
Pray gods they change for worse!

ŒNONE. Fair and fair, etc.
PARIS. Fair and fair, etc.
Thy love is fair, etc.
ŒNONE. My love can pipe, my love can sing,
My love can many a pretty thing,
And of his lovely praises ring
My merry, merry, merry roundelays,
Amen to Cupid's curse,—
They that do change, etc.
PARIS. They that do change, etc.
AMBO. Fair and fair, etc.

Geo. Peele.

LXX

A MADRIGAL

LIKE the Idalian queen,
Her hair about her eyne,
With neck and breast's ripe apples to be seen,
At first glance of the morn
In Cyprus' gardens gathering those fair flow'rs
Which of her blood were born,
I saw, but fainting saw, my paramours.

The Graces naked danced about the place,
The winds and trees amazed
With silence on her gazed,
The flower did smile, like those upon her face;
And as their aspen stalks those fingers band,
That she might read my case,
A hyacinth I wished me in her hand.
Drummond of Hawthornden.

LXXI

BEAUTY BATHING

Beauty sat bathing by a spring,
　Where fairest shades did hide her;
The winds blew calm, the birds did sing,
　The cool streams ran beside her.
My wanton thoughts enticed mine eye
　To see what was forbidden:
But better memory said Fie;
　So vain desire was chidden—
　　　　Hey nonny nonny O!
　　　　Hey nonny nonny!

Into a slumber then I fell,
　And fond imagination
Seemed to see, but could not tell,
　Her feature or her fashion:
But ev'n as babes in dreams do smile,
　And sometimes fall a-weeping,
So I awaked as wise that while
　As when I fell a-sleeping.
Anthony Munday.

LXXII

DISCREET

'Open the door!   Who's there within?
The fairest of thy mother's kin,
O come, come, come abroad
    And hear the shrill birds sing,
    The air with tunes that load!
It is too soon to go to rest,
The sun not midway yet to west,
    The day doth miss thee
And will not part until it kiss thee.'

'Were I as fair as you pretend,
Yet to an unknown seld-seen [1] friend,
I dare not ope the door:
    To hear the sweet birds sing
    Oft proves a dangerous thing.
The sun may run his wonted race
And yet not gaze on my poor face;
    The day may miss me:
Therefore depart; you shall not kiss me.'

Anon.

LXXIII

THE WAKENING

On a time the amorous Silvy
Said to her shepherd, 'Sweet, how do ye?
Kiss me this once and then God be with ye,
                My sweetest dear!
Kiss me this once and then God be with ye,
For now the morning draweth near.'

[1] Seldom seen.

With that, her fairest bosom showing,
Op'ning her lips, rich perfumes blowing,
She said, 'Now kiss me and be going,
　　　　　　My sweetest dear !
Kiss me this once and then be going,
For now the morning draweth near.'

With that the shepherd waked from sleeping,
And spying that the day was peeping,
He said, 'Now take my soul in keeping,
　　　　　　My sweetest dear !
Kiss me and take my soul in keeping,
Since I must go, now day is near.'

Anon.

LXXIV

HYMN TO PAN

Sing his praises that doth keep
　　Our flocks from harm,
Pan, the father of our sheep ;
　　And arm in arm
Tread we softly in a round,
Whilst the hollow neighbouring ground
Fills the music with her sound.

Pan, O great god Pan, to thee
　　Thus do we sing !
Thou who keep'st us chaste and free
　　As the young spring :

Ever by thy honour spoke
From that place the morn is broke
To that place day doth unyoke !

J. Fletcher.

LXXV

HYMN TO DIANA

Queen and huntress, chaste and fair,
  Now the sun is laid to sleep,
Seated in thy silver chair,
  State in wonted manner keep :
    Hesperus entreats thy light,
    Goddess excellently bright.

Earth, let not thy envious shade
  Dare itself to interpose ;
Cynthia's shining orb was made
  Heaven to clear when day did close :
    Bless us then with wishèd sight,
    Goddess excellently bright.

Lay thy bow of pearl apart,
  And thy crystal-shining quiver ;
Give unto the flying hart
  Space to breathe, how short soever :
    Thou that mak'st a day of night,—
    Goddess excellently bright.

B. Jonson.

LXXVI

THE CHASE

ART thou gone in haste ?
  I 'll not forsake thee ;
Runn'st thou ne'er so fast,
  I 'll overtake thee :
O'er the dales, o'er the downs,
  Through the green meadows,
From the fields through the towns,
  To the dim shadows.

All along the plain,
  To the low fountains,
Up and down again
  From the high mountains ;
Echo then shall again
  Tell her I follow,
And the floods to the woods
  Carry my holla !
      Holla !
Ce ! la ! ho ! ho ! hu !

Wm. Rowley.

LXXVII

ANTIQUE COURTSHIP

IN time of yore when shepherds dwelt
  Upon the mountain rocks ;
And simple people never felt
  The pain of lovers' mocks ;

But little birds would carry tales
   'Twixt Susan and her sweeting,
And all the dainty nightingales
   Did sing at lovers' meeting:
Then might you see what looks did pass
   Where shepherds did assemble,
And where the life of true love was
   When hearts could not dissemble.

Then *yea* and *nay* was thought an oath
   That was not to be doubted;
And when it came to *faith* and *troth*
   We were not to be flouted.
Then did they talk of curds and cream,
   Of butter, cheese, and milk;
There was no speech of sunny beam
   Nor of the golden silk.
Then for a gift a row of pins,
   A purse, a pair of knives,
Was all the way that love begins;
   And so the shepherd wives.

But now we have so much ado,
   And are so sore aggrieved,
That when we go about to woo
   We cannot be believed.
Such choice of jewels, rings, and chains,
   That may but favour move,
And such intolerable pains
   Ere one can hit on love;

That if I still shall bide this life
  'Twixt love and deadly hate,
I will go learn the country life,
  Or leave the lover's state.

N. Breton.

LXXVIII

ROSALIND'S MADRIGAL

LOVE in my bosom, like a bee,
    Doth suck his sweet :
Now with his wings he plays with me,
    Now with his feet.
  Within mine eyes he makes his nest,
  His bed amidst my tender breast ;
  My kisses are his daily feast,
  And yet he robs me of my rest :
      Ah ! wanton, will ye ?

And if I sleep, then percheth he
    With pretty flight,
And makes his pillow of my knee
    The livelong night.
  Strike I my lute, he tunes the string ;
  His music plays if so I sing ;
  He lends me every lovely thing,
  Yet cruel he my heart doth sting :
      Whist, wanton, still ye !

Else I with roses every day
    Will whip you hence,
And bind you, when you long to play,
    For your offence.
I 'll shut mine eyes to keep you in ;
I 'll make you fast it for your sin ;
I 'll count your power not worth a pin.
—Alas ! what hereby shall I win
    If he gainsay me ?

What if I beat the wanton boy
    With many a rod?
He will repay me with annoy,
    Because a god.
Then sit thou safely on my knee ;
Then let thy bower my bosom be ;
Lurk in mine eyes, I like of thee ;
O Cupid, so thou pity me,
    Spare not, but play thee !

T. Lodge.

LXXIX

THE SHEPHERD'S DESCRIPTION OF LOVE

MELIBŒUS.   SHEPHERD, what 's Love, I pray thee tell ?
FAUSTUS.   It is that fountain and that well
    Where pleasures and repentance dwell ;
    It is perhaps that sauncing bell[1]
      That tolls all into heaven or hell :
      And this is Love, as I heard tell.

[1] Saint's bell, *quod ad sancta vocat.* Another form is 'sacring bell,' the bell sounded at the elevation of the Host.

MEL.   Yet what is Love, I prithee say?
FAUST. It is a work on holiday;
      It is December matched with May,
      When lusty bloods in fresh array
         Hear ten months after of the play:
         And this is Love, as I hear say.

MEL.   Yet what is Love, good Shepherd, sain?[1]
FAUST. It is a sunshine mix'd with rain;
      It is a toothache, or like pain;
      It is a game where none doth gain;
         The lass saith no, and would full fain;
         And this is Love, as I hear sain.

MEL.   Yet, Shepherd, what is Love, I pray?
FAUST. It is a yea, it is a nay;
      A pretty kind of sporting fray;
      It is a thing will soon away;
         Then, nymphs, take vantage while ye
            may:
         And this is Love, as I hear say.

MEL.   Yet what is Love, good Shepherd, show?
FAUST. A thing that creeps; it cannot go;
      A prize that passeth to and fro;
      A thing for one, a thing for moe;
         And he that proves shall find it so:
         And, Shepherd, this is Love, I trow.
                Sir W. Raleigh.

---

[1] Say.

LXXX

YOUNGLING LOVE

Tell me where is fancy bred,
Or in the heart or in the head?
How begot, how nourishèd?
   Reply, reply.
It is engendered in the eyes,
With gazing fed; and fancy dies
In the cradle where it lies.
   Let us all ring fancy's knell:
   I 'll begin it,—Ding, dong, bell.
All. Ding dong, bell.

Shakespeare.

LXXXI

LOVE SICKNESS

Love is a sickness full of woes,
  All remedies refusing;
A plant that with most cutting grows,
  Most barren with best using.
     Why so?
More we enjoy it, more it dies;
If not enjoy'd, it sighing cries—
     Heigh ho!

Love is a torment of the mind,
  A tempest everlasting;
And Jove hath made it of a kind
Not well, nor full, nor fasting.
     Why so?

More we enjoy it, more it dies ;
If not enjoy'd, it sighing cries—
          Heigh ho !
            S. Daniel.

LXXXII

HEY, DOWN A DOWN

Hey, down a down !' did Dian sing
  Amongst her virgins sitting ;
' Than love there is no vainer thing,
  For maidens most unfitting.'
And so think I, with a down, down, derry.

When women knew no woe,
  But lived themselves to please,
Men's feigning guiles they did not know,
  The ground of their disease.
Unborn was false suspect ;
  No thought of jealousy ;
From wanton toys and fond affect,
  The virgin's life was free.
        ' Hey, down a down !' . . .

At length men usèd charms
  To which what maids gave ear,
Embracing gladly endless harms,
  Anon enthrallèd were.
Thus women welcomed woe
  Disguised in name of love,
A jealous hell, a painted show :
  So shall they find that prove.

' Hey, down a down !' did Dian sing,
    Amongst her virgins sitting ;
'Than love there is no vainer thing,
    For maidens most unfitting.'
And so think I, with a down, down, derry !'

Anon.

LXXXIII

A COUNSEL FOR MAIDS

NEVER love unless you can
Bear with all the faults of man !
Men sometimes will jealous be,
Though but little cause they see,
And hang the head as discontent,
And speak what straight they will repent.

Men that but one Saint adore,
Make a show of love to more ;
Beauty must be scorn'd in none,
Though but truly served in one :
For what is courtship but disguise ?
True hearts may have dissembling eyes.

Men, when their affairs require,
Must awhile themselves retire ;
Sometimes hunt and sometimes hawk,
And not ever sit and talk :
If these and such-like you can bear,
Then like and love, and never fear !

T. Campion.

LXXXIV

Thus saith my Chloris bright,
When we of love sit down and talk together :—
'Beware of Love, dear; Love is a walking sprite,
And Love is this and that,
And, O, I know not what,
And comes and goes again I wot not whither.'
No, no,—these are but bugs [1] to breed amazing,
For in her eyes I saw his torchlight blazing.

Anon.

LXXXV

FANCY AND DESIRE

Come hither, shepherd's swain !
'Sir, what do you require ?'
I pray thee, shew to me thy name !
'My name is Fond Desire.'

When wert thou born, Desire ?
'In pomp and prime of May.'
By whom, sweet boy, wert thou begot ?
'By fond Conceit, men say.'

Tell me who was thy nurse ?
'Fresh Youth, in sugar'd joy.'
What was thy meat and daily food
'Sad sighs, with great annoy.'

[1] Bugbears.

What hadst thou then to drink?
  'Unfeignèd lovers' tears.'
What cradle wert thou rockèd in?
  'In hope devoid of fears.'

What lull'd thee then asleep?
  'Sweet speech, which likes me best.'
Tell me where is thy dwelling-place?
  'In gentle hearts I rest.'

What thing doth please thee most?
  'To gaze on beauty still.'
Whom dost thou think to be thy foe?
  'Disdain of my good-will.'

Doth company displease?
  'Yes, surely, many one.'
Where doth Desire delight to live?
  'He loves to live alone.'

Doth either time or age
  Bring him into decay?
'No, no! Desire both lives and dies
  A thousand times a day.'

Then, Fond Desire, farewell!
  Thou art no mate for me;
I should be loth, methinks, to dwell
  With such a one as thee.

Ed. Vere, Earl of Oxford.

LXXXVI

CASSANDRA

The sea hath many thousand sands,
The sun hath motes as many;
The sky is full of stars, and Love
As full of woes as any:
Believe me, that do know the elf,
And make no trial by thyself.

It is in truth a pretty toy
For babes to play withal;
But O, the honies of our youth
Are oft our age's gall!
Self-proof in time will make thee know
He was a prophet told thee so:

A prophet that, Cassandra-like,
Tells truth without belief;
For headstrong youth will run his race,
Although his goal be grief:
Love's martyr, when his heat is past,
Proves Care's confessor at the last.

Anon.

LXXXVII

FIRST LOVE

1

If thou long'st so much to learn, sweet boy, what
    'tis to love,
Do but fix thy thoughts on me, and thou shalt
    quickly prove:

> Little suit at first shall win
> Way to thy abasht desire,
> But then will I hedge thee in,
> Salamander-like with fire.

With thee dance I will, and sing, and thy fond
> dalliance bear;
We the grovy hills will climb and play the wantons
> there;
> Other whiles we'll gather flowers,
> Lying dallying on the grass;
> And thus our delightful hours
> Full of waking dreams shall pass.

When thy joys were thus at height, my love should
> turn from thee,
Old acquaintance then should grow as strange as
> strange might be:
> Twenty rivals thou shouldst find
> Breaking all their hearts for me,
> While to all I'll prove more kind
> And more forward than to thee.

Thus thy silly youth, enraged, would soon my love
> defy;
But alas, poor soul, too late! clipt wings can never
> fly.
> Those sweet hours which we had pass'd,
> Call'd to mind, thy heart would burn;
> And couldst thou fly ne'er so fast,
> They would make thee straight return.

T. Campion.

LXXXVIII

2

Silly boy, 'tis full moon yet, thy night as day shines
   clearly ;
Had thy youth but wit to fear, thou couldst not love
   so dearly.
Shortly will thou mourn when all thy pleasures are
   bereavèd ;
Little knows he how to love that never was deceivèd.

This is thy first maiden flame, that triumphs yet
   unstainèd ;
All is artless now you speak, not one word yet is
   feignèd ;
All is heaven that you behold, and all your thoughts
   are blessèd ;
But no spring can want his fall, each Troilus hath
   his Cressid.

Thy well-order'd locks ere long shall rudely hang
   neglected ;
And thy lively pleasant cheer read grief on earth
   dejected.
Much then wilt thou blame thy Saint, that made
   thy heart so holy,
And with sighs confess, in love that too much faith
   is folly.

Yet be just and constant still ! Love may beget a
   wonder,
Not unlike a summer's frost, or winter's fatal
   thunder.

He that holds his sweetheart true unto his day of
    dying,
Lives, of all that ever breath'd, most worthy the
    envỳing.

                        T. Campion.

LXXXIX

Love guards the roses of thy lips
    And flies about them like a bee ;
If I approach he forward skips,
    And if I kiss he stingeth me.

Love in thine eyes doth build his bower,
    And sleeps within his pretty shrine ; [1]
And if I look the boy will lower,
    And from their orbs shoot shafts divine.

Love works thy heart within his fire,
    And in my tears doth firm the same ;
And if I tempt it will retire,
    And of my plaints doth make a game.

Love, let me cull her choicest flowers ;
    And pity me, and calm her eye ;
Make soft her heart, dissolve her lowers ;
    Then will I praise thy deity.

But if thou do not, Love, I'll truly serve her
    In spite of thee, and by firm faith deserve her.

                        T. Lodge.

[1] *v.l.* 'their pretty shine.'

XC

A CONSPIRACY

SWEET Love, if thou wilt gain a monarch's glory,
Subdue her heart who makes me glad and sorry:
    Out of thy golden quiver
    Take thou thy strongest arrow
    That will through bone and marrow,
    And me and thee of grief and fear deliver :—
But come behind, for if she look upon thee,
Alas! poor Love, then thou art woe-begone thee !

Anon.

XCI

CARDS AND KISSES

CUPID and my Campaspe play'd
At cards for kisses—Cupid paid:
He stakes his quiver, bow, and arrows,
His mother's doves, and team of sparrows ;
Loses them too ; then down he throws
The coral of his lip, the rose
Growing on 's cheek (but none knows how);
With these, the crystal of his brow,
And then the dimple of his chin :
All these did my Campaspe win.
At last he set her both his eyes—
She won, and Cupid blind did rise.
    O Love ! has she done this for thee ?
    What shall, alas ! become of me ?

John Lyly.

XCII

O Cupid! monarch over kings,
Wherefore hast thou feet and wings?
It is to show how swift thou art
When thou wound'st a tender heart!
Thy wings being clipt, and feet held still,
Thy bow so many could not kill.

It is all one in Venus' wanton school,
Who highest sits, the wise man or the fool.
     Fools in love's college
     Have far more knowledge
     To read a woman over
     Than a neat prating lover:
       Nay, 'tis confest
     That fools please women best.

John Lyly.

XCIII

THE KISS

O, that joy so soon should waste!
     Or so sweet a bliss
     As a kiss
Might not for ever last!
So sugar'd, so melting, so soft, so delicious,
     The dew that lies on roses,
When the morn herself discloses,
     Is not so precious.

O, rather than it would I smother,
Were I to taste such another,
   It should be my wishing
   That I might die kissing.

B. Jonson.

XCIV

Come you pretty false-eyed wanton,
   Leave your crafty smiling!
Think you to escape me now
   With slipp'ry words beguiling?
No; you mock'd me t' other day;
When you got loose, you fled away;
But, since I have caught you now,
   I'll clip your wings for flying:
Smoth'ring kisses fast I'll heap,
   And keep you so from crying.

Sooner may you count the stars
   And number hail down-pouring,
Tell the osiers of the Thames,
   Or Goodwin sands devouring,
Than the thick-shower'd kisses here
Which now thy tirèd lips must bear.
Such a harvest never was
   So rich and full of pleasure,
But 'tis spent as soon as reap'd,
   So trustless is Love's treasure.

T. Campion.

XCV

TO ELECTRA

I DARE not ask a kiss,
   I dare not beg a smile,
Lest having that, or this,
   I might grow proud the while.

No, no, the utmost share
   Of my desire shall be
Only to kiss the air
   That lately kissèd thee.

Herrick.

XCVI

BASIA

TURN back, you wanton flyer,
And answer my desire
   With mutual greeting.
Yet bend a little nearer,—
True beauty still shines clearer
   In closer meeting.
Hearts with hearts delighted
Should strive to be united
   Each other's arms with arms enchaining:
Hearts with a thought,
Rosy lips with a kiss still entertaining.

What harvest half so sweet is
As still to reap the kisses
     Grown ripe in sowing ?
And straight to be receiver
Of that which thou art giver,
     Rich in bestowing ?
There 's no strict observing
Of times' or seasons' swerving,
     There is ever one fresh spring abidiug ;
Then what we sow,
     With our lips let's reap, love's gains dividing.
                                   T. Campion.

XCVII

SONG OF THE SIRENS

STEER, hither steer your wingèd pines,
     All beaten mariners !
Here lie Love's undiscover'd mines,
     A prey to passengers ;—
Perfumes far sweeter than the best
Which make the Phœnix' urn and nest.
     Fear not your ships,
Nor any to oppose you save our lips ;
     But come on shore
Where no joy dies till Love hath gotten more.

For swelling waves our panting breasts,
     Where never storms arise,
Exchange, and be awhile our guests
     For stars gaze on our eyes :

The compass Love shall hourly sing,
And as he goes about the ring,
   We will not miss
To tell each point he nameth with a kiss.
   Then come on shore,
Where no joy dies till Love hath gotten more.
Wm. Browne.

XCVIII

ULYSSES AND THE SIREN

SIREN

COME, worthy Greek! Ulysses, come,
   Possess these shores with me :
The winds and seas are troublesome
   And here we may be free.
Here may we sit and view their toil
   That travail in the deep,
And joy the day in mirth the while,
   And spend the night in sleep.

ULYSSES

Fair Nymph, if fame or honour were
   To be attain'd with ease,
Then would I come and rest with thee,
   And leave such toils as these.
But here it dwells, and here must I
   With danger seek it forth :
To spend the time luxuriously
   Becomes not men of worth.

Siren

Ulysses, O be not deceived
  With that unreal name;
This honour is a thing conceived
  And rests on others' fame:
Begotten only to molest
  Our peace, and to beguile
The best thing of our life—our rest,
  And give us up to toil.

Ulysses

Delicious Nymph, suppose there were
  No honour nor report,
Yet manliness would scorn to wear
  The time in idle sport:
For toil doth give a better touch
  To make us feel our joy,
And ease finds tediousness as much
  As labour yields annoy.

Siren

Then pleasure likewise seems the shore
  Whereto tends all your toil,
Which you forgo to make it more,
  And perish oft the while.
Who may disport them diversely
  Find never tedious day,
And ease may have variety
  As well as action may.

Ulysses

But natures of the noblest frame
    These toils and dangers please ;
And they take comfort in the same
    As much as you in ease ;
And with the thought of actions past
    Are recreated still :
When Pleasure leaves a touch at last
    To show that it was ill.

Siren

That doth *Opinion* only cause
    That 's out of *Custom* bred,
Which makes us many other laws
    Than ever *Nature* did.
No widows wail for our delights,
    Our sports are without blood ;
The world we see by warlike wights
    Receives more hurt than good.

Ulysses

But yet the state of things require
    These motions of unrest :
And these great spirits of high desire
    Seem born to turn them best :
To purge the mischiefs that increase
    And all good order mar,
For oft we see a wicked peace
    To be well changed for war.

Siren

Well, well, Ulysses, then I see
  I shall not have thee here:
And therefore I will come to thee,
  And take my fortune there.
I must be won, that cannot win,
  Yet lost were I not won,
For beauty hath created been
T' undo, or be undone.

S. Daniel.

XCIX

WISHES TO HIS SUPPOSED MISTRESS

Whoe'er she be
That not impossible She
That shall command my heart and me;

Where'er she lie,
Lock'd up from mortal eye
In shady leaves of destiny;

Till that ripe birth
Of studied Fate step forth
And teach her fair steps to our earth;

Till that divine
Idea take a shrine
Of crystal flesh, through which to shine;

Meet you her, my Wishes,
Bespeak her to my blisses,
And be ye call'd my absent kisses.

I wish her Beauty,
That owes not all its duty
To gaudy tire, or glist'ring shoe-tie :

Something more than
Taffata or tissue can,
Or rampant feather, or rich fan.

A Face, that 's best
By its own beauty drest,
And can alone command the rest :

A Face made up
Out of no other shop
Than what Nature's white hand sets ope.

A Cheek, where youth
And blood, with pen of truth,
Write what the reader sweetly rueth.

A Cheek where grows
More than a morning rose,
Which to no box his being owes.

Lips, where all day
A lover's kiss may play,
Yet carry nothing thence away.

Eyes, that displace
The neighbour diamond, and outface
That sunshine by their own sweet grace.

Tresses, that wear
Jewels but to declare
How much themselves more precious are :

Whose native ray
Can tame the wanton day
Of gems that in their bright shades play.

Each ruby there,
Or pearl that dare appear,
Be its own blush, be its own tear.

A well tamed Heart,
For whose more noble smart
Love may be long choosing a dart.

Sydneian showers
Of sweet discourse, whose powers
Can crown old Winter's head with flowers.

Soft silken hours,
Open suns, shady bowers,
'Bove all, nothing within that lowers.

Whate'er delight
Can make Day's forehead bright,
Or give down to the wings of night.

Days that need borrow
No part of their good morrow,
From a fore-spent night of sorrow :

Days that, in spite
Of darkness, by the light
Of a clear mind are day all night.

Life that dares send
A challenge to his end,
And when it comes, say Welcome, friend !

I wish her store
Of worth may leave her poor
Of wishes ; and I wish—no more.

Now, if Time knows
That Her, whose radiant brows
Weave them a garland of my vows ;

Her that dares be
What these lines wish to see ;
I seek no further, it is She.

'Tis She, and here,
Lo ! I unclothe and tear
My Wish's cloudy character.

May she enjoy it,
Whose merit dare apply it,
But modesty dares still deny it !

Such work as this is
Shall fix my flying wishes,
And determine them to kisses.

Let her full glory,
My fancies fly before ye,
Be ye my fictions—but her story.

Rich. Crashaw.

c

FLOS FLORUM

Me so oft my fancy drew
Here and there, that I ne'er knew
Where to place desire before
So that range it might no more;
But as he that passeth by
Where, in all her jollity,
Flora's riches in a row
Doth in seemly order grow,
And a thousand flowers stand
Bending as to kiss his hand;
Out of which delightful store
One he may take and no more;
Long he pausing doubteth whether
Of those fair ones he should gather.

First the Primrose courts his eyes,
Then a Cowslip he espies;
Next the Pansy seems to woo him,
Then Carnations bow unto him;
Which whilst that enamour'd swain
From the stalk intends to strain,
As half-fearing to be seen
Prettily her leaves between
Peeps the Violet, pale to see
That her virtues slighted be;
Which so much his liking wins
That to seize her he begins.

Yet before he stoop'd so low
He his wanton eye did throw
On a stem that grew more high,
And the Rose did there espy.
Who, beside her precious scent,
To procure his eyes content
Did display her goodly breast,
Where he found at full express'd
All the good that Nature showers
On a thousand other flowers;
Wherewith he affected takes it,
His belovèd flower he makes it,
And without desire of more
Walks through all he saw before.

So I wandering but erewhere
Through the garden of this isle,
Saw rich beauties I confess,
And in number numberless.
Yea, so differing lovely too,
That I had a world to do
Ere I could set up my rest,
Where to choose and choose the best.

Thus I fondly fear'd, till Fate
(Which I must confess in that
Did a greater favour to me
Than the world can malice do me)
Show'd to me that matchless flower,
Subject for this song of our;

Whose perfection having eyed,
Reason instantly espied
That Desire, which ranged abroad,
There would find a period :
And no marvel if it might,
For it there hath all delight,
And in her hath nature placed
What each several fair one graced.

Let who list for me advance
The admirèd flowers of France,
Let who will praise and behold
The reservèd Marigold ;
Let the sweet-breath'd Violet now
Unto whom she pleaseth bow ;
And the fairest Lily spread
Where she will her golden head ;
I have such a flower to wear
That for those I do not care.

Let the young and happy swains
Playing on the Britain plains
Court unblamed their shepherdesses,
And with their gold curlèd tresses
Toy uncensured, until I
Grudge at their prosperity.

Let all times, both present, past,
And the age that shall be last,
Vaunt the beauties they bring forth.
I have found in one each worth,

That content I neither care
What the best before me were;
Nor desire to live and see
Who shall fair hereafter be;
For I know the hand of Nature
Will not make a fairer creature.

G. Wither.

CI

SPRING SONG

Now each creature joys the other,
  Passing happy days and hours;
One bird reports unto another
  In the fall of silver showers;
Whilst the Earth, our common mother,
  Hath her bosom deck'd with flowers.

Whilst the greatest torch of heaven
  With bright rays warms Flora's lap,
Making nights and days both even,
  Cheering plants with fresher sap;
My field of flowers quite bereaven,
  Wants refresh of better hap.

Echo, daughter of the air,
  Babbling guest of rocks and hills,
Knows the name of my fierce fair,
  And sounds the accents of my ills.
Each thing pities my despair,
  Whilst that she her lover kills.

Whilst that she—O cruel maid !—
  Doth me and my love despise,
My life's flourish is decay'd,
  That depended on her eyes :
But her will must be obey'd—
  And well he ends, for love who dies.
S. Daniel.

CII

DESCRIPTION OF SPRING

WHEREIN EACH THING RENEWS, SAVE ONLY THE LOVER

THE soote season, that bud and bloom forth brings,
With green hath clad the hill and eke the vale :
The nightingale with feathers new she sings ;
The turtle to her make hath told her tale.

Summer is come, for every spray now springs :
The hart hath hung his old head on the pale ;
The buck in brake his winter coat he flings ;
The fishes flete with new repairèd scale.

The adder all her slough away she slings ;
The swift swallow pursueth the flies smale ;
The busy bee her honey now she mings ;[1]
Winter is worn that was the flowers' bale.

And thus I see among these pleasant things
Each care decays, and yet my sorrow springs.
Earl of Surrey.

[1] Mingles, mixes.

CIII

PHILOMELA

1

THE Nightingale, as soon as April bringeth
  Unto her rested sense a perfect waking,
While late-bare Earth, proud of new clothing,
    springeth,
   Sings out her woes, a thorn her song-book making;
      And mournfully bewailing,
      Her throat in tunes expresseth
      What grief her breast oppresseth,
For Tereus' force on her chaste will prevailing.

    O Philomela fair, O take some gladness
    That here is juster cause of plaintful sadness!
      Thine earth now springs, mine fadeth;
    Thy thorn without, my thorn my heart invadeth.

Alas! she hath no other cause of anguish
  But Tereus' love, on her by strong hand wroken;
Wherein she suffering, all her spirits languish,
   Full womanlike complains her will was broken.
      But I, who, daily craving,
      Cannot have to content me,
      Have more cause to lament me,
Since wanting is more woe than too much having.

    O Philomela fair, O take some gladness
    That here is juster cause of plaintful sadness!
      Thine earth now springs, mine fadeth;
    Thy thorn without, my thorn my heart invadeth.

Sir P. Sidney.

CIV

2

As it fell upon a day
In the merry month of May,
Sitting in a pleasant shade
Which a grove of myrtles made,
Beasts did leap and birds did sing,
Trees did grow and plants did spring;
Everything did banish moan
Save the Nightingale alone:
She, poor bird as all forlorn
Lean'd her breast up-till a thorn,
And there sung the dolefull'st ditty,
That to hear it was great pity.
Fie, fie, fie! now would she cry;
Tereu, Tereu! by and by;
That to hear her so complain
Scarce I could from tears refrain;
For her griefs so lively shown
Made me think upon mine own.
Ah! thought I, thou mourn'st in vain,
None takes pity on thy pain:
Senseless trees they cannot hear thee,
Ruthless beasts they will not cheer thee:
King Pandion he is dead,
All thy friends are lapp'd in lead;
All thy fellow birds do sing
Careless of thy sorrowing:
Even so, poor bird, like thee,
None alive will pity me.

R. Barnefield.

CV

THE FAITHLESS SHEPHERDESS

WHILE that the sun with his beams hot
　Scorchèd the fruits in vale and mountain,
Philon the shepherd, late forgot,
　Sitting beside a crystal fountain
　　In shadow of a green oak tree,
　　Upon his pipe this song play'd he:
Adieu, Love, adieu, Love, untrue Love!
Untrue Love, untrue Love, adieu, Love!
Your mind is light, soon lost for new love.

So long as I was in your sight
　I was your heart, your soul, your treasure;
And evermore you sobb'd and sigh'd
　Burning in flames beyond all measure:
　　—Three days endured your love to me,
　　And it was lost in other three!
Adieu, Love, adieu, Love, untrue Love!
Untrue Love, untrue Love, adieu, Love!
Your mind is light, soon lost for new love.

Another shepherd you did see
　To whom your heart was soon enchainèd;
Full soon your love was leapt from me,
　Full soon my place he had obtainèd.
　　Soon came a third your love to win,
　　And we were out and he was in.
Adieu, Love, adieu, Love, untrue Love!
Untrue Love, untrue Love, adieu, Love!
Your mind is light, soon lost for new love.

Sure you have made me passing glad
  That you your mind so soon removèd,
Before that I the leisure had
  To choose you for my best belovèd:
    For all my love was pass'd and done
    Two days before it was begun.
Adieu, Love, adieu, Love, untrue Love!
Untrue Love, untrue Love, adieu, Love!
Your mind is light, soon lost for new love.

Anon.

CVI

SHORT SUNSHINE

Full many a glorious morning have I seen
Flatter the mountain tops with sovran eye,
Kissing with golden face the meadows green,
Gilding pale streams with heavenly alchemy;

Anon permit the basest clouds to ride
With ugly rack on his celestial face,
And from the forlorn world his visage hide,
Stealing unseen to west with this disgrace.

E'en so my sun one early morn did shine
With all-triumphant splendour on my brow;
But out, alack! he was but one hour mine,
The region cloud hath mask'd him from me now.

Yet him for this my love no whit disdaineth;
Suns of the world may stain when heaven's sun
  staineth.

Shakespeare.

CVII

A MADRIGAL

The earth, late choked with showers,
  Is now array'd in green ;
Her bosom springs with flowers,
  The air dissolves her teen,
The heavens laugh at her glory :
Yet bide I sad and sorry.

The woods are deckt with leaves,
  And trees are clothèd gay,
And Flora, crown'd with sheaves,
  With oaken boughs doth play :
Where I am clad in black,
The token of my wrack.

The birds upon the trees
  Do sing with pleasant voices,
And chant in their degrees
  Their loves and lucky choices :
When I, whilst they are singing,
With sighs mine arms am wringing.

The thrushes seek the shade,
  And I my fatal grave ;
Their flight to heaven is made,
  My walk on earth I have :
They free, I thrall ; they jolly,
I sad and pensive wholly.

                              T. Lodge.

CVIII

TO DAFFODILS

Fair daffodils, we weep to see
You haste away so soon ;
As yet the early-rising sun
Has not attain'd his noon.
Stay, stay
Until the hasting day
Has run
But to the evensong ;
And, having prayed together, we
Will go with you along.

We have short time to stay, as you,
We have as short a spring ;
As quick a growth to meet decay,
As you, or anything.
We die
As your hours do, and dry
Away,
Like to the summer's rain ;
Or as the pearls of morning's dew,
Ne'er to be found again.

Herrick.

CIX

THE BLOSSOM

Little think'st thou, poor flower,
Whom I have watched six or seven days,
And seen thy birth, and seen what every hour
Gave to thy growth, thee to this height to raise,

And now dost laugh and triumph on this bough,
    —Little think'st thou
That it will freeze anon, and that I shall
To-morrow find thee fall'n, or not at all.

Little think'st thou, poor heart,
That labourest yet to nestle thee,
And think'st by hovering here to get a part
In a forbidden or forbidding tree,
And hop'st her stiffness by long siege to bow,
    —Little think'st thou
That thou, to-morrow, ere the sun doth wake,
Must with the sun and me a journey take.

J. Donne.

CX

TO BLOSSOMS

Fair pledges of a fruitful tree,
    Why do ye fall so fast ?
    Your date is not so past
But you may stay yet here awhile
    To blush and gently smile,
      And go at last.

What ! were ye born to be
    An hour or half's delight,
    And so to bid good night ?
'Twas pity Nature brought you forth
    Merely to show your worth
      And lose you quite.

But you are lovely leaves, where we
   May read how soon things have
   Their end, though ne'er so brave :
And after they have shown their pride
   Like you awhile, they glide
      Into the grave.

Herrick.

CXI

TO VIOLETS

WELCOME, maids of honour,
    You do bring
    In the Spring,
And wait upon her.

She has virgins many,
    Fresh and fair ;
    Yet you are
More sweet than any.

You 're the maiden posies,
    And so graced
    To be placed
'Fore damask roses.

Yet, though thus respected,
    By-and-by
    Ye do lie,
Poor girls, neglected.

Herrick.

CXII

THE ROSE

A Rose, as fair as ever saw the North,
Grew in a little garden all alone;
A sweeter flower did Nature ne'er put forth,
Nor fairer garden yet was never known:

The maidens danced about it morn and noon,
And learnèd bards of it their ditties made;
The nimble fairies by the pale-faced moon
Water'd the root and kiss'd her pretty shade.

But well-a-day !—the gardener careless grew;
The maids and fairies both were kept away,
And in a drought the caterpillars threw
Themselves upon the bud and every spray.

God shield the stock ! If heaven send no supplies,
The fairest blossom of the garden dies.

Wm. Browne.

CXIII

THE FUNERAL RITES OF THE ROSE

The Rose was sick and smiling died;
And, being to be sanctified,
About the bed there sighing stood
The sweet and flowery sisterhood:
Some hung the head, while some did bring,
To wash her, water from the spring;
Some laid her forth, while others wept,
But all a solemn fast there kept:

The holy sisters, some among,
The sacred dirge and trental [1] sung.
But ah ! what sweets smelt everywhere,
As Heaven had spent all perfumes there.
At last, when prayers for the dead
And rites were all accomplishèd,
They, weeping, spread a lawny loom,
And closed her up as in a tomb.

Herrick.

CXIV

A SUMMER'S EVENING

CLEAR had the day been from the dawn,
　All chequer'd was the sky,
The clouds, like scarfs of cobweb lawn,
　Veil'd heaven's most glorious eye.

The wind had no more strength than this,
　—That leisurely it blew—
To make one leaf the next to kiss
　That closely by it grew.

The rills, that on the pebbles play'd,
　Might now be heard at will ;
This world the only music made,
　Else everything was still.

The flowers, like brave embroider'd girls,
　Look'd as they most desired
To see whose head with orient pearls
　Most curiously was tyred.

----

[1] *Trental,* a service for the dead, of thirty masses, usually celebrated upon as many different days.

And to itself the subtle air
  Such sovereignty assumes,
That it receiv'd too large a share
  From Nature's rich perfumes.

M. Drayton.

CXV

ROSALINE

LIKE to the clear in highest sphere
  Where all imperial glory shines,
Of selfsame colour is her hair
  Whether unfolded or in twines:
    Heigh ho, fair Rosaline!
Her eyes are sapphires set in snow,
  Resembling heaven by every wink;
The gods do fear whenas they glow,
  And I do tremble when I think
    Heigh ho, would she were mine!

Her cheeks are like the blushing cloud
  That beautifies Aurora's face,
Or like the silver crimson shroud
  That Phœbus' smiling looks doth grace:
    Heigh ho, fair Rosaline!
Her lips are like two budded roses
  Whom ranks of lilies neighbour nigh,
Within whose bounds she balm encloses
  Apt to entice a deity:
    Heigh ho, would she were mine!

Her neck is like a stately tower
  Where Love himself imprison'd lies,
To watch for glances every hour
  From her divine and sacred eyes:
    Heigh ho, fair Rosaline!
Her paps are centres of delight,
  Her breasts are orbs of heavenly frame,
Where Nature moulds the dew of light
  To feed perfection with the same:
    Heigh ho, would she were mine!

With orient pearl, with ruby red,
  With marble white, with sapphire blue,
Her body every way is fed,
  Yet soft in touch and sweet in view:
    Heigh ho, fair Rosaline!
Nature herself her shape admires;
  The Gods are wounded in her sight;
And Love forsakes his heavenly fires
  And at her eyes his brand doth light:
    Heigh ho, would she were mine!

Then muse not, Nymphs, though I bemoan
  The absence of fair Rosaline,
Since for a fair there's fairer none,
  Nor for her virtues so divine:
    Heigh ho, fair Rosaline!
Heigh ho, my heart! would God that she
  were mine!

                                   T. Lodge.

CXVI

BEAUTY AND RHYME

1

When in the chronicle of wasted time
I see descriptions of the fairest wights,
And beauty making beautiful old rhyme
In praise of ladies dead and lovely knights;

Then, in the blazon of sweet beauty's best,
Of hand, of foot, of lip, of eye, of brow,
I see their antique pen would have exprest
Even such a beauty as you master now.

So all their praises are but prophecies
Of this our time, all you prefiguring;
And for they look'd but with divining eyes,
They had not skill enough your worth to sing:

For we, who now behold these present days,
Have eyes to wonder, but lack tongues to praise.
Shakespeare.

CXVII

2

Let others sing of Knights and Paladines
In aged accents and untimely words,
Paint shadows in imaginary lines,
Which well the reach of their high wit records:

But I must sing of thee, and those fair eyes
Authentic shall my verse in time to come,
When yet th' unborn shall say, Lo, where she lies!
Whose beauty made him speak, that else was dumb!

These are the arcs, the trophies I erect,
That fortify thy name against old age ;
And these thy sacred virtues must protect
Against the Dark, and Time's consuming rage.

Though th' error of my youth in them appear,
Suffice, they show I lived, and loved thee dear.
S. Daniel.

CXVIII

3

One day I wrote her name upon the strand,
But came the waves and washèd it away :
Again I wrote it with a second hand,
But came the tide and made my pains his prey.

Vain man (said she) that dost in vain assay
A mortal thing so to immortalise ;
For I myself shall like to this decay,
And eke my name be wipèd out likewise.

Not so (quod I); let baser things devise
To die in dust, but you shall live by fame ;
My verse your virtues rare shall eternise,
And in the heavens write your glorious name :

Where, whenas Death shall all the world subdue,
Our love shall live, and later life renew.
Spenser.

CXIX

IF thou survive my well-contented day
When that churl Death my bones with dust shall
          cover,
And shall by fortune once more re-survey
These poor rude lines of thy deceasèd lover,

Compare them with the bettering of the time,
And though they be outstripp'd by every pen,
Reserve them for my love, not for their rhyme,
Exceeded by the height of happier men.

O then vouchsafe me but this loving thought:
'Had my friend's Muse grown with this growing
          age,
A dearer birth than this his love had brought
To march in ranks of better equipage:

But since he died, and poets better prove,
Theirs for their style I 'll read, his for his love.'
                              Shakespeare.

CXX

NOT mine own fears, nor the prophetic soul
Of the wide world dreaming on things to come,
Can yet the lease of my true love control,
Supposed as forfeit to a confined doom.

The mortal moon hath her eclipse endured,
And the sad augurs mock their own presage;
Incertainties now crown themselves assured,
And peace proclaims olives of endless age.

Now with the drops of this most balmy time
My love looks fresh, and Death to me subscribes,
Since spite of him I'll live in this poor rhyme,
While he insults o'er dull and speechless tribes:

And thou in this shalt find thy monument
When tyrants' crests and tombs of brass are spent.

Shakespeare.

CXXI

THERE IS NONE, O, NONE BUT YOU

There is none, O, none but you,
   That from me estrange your sight,
Whom mine eyes affect to view
   Or chainèd ears hear with delight.

Other beauties others move,
   In you I all graces find;
Such is the effect of Love,
   To make them happy that are kind.

Women in frail beauty trust,
   Only seem you fair to me;
Yet prove truly kind and just,
   For that may not dissembled be.

Sweet, afford me then your sight!
  That, surveying all your looks,
Endless volumes I may write
  And fill the world with envied books:

Which when after-ages view,
  All shall wonder and despair,—
Woman to find a man so true,
  Or man a woman half so fair.

T. Campion.

CXXII

A PRAISE OF HIS LADY

Give place, you ladies, and begone!
  Boast not yourselves at all!
For here at hand approacheth one
  Whose face will stain you all.

The virtue of her lively looks
  Excels the precious stone;
I wish to have none other books
  To read or look upon.

In each of her two crystal eyes
  Smileth a naked boy;
It would you all in heart suffice
  To see that lamp of joy.

I think Nature hath lost the mould
    Where she her shape did take;
Or else I doubt if Nature could
    So fair a creature make.

She may be well compared
    Unto the Phœnix kind,
Whose like was never seen nor heard
    That any man can find.

In life she is Diana chaste,
    In truth Penelope;
In word and eke in deed steadfast.
    —What will you more we say?

If all the world were sought so far,
    Who could find such a wight?
Her beauty twinkleth like a star
    Within the frosty night.

Her roseal colour comes and goes
    With such a comely grace,
More ruddier, too, than doth the rose,
    Within her lively face.

At Bacchus' feast none shall her meet,
    Ne at no wanton play,
Nor gazing in an open street,
    Nor gadding as a stray.

The modest mirth that she doth use
  Is mix'd with shamefastness;
All vice she wholly doth refuse,
  And hateth idleness.

O Lord! it is a world to see
  How virtue can repair,
And deck her in such honesty,
  Whom Nature made so fair.

Truly she doth so far exceed
  Our women nowadays,
As doth the gillyflower a weed;
  And more a thousand ways.

How might I do to get a graff
  Of this unspotted tree?
—For all the rest are plain but chaff,
  Which seem good corn to be.

This gift alone I shall her give;
  When death doth what he can,
Her honest fame shall ever live
  Within the mouth of man.

John Heywood.

CXXIII

ELIZABETH OF BOHEMIA

You meaner beauties of the night,
  That poorly satisfy our eyes
More by your number than your light,
  You common people of the skies;
What are you when the moon shall rise?

You curious chanters of the wood
   That warble forth Dame Nature's lays,
Thinking your passions understood
   By your weak accents ; what's your praise
When Philomel her voice shall raise ?

You violets that first appear
   By your pure purple mantles known
Like the proud virgins of the year,
   As if the spring were all your own ;
What are you when the rose is blown ?

So, when my mistress shall be seen
   In form and beauty of her mind,
By virtue first, then choice, a Queen,
   Tell me, if she were not design'd
Th' eclipse and glory of her kind.
                    Sir H. Wotton.

CXXIV

THERE is a Lady sweet and kind,
Was never face so pleased my mind ;
I did but see her passing by,
And yet I love her till I die.

Her gesture, motion, and her smiles,
Her wit, her voice my heart beguiles,
Beguiles my heart, I know not why,
And yet I love her till I die.

Cupid is wingèd and doth range,
Her country so my love doth change :
But change she earth, or change she sky,
Yet will I love her till I die.

Anon.

CXXV

HIS SUPPOSED MISTRESS

If I freely may discover
What would please me in my lover,
　I would have her fair and witty,
　Savouring more of court than city ;
　A little proud, but full of pity ;
　Light and humorous in her toying ;
　Oft building hopes and soon destroying ;
　Long, but sweet in the enjoying ;
Neither too easy, nor too hard :
All extremes I would have barr'd.

She should be allowed her passions,
So they were but used as fashions ;
　Sometimes froward and then frowning,
　Sometimes sickish and then swowning,
　Every fit with change still crowning.
　Purely jealous I would have her,
　Then only constant when I crave her :
　'Tis a virtue should not save her.
Thus nor her delicates would cloy me,
Neither her peevishness annoy me.

B. Jonson.

CXXVI

SILVIA

Who is Silvia?   What is she,
  That all our swains commend her?
Holy, fair and wise is she;
  The heaven such grace did lend her.
That she might admired be.

Is she kind as she is fair?
  For beauty lives with kindness:
Love doth to her eyes repair,
  To help him of his blindness;
And, being help'd, inhabits there.

Then to Silvia let us sing,
  That Silvia is excelling;
She excels each mortal thing
  Upon the dull earth dwelling:
To her let us garlands bring.

Shakespeare.

CXXVII

BEAUTY CLEAR AND FAIR

Beauty clear and fair,
    Where the air
Rather like a perfume dwells;
  Where the violet and the rose
  Their blue veins and blush disclose,
And come to honour nothing else:

Where to live near
    And planted there
Is to live, and still live new;
    Where to gain a favour is
    More than light, perpetual bliss,—
Make me live by serving you.

Dear, again back recall
    To this light,
A stranger to himself and all!
    Both the wonder and the story
    Shall be yours, and eke the glory;
I am your servant, and your thrall.

J. Fletcher.

CXXVIII

A COMPARISON

1

Mark when she smiles with amiable cheer,
And tell me whereto can ye liken it—
When on each eyelid sweetly do appear
An hundred Graces as in shade to sit?

Likest it seemeth to my simple wit
Unto the fair sunshine in summer's day,
That, when a dreadful storm away is flit,
Through the broad world doth spread his goodly
    ray:

At sight whereof each bird that sits on spray,
And every beast that to his den was fled,
Comes forth afresh out of their late dismay,
And to the light lift up their drooping head.

So my storm-beaten heart likewise is cheer'd
With that sunshine when cloudy looks are clear'd.
                                        Spenser.

CXXIX

2

SHALL I compare thee to a summer's day?
Thou art more lovely and more temperate :
Rough winds do shake the darling buds of May,
And summer's lease hath all too short a date :

Sometime too hot the eye of heaven shines,
And often is his gold complexion dimm'd ;
And every fair from fair sometime declines,
By chance or nature's changing course untrimm'd.

But thy eternal summer shall not fade
Nor lose possession of that fair thou owest ;
Nor shall death brag thou wanderest in his shade,
When in eternal lines to time thou growest :

So long as men can breathe, or eyes can see,
So long lives this, and this gives life to thee.
                                        Shakespeare.

CXXX

SONG

Ask me no more where Jove bestows,
When June is past, the fading rose;
For in your beauty's orient deep
These flowers, as in their causes, sleep.

Ask me no more whither do stray
The golden atoms of the day;
For in pure love heaven did prepare
Those powders to enrich your hair.

Ask me no more whither doth haste
The nightingale when May is past;
For in your sweet dividing throat
She winters and keeps warm her note.

Ask me no more where those stars light
That downwards fall in dead of night;
For in your eyes they sit, and there
Fixèd become as in their sphere.

Ask me no more if east or west
The Phœnix builds her spicy nest;
For unto you at last she flies,
And in your fragrant bosom dies.

T. Carew.

CXXXI

CHERRY-RIPE

1

CHERRY-RIPE, ripe, ripe, I cry,
Full and fair ones; come and buy.
If so be you ask me where
They do grow, I answer: There
Where my Julia's lips do smile;
There's the land, or cherry-isle,
Whose plantations fully show
All the year where cherries grow.

Herrick.

CXXXII

2

THERE is a garden in her face
  Where roses and white lilies blow;
A heavenly paradise is that place
  Wherein all pleasant fruits do flow:
    There cherries grow that none may buy
    Till 'Cherry-ripe' themselves do cry.

Those cherries fairly do enclose
  Of orient pearl a double row,
Which when her lovely laughter shows,
  They look like rose-buds fill'd with snow;
    Yet them nor peer nor prince may buy
    Till 'Cherry-ripe' themselves do cry.

I

Her eyes like angels watch them still;
  Her brows like bended bows do stand,
Threat'ning with piercing frowns to kill
  All that attempt with eye or hand
    Those sacred cherries to come nigh,
      Till 'Cherry-ripe' themselves do cry.
                                    T. Campion.

CXXXIII

DRESS AND UNDRESS

My Love in her attire doth show her wit,
  It doth so well become her;
For every season she hath dressings fit,
  For Winter, Spring, and Summer.
    No beauty she doth miss
      When all her robes are on:
    But Beauty's self she is
      When all her robes are gone.
                                    Anon.

CXXXIV

SIMPLEX MUNDITIIS

STILL to be neat, still to be drest,
As you were going to a feast;
Still to be powder'd, still perfumed:
Lady, it is to be presumed,
Though art's hid causes are not found,
All is not sweet, all is not sound.

Give me a look, give me a face
That makes simplicity a grace;
Robes loosely flowing, hair as free:
Such sweet neglect more taketh me
Than all th' adulteries of art;
They strike mine eyes, but not my heart.

B. Jonson.

CXXXV

ART ABOVE NATURE: TO JULIA

When I behold a forest spread
With silken trees upon thy head,
And when I see that other dress
Of flowers set in comeliness;
When I behold another grace
In the ascent of curious lace,
Which like a pinnacle doth show
The top, and the top-gallant too;
Then, when I see thy tresses bound
Into an oval, square, or round,
And knit in knots far more than I
Can tell by tongue, or true-love tie;
Next, when those lawny films I see
Play with a wild civility,
And all those airy silks to flow,
Alluring me, and tempting so:
I must confess mine eye and heart
Dotes less of Nature than on Art.

Herrick.

CXXXVI

DELIGHT IN DISORDER

A SWEET disorder in the dress
Kindles in clothes a wantonness:
A lawn about the shoulders thrown
Into a fine distraction:
An erring lace, which here and there
Enthrals the crimson stomacher:
A cuff neglectful, and thereby
Ribbons to flow confusedly:
A winning wave, deserving note,
In the tempestuous petticoat:
A careless shoe-string, in whose tie
I see a wild civility:
Do more bewitch me than when art
Is too precise in every part.

Herrick.

CXXXVII

UPON JULIA'S CLOTHES

WHENAS in silks my Julia goes,
Then, then, methinks, how sweetly flows
The liquefaction of her clothes!

Next, when I cast mine eyes and see
That brave vibration each way free,
—O how that glittering taketh me!

Herrick.

CXXXVIII

THE COMPLETE LOVER

1. *He*

For her gait, if she be walking;
Be she sitting, I desire her
For her state's sake; and admire her
For her wit if she be talking;
 Gait and state and wit approve her;
 For which all and each I love her.

Be she sullen, I commend her
For a modest.   Be she merry,
For a kind one her prefer I.
Briefly, everything doth lend her
 So much grace, and so approve her,
 That for everything I love her.

Wm. Browne.

CXXXIX

2. *She*

Love not me for comely grace,
For my pleasing eye or face,
Nor for any outward part,
No, nor for a constant heart:
 For these may fail or turn to ill,
  So thou and I shall sever:
Keep, therefore, a true woman's eye,
And love me still but know not why—
 So hast thou the same reason still
  To doat upon me ever!

Anon.

CXL

MY LADY'S HAND

O GOODLY hand !
Wherein doth stand
    My heart distraught in pain ;
Dear hand, alas !
In little space
    My life thou dost restrain.

O fingers slight !
Departed right,
    So long, so small, so round ;
Goodly begone,
And yet a bone,
    Most cruel in my wound.

With lilies white
And roses bright
    Doth strain thy colour fair ;
Nature did lend
Each finger's end
    A pearl for to repair.

Consent at last,
Since that thou hast
    My heart in thy demesne,

For service true
On me to rue,
 And reach me love again.

And if not so,
There with more woe
 Enforce thyself to strain
This simple heart,
That suffer'd smart,
 And rid it out of pain.
     Sir Thomas Wyat.

CXLI

HER HAIR

THERE's her hair with which Love angles
And beholders' eyes entangles;
For in those fair curled snares,
They are hamper'd unawares,
And compell'd to swear a duty
To her sweet enthralling beauty.
In my mind 'tis the most fair
That was ever callèd hair;
Somewhat brighter than a brown,
And her tresses waving down
At full length, and so dispread,
Mantle her from foot to head.
     Geo. Wither.

CXLII

A DOUBLE DOUBTING

Lady, when I behold the roses sprouting,
  Which clad in damask mantles deck the arbours,
  And then behold your lips where sweet love
    harbours,
My eyes present me with a double doubting:
For viewing both alike, hardly my mind supposes
Whether the roses be your lips, or your lips the roses.

Anon.

CXLIII

  Rose-cheek'd *Laura*, come;
Sing thou smoothly with thy beauty's
Silent music, either other
    Sweetly gracing.

  Lovely forms do flow
From concent divinely framèd:
Heaven is music, and thy beauty's
    Birth is heavenly.

  These dull notes we sing
Discords need for helps to grace them;
Only beauty purely loving
    Knows no discord;

  But still moves delight,
Like clear springs renew'd by flowing
Ever perfect, ever in them-
    selves eternal.

T. Campion.

CXLIV

CHLORIS IN THE SNOW

I saw fair *Chloris* walk alone,
When feather'd rain came softly down,
As Jove descending from his Tower
To court her in a silver shower:
The wanton snow flew to her breast,
Like pretty birds into their nest,
But, overcome with whiteness there,
For grief it thaw'd into a tear:
  Thence falling on her garment's hem,
  To deck her, froze into a gem.

Anon.

CXLV

Pretty twinkling starry eyes,
How did Nature first devise
Such a sparkling in your sight
As to give Love such delight
As to make him, like a fly,
Play with looks until he die?

N. Breton.

CXLVI

TO DIANEME

Sweet, be not proud of those two eyes
Which starlike sparkle in their skies;
Nor be you proud that you can see
All hearts your captives, yours yet free;

Be you not proud of that rich hair
Which wantons with the love-sick air;
Whenas that ruby which you wear,
Sunk from the tip of your soft ear,
Will last to be a precious stone
When all your world of beauty's gone.

Herrick.

CXLVII

TO CELIA

Drink to me only with thine eyes,
  And I will pledge with mine;
Or leave a kiss but in the cup
  And I 'll not look for wine.
The thirst that from the soul doth rise
  Doth ask a drink divine;
But might I of Jove's nectar sup,
  I would not change for thine.

I sent thee late a rosy wreath,
  Not so much honouring thee
As giving it a hope that there
  It could not wither'd be;
But thou thereon didst only breathe
  And sent'st it back to me;
Since when it grows, and smells, I swear,
  Not of itself but thee!

B. Jonson.

CXLVIII

A MADRIGAL

WHEN in her face mine eyes I fix,
A fearful boldness takes my mind,
Sweet honey Love with gall doth mix,
    And is unkindly kind :
        It seems to breed,
        And is indeed
    A special pleasure to be pined.
      No danger then I dread :
For though I went a thousand times to Styx,
I know she can revive me with her eye
As many looks, as many lives to me :
    And yet had I a thousand hearts,
    As many looks, as many darts,
      Might make them all to die.

W. Alexander, Earl of Stirling.

CXLIX

HEART'S HIDING

SWEET Love, mine only treasure,
    For service long unfeignèd,
    Wherein I nought have gainèd
Vouchsafe this little pleasure,
    To tell me in what part
    My mistress keeps her heart.

If in her hair so slender
    Like golden nets entwinèd
    Which fire and art have 'finèd,
Her thrall my heart I render
    For ever to abide
    With locks so dainty tied.

If in her eyes she bind it,
    Wherein that fire was framèd
    By which it is inflamèd,
I dare not look to find it :
    I only wish it sight
    To see that pleasant light.

But if her breast have deignèd
    With kindness to receive it,
    I am content to leave it,
Though death thereby were gainèd.
    Then, Lady, take your own
    That lives for you alone.

                          A. W.

CL

So sweet is thy discourse to me,
    And so delightful is thy sight,
As I taste nothing right but thee.
O why invented Nature light ?
    Was it alone for Beauty's sake,
That her graced words might better take ?

No more can I old joys recall :
  They now to me become unknown,
Not seeming to have been at all.
Alas ! how soon is this Love grown
  To such a spreading height in me
  As with it all must shadow'd be !

T. Campion.

CLI

DEVOTION

FAIN would I change that note
To which fond Love hath charm'd me
Long long to sing by rote,
Fancying that that harm'd me :
Yet when this thought doth come,
' Love is the perfect sum
    Of all delight,'
I have no other choice
Either for pen or voice
    To sing or write.

O Love, they wrong thee much
That say thy sweet is bitter,
When thy rich fruit is such
As nothing can be sweeter.
Fair house of joy and bliss,
Where truest pleasure is,
    I do adore thee :
I know thee what thou art,
 I serve thee with my heart,
    And fall before thee.

Anon.

CLII

A RECANTATION

O Love, sweet Love, O high and heavenly Love!
The court of pleasures, paradise of rest,
Without whose circuit all things bitter prove,
Within whose ceinture every wretch is blest:
    O grant me pardon, sacred deity,
    I do recant my former heresy!

And thou, the dearest idol of my thought,
Whom love I did, and do, and always will:
O pardon what my coy disdain hath wrought,
My coy disdain, the author of this ill:
    And for the pride that I have show'd before,
    By Love I swear I'll love thee ten times more.
Anon.

CLIII

VIA AMORIS

Highway, since you my chief Parnassus be,
And that my Muse, to some ears not unsweet,
Tempers her words to trampling horses' feet
More oft than to a chamber-melody,—

Now blessèd you bear onward blessèd me
To her, where I my heart, safe-left, shall meet;
My Muse and I must you of duty greet
With thanks and wishes, wishing thankfully;

Be you still fair, honour'd by public heed ;
By no encroachment wrong'd, nor time forgot ;
Nor blamed for blood, nor shamed for sinful deed ;
And that you know I envy you no lot

Of highest wish, I wish you so much bliss,
Hundreds of years you Stella's feet may kiss !
Sir P. Sidney.

CLIV

COMFORT

1

WHEN in disgrace with fortune and men's eyes
I all alone beweep my outcast state,
And trouble deaf heaven with my bootless cries,
And look upon myself, and curse my fate,

Wishing me like to one more rich in hope,
Featured like him, like him with friends possest,
Desiring this man's art and that man's scope,
With what I most enjoy contented least,

Yet in these thoughts myself almost despising,—
Haply I think on Thee : and then my state,
Like to the lark at break of day arising
From sullen earth, sings hymns at heaven's gate ;

For thy sweet love remember'd such wealth brings
That then I scorn to change my fate with kings.
Shakespeare.

CLV

2

WHEN to the sessions of sweet silent thought
I summon up remembrance of things past,
I sigh the lack of many a thing I sought,
And with old woes new wail my dear time's waste:

Then can I drown an eye, unused to flow,
For precious friends hid in death's dateless night,
And weep afresh love's long-since cancell'd woe,
And moan th' expense of many a vanish'd sight:

Then can I grieve at grievances foregone,
And heavily from woe to woe tell o'er
The sad account of fore-bemoanèd moan,
Which I new pay as if not paid before.

But if the while I think on thee, dear Friend,
All losses are restored and sorrows end.

Shakespeare.

CLVI

3

THY bosom is endearèd with all hearts
Which I, by lacking, have supposèd dead:
And there reigns Love,and all Love's loving parts,
And all those friends which I thought burièd.

How many a holy and obsequious tear
Hath dear religious love stol'n from mine eye,
As interest for the dead!—which now appear
But things removed that hidden in thee lie.

Thou art the grave where buried love doth live,
Hung with the trophies of my lovers gone,
Who all their parts of me to thee did give :
—That due of many·now is thine alone :

Their images I loved I view in thee,
And thou, all they, hast all the all of me.
Shakespeare.

CLVII

THE INTERPRETER

Though others may her brow adore
Yet more must I, that therein see far more
Than any other's eyes have power to see :
      She is to me
More than to any others she can be !

I can discern more secret notes
That in the margin of her cheek Love quotes,
Than any else beside have art to read :
      No looks proceed
From those fair eyes but to me wonder breed.
Anon.

CLVIII

THE UNFADING BEAUTY

He that loves a rosy cheek,
   Or a coral lip admires,
Or from star-like eyes doth seek
   Fuel to maintain his fires :

As old Time makes these decay,
So his flames must waste away.

But a smooth and steadfast mind,
    Gentle thoughts and calm desires,
Hearts with equal love combined,
    Kindle never-dying fires :—
Where these are not, I despise
Lovely cheeks or lips or eyes.

T. Carew.

CLIX

YEA OR NAY

1

Madam, withouten many words
    Once I am sure you will or no;
And if you will, then leave your boards,[1]
    And use your wit and show it so.

For with a beck you shall me call;
    And if of one that burns alway
You have pitie or ruth at all,
    Answer him fair with yea or nay.

If it be yea, I shall be fain;
    If it be nay, friends as before;
You shall another man obtain,
    And I mine own, and yours no more.

Sir Thomas Wyat.

---

[1] Tackings to and fro. A vessel tacking is still said to 'make boards.'

CLX

2

MAID, will ye love me, yea or no?
Tell me the truth, and let me go.
It can be no less than a sinful deed,
Trust me truly,
To linger a lover that looks to speed
In due time duly.

You maids, that think yourselves as fine
As Venus and all the Muses nine,
The Father himself when He first made man,
Trust me truly,
Made you for his help, when the world began,
In due time duly.

Then sith God's will was even so,
Why should you disdain your lover tho?[1]
But rather with a willing heart
Love him truly:
For in so doing you do but your part;
Let reason rule ye.

Consider, Sweet, what sighs and sobs
Do nip my heart with cruel throbs,
And all, my Dear, for love of you,
Trust me truly;
But I hope that you will some mercy show
In due time duly.

Anon.

[1] Then.

CLXI

THE PRIMROSE

Ask me why I send you here
This firstling of the infant year?
Ask me why I send to you
This Primrose, all bepearl'd with dew?
I straight whisper to your ears:
The sweets of love are wash'd with tears.

Ask me why this flower does show
So yellow-green and sickly too?
Ask me why the stalk is weak
And bending, yet it doth not break?
I will answer: These discover
What doubts and fears are in a lover.

T. Carew or *R. Herrick.*

CLXII

LOVE'S CASUISTRY

1

If love make me forsworn, how shall I swear to love?
Ah, never faith could hold, if not to beauty vow'd!
Though to myself forsworn, to thee I'll faithful prove;
Those thoughts to me were oaks, to thee like
    osiers bow'd.

Study his bias leaves and makes his book thine eyes,
Where all those pleasures live that art would
    comprehend;
If knowledge be the mark, to know thee shall suffice;
Well learnèd is that tongue that well can thee
    commend;

All ignorant that soul that sees thee without
    wonder;
Which is to me some praise that I thy parts admire.
Thy eye Jove's lightning bears, thy voice his dread-
    ful thunder,
Which, not to anger bent, is music and sweet fire.

Celestial as thou art, O pardon love this wrong
That sings heaven's praise with such an earthly
    tongue.

Shakespeare.

CLXIII

2

Did not the heavenly rhetoric of thine eye,
'Gainst whom the world cannot hold argument,
Persuade my heart to this false perjury?
Vows for thee broke deserve not punishment.

A woman I forswore; but I will prove,
Thou being a goddess, I forswore not thee:
My vow was earthly, thou a heavenly love;
Thy grace being gain'd cures all disgrace in me.

Vows are but breath, and breath a vapour is:
Then thou, fair sun, which on my earth dost shine,
Exhal'st this vapour-vow; in thee it is:
If broken then, it is no fault of mine;

If by me broke, what fool is not so wise
To lose an oath to win a paradise?

Shakespeare.

CLXIV

THE GIFT

FAIN would I have a pretty thing
    To give unto my Lady:
I name no thing, nor I mean no thing,
    But as pretty a thing as may be.

Twenty journeys would I make,
    And twenty ways would hie me,
To make adventure for her sake,
    To set some matter by me:
        But fain would I have . . .

Some do long for pretty knacks,
    And some for strange devices:
God send me that my Lady lacks,
    I care not what the price is.
        Thus fain . . .

I walk the town and tread the street,
    In every corner seeking

The pretty thing I cannot meet,
  That 's for my Lady's liking :
                For fain . . .

The mercers pull me, going by,
  The silk-wives say 'What lack ye ?'
'The thing you have not,' then say I :
  'Ye foolish knaves, go pack ye !'
                But fain . . .

It is not all the silk in Cheap,
  Nor all the golden treasure ;
Nor twenty bushels on a heap
  Can do my Lady pleasure.
                But fain . . .

But were it in the wit of man
  By any means to make it,
I could for money buy it then,
  And say, 'Fair Lady, take it !'
                Thus fain . . .

O Lady, what a luck is this,
  That my good willing misseth
To find what pretty thing it is
  That my Good Lady wisheth !
       Thus fain would I have had this
          pretty thing
         To give unto my Lady ;
      I said no harm, nor I meant no harm,
      But as pretty a thing as may be.
                    Anon.

CLXV

TO HIS BOOK

HAPPY ye leaves whenas those lily hands,
Which hold my life in their dead-doing might,
Shall handle you, and hold in love's soft bands,
Like captives trembling at the victor's sight:

And happy lines, on which with starry light
Those lamping eyes will deign sometime to look
And read the sorrows of my dying sprite,
Written with tears in heart's close bleeding book:

And happy rhymes, bathed in the second book
Of *Helicon*, whence she derivèd is,
When ye behold that angel's blessèd look,
My soul's long lackèd food, my heaven's bliss:

Leaves, lines, and rhymes, seek her to please alone,
Whom if ye please, I care for other none.

Spenser.

CLXVI

UPON JULIA'S RECOVERY

DROOP, droop no more, or hang the head,
Ye roses almost witherèd;
Now strength and newer purple get,
Each here declining violet;
O primroses! let this day be
A resurrection unto ye,

And to all flowers allied in blood,
Or sworn to that sweet sisterhood :
For health on Julia's cheek hath shed
Claret and cream comminglèd ;
And those her lips do now appear
As beams of coral, but more clear.

Herrick.

CLXVII

THE BRACELET: TO JULIA

WHY I tie about thy wrist,
    Julia, this silken twist ;
    For what other reason is 't
But to show thee how, in part,
Thou my pretty captive art ?
But thy bond-slave is my heart :
'Tis but silk that bindeth thee,
Knap the thread and thou art free ;
But 'tis otherwise with me :
—I am bound and fast bound, so
That from thee I cannot go ;
If I could, I would not so.

Herrick.

CLXVIII

TO DAISIES, NOT TO SHUT SO SOON

SHUT not so soon ; the dull-eyed night
    Has not as yet begun
To make a seizure on the light,
    Or to seal up the sun.

No marigolds yet closed are,—
  No shadows great appear;
Nor doth the early shepherd's star
  Shine like a spangle here.

Stay but till my Julia close
  Her life-begetting eye,
And let the whole world then dispose
  Itself to live or die.

Herrick.

CLXIX

THE NIGHT-PIECE : TO JULIA

HER eyes the glow-worm lend thee,
The shooting stars attend thee;
    And the elves also,
    Whose little eyes glow
Like the sparks of fire, befriend thee.

No Will-o'-the-wisp mislight thee,
Nor snake nor slow-worm bite thee;
    But on, on thy way
    Not making a stay,
Since ghost there's none to affright thee.

Let not the dark thee cumber :
What though the moon does slumber?
    The stars of the night
    Will lend thee their light
Like tapers clear without number.

Then, Julia, let me woo thee,
Thus, thus to come unto me ;
And when I shall meet
Thy silvr'y feet
My soul I 'll pour into thee.

Herrick.

CLXX

LOVE SEES BY NIGHT

O Night, O jealous Night, repugnant to my measures !
  O Night so long desired, yet cross to my content !
There 's none but only thou that can perform my
    pleasures,
  Yet none but only thou that hind'reth my intent.

Thy beams, thy spiteful beams, thy lamps that burn
    too brightly,
  Discover all my trains, and naked lay my drifts,
That night by night I hope, yet fail my purpose
    nightly ;
  Thy envious glaring gleam defeateth so my shifts.

Sweet Night, withhold thy beams, withhold them
    till to-morrow !
  Whose joy's in lack so long a hell of torment
    breeds.
Sweet Night, sweet gentle Night, do not prolong
    my sorrow :
  Desire is guide to me, and Love no lodestar needs.

Let sailors gaze on Stars and Moon so freshly shining;
  Let them that miss the way be guided by the
    light;
I know my Lady's bower, there needs no more
    divining; ·
  Affection sees in dark, and Love hath eyes by
    night.

Dame Cynthia, couch awhile! hold in thy horns for
    shining,
  And glad not low'ring Night with thy too glorious
    rays;
But be she dim and dark, tempestuous and repining,
  That in her spite my sport may work thy endless
    praise.

And when my will is wrought, then, Cynthia, shine,
    good lady,
  All other nights and days in honour of that night,
That happy, heavenly night, that night so dark and
    shady,
  Wherein my Love had eyes that lighted my
    delight.

Anon.

CLXXI

SLEEPING

Sleep, angry beauty, sleep and fear not me:
  For what a sleeping lion dares provoke?
It shall suffice me here to sit and see
  Those lips shut up that never kindly spoke:

What sight can more content a lover's mind
Than beauty seeming harmless, if not kind?

My words have charm'd her, for secure she sleeps,
   Though guilty much of wrong done to my love;
And in her slumber, see ! she close-eyed weeps !
   Dreams often more than waking passions move.
Plead, Sleep, my cause, and make her soft like thee,
That she in peace may wake and pity me !

T. Campion.

CLXXII

SLEEP

Come, Sleep; O Sleep ! the certain knot of peace,
The baiting-place of wit, the balm of woe,
The poor man's wealth, the prisoner's release,
Th' indifferent judge between the high and low ;

With shield of proof shield me from out the prease [1]
Of those fierce darts Despair at me doth throw :
O make in me those civil wars to cease ;
I will good tribute pay, if thou do so.

Take thou of me smooth pillows, sweetest bed,
A chamber deaf of noise and blind of light,
A rosy garland and a weary head ;
And if these things, as being thine by right,

Move not thy heavy grace, thou shalt in me
Livelier than elsewhere Stella's image see.

Sir P. Sidney.

[1] Press.

CLXXIII

INVOCATION TO SLEEP

CARE-CHARMING Sleep, thou easer of all woes,
Brother to Death, sweetly thyself dispose
On this afflicted prince ; fall like a cloud
In gentle showers ; give nothing that is loud
Or painful to his slumbers ; easy, light,
And as a purling stream, thou son of Night
Pass by his troubled senses ; sing his pain
Like hollow murmuring wind or silver rain ;
In to this prince gently, O gently, slide,
And kiss him into slumbers like a bride.

J. Fletcher.

CLXXIV

ANOTHER

CARE-CHARMER Sleep, son of the sable Night,
Brother to Death, in silent darkness born,
Relieve my languish and restore the light ;
With dark forgetting of my care, return :

And let the day be time enough to mourn
The shipwreck of my ill-adventured youth :
Let waking eyes suffice to wail their scorn,
Without the torment of the night's untruth.

Cease dreams, the images of day's desires,
To model forth the passions of the morrow;
Never let rising Sun approve you liars,
To add more grief to aggravate my sorrow.

Still let me sleep, embracing clouds in vain,
And never wake to feel the day's disdain.
S. Daniel.

CLXXV

MORTIS IMAGO

Sleep, Silence' child, sweet father of soft rest,
Prince, whose approach peace to all mortals brings,
Indifferent host to shepherds and to kings,
Sole comforter of minds with grief opprest;

Lo, by thy charming rod all breathing things
Lie slumb'ring, with forgetfulness possest,
And yet o'er me to spread thy drowsy wings
Thou spares, alas! who cannot be thy guest.

Since I am thine, O come! but with that face
To inward light which thou art wont to show,
With feignèd solace ease a true-felt woe;
Or if, deaf god, thou do deny that grace,

Come as thou wilt, and what thou wilt bequeath,
I long to kiss the image of my death.
Drummond of Hawthornden.

CLXXVI

THE DREAM

THE ivory, coral, gold,
Of breast, of lips, of hair,
So lively Sleep doth show to inward sight,
That wake I think I hold
No shadow, but my Fair:
Myself so to deceive,
With long-shut eyes I shun the irksome light.
Such pleasure thus I have,
Delighting in false gleams,
If Death Sleep's brother be,
    And souls relieved of sense have so sweet dreams,
    That I would wish me thus to dream and die.
Drummond of Hawthornden.

CLXXVII

A SWEET PASTORAL

GOOD Muse, rock me asleep
  With some sweet harmony;
The weary eye is not to keep
  Thy wary company.

Sweet Love, begone awhile;
  Thou know'st my heaviness;
Beauty is born but to beguile
  My heart of happiness.

See how my little flock,
  That loved to feed on high,
Do headlong tumble down the rock
  And in the valley die.

The bushes and the trees
  That were so fresh and green,
Do all their dainty colour leese,[1]
  And not a leaf is seen.

The blackbird and the thrush
  That made the woods to ring,
With all the rest are now at hush
  And not a note they sing.

Sweet Philomel, the bird
  That hath the heavenly throat,
Doth now, alas ! not once afford
  Recording of a note.

The flowers have had a frost,
  Each herb hath lost her savour,
And Phyllida the fair hath lost
  The comfort of her favour.

Now all these careful sights
  So kill me in conceit,
That how to hope upon delights,
  It is but mere deceit.

And therefore, my sweet Muse,
  Thou know'st what help is best ;
Do now thy heavenly cunning use
  To set my heart at rest :

And in a dream bewray
  What fate shall be my friend,
Whether my life shall still decay,
  Or when my sorrow end.

N. Breton.

[1] Lose.

CLXXVIII

ORPHEUS

Orpheus with his lute made trees
And the mountain tops that freeze
  Bow themselves when he did sing :
To his music plants and flowers
Ever sprung ; as sun and showers
  There had made a lasting spring.

Every thing that heard him play,
Even the billows of the sea,
  Hung their heads and then lay by.
In sweet music is such art,
Killing care and grief of heart
  Fall asleep, or hearing, die.

Shakespeare.

CLXXIX

TO MUSIC, TO BECALM HIS FEVER

Charm me asleep and melt me so
  With thy delicious numbers
That, being ravisht, hence I go
  Away in easy slumbers.
    Ease my sick head,
    And make my bed,
Thou power that canst sever
    From me this ill,
    And quickly still,
    Though thou not kill,
     My fever.

Thou sweetly canst convert the same
From a consuming fire
Into a gentle licking flame,
And make it thus expire.
Then make me weep
My pains asleep;
And give me such reposes
That I, poor I,
May think thereby
I live and die
'Mongst roses.

Fall on me like the silent dew,
Or like those maiden showers
Which, by the peep of day, do strew
A baptim o'er the flowers.
Melt, melt my pains
With thy soft strains;
That, having ease me given,
With full delight
I leave this light,
And take my flight
For Heaven.

Herrick.

CLXXX

CHURCH MUSIC

Sweetest of sweets, I thank you : when displeasure
Did through my body wound my mind,
You took me thence, and in your house of pleasure
A dainty lodging me assign'd.

Now I in you without a body move,
   Rising and falling with your wings;
We both together sweetly live and love,
   Yet say sometimes, *God help poor kings !*

Comfort, I 'll die; for if you post from me
   Sure I shall do so and much more;
But if I travel in your company,
   You know the way to Heaven's door.

Geo. Herbert.

CLXXXI

TEARS

Weep you no more, sad fountains;
   What need you flow so fast ?
Look how the snowy mountains
   Heaven's sun doth gently waste !
But my Sun's heavenly eyes
     View not your weeping,
   That now lies sleeping
Softly, now softly lies
     Sleeping.

Sleep is a reconciling,
   A rest that peace begets;
Doth not the sun rise smiling
   When fair at even he sets ?
Rest you then, rest, sad eyes !
     Melt not in weeping
     While she lies sleeping
Softly, now softly lies
     Sleeping.   *Anon.*

CLXXXII

Slow, slow, fresh fount, keep time with my salt tears;
  Yet slower, yet; O faintly, gentle springs!
List to the heavy part the music bears,
  Woe weeps out her division when she sings.
        Droop herbs and flowers;
        Fall grief in showers;
        Our beauties are not ours:
            O, I could still,
  Like melting snow upon some craggy hill,
          Drop, drop, drop, drop,
Since Nature's pride is now a withered daffodil.
                                    B. Jonson.

CLXXXIII

IN TEARS HER TRIUMPH

So sweet a kiss the golden sun gives not
  To those fresh morning drops upon the rose,
As thy eye-beams, when their fresh rays have smote
  The night of dew that on my cheek down flows:
Nor shines the silver moon one half so bright
  Through the transparent bosom of the deep,
As doth thy face through tears of mine give light:
  Thou shin'st in every tear that I do weep;
No drop but as a coach doth carry thee,
  So ridest thou triumphing in my woe:
Do but behold the tears that swell in me,
  And they thy glory through my grief will show:

But do not love thyself; then thou wilt keep
My tears for glasses, and still make me weep.
O queen of queens! how far dost thou excel,
No thought can think, nor tongue of mortal tell!

Shakespeare.

CLXXXIV

IN TEARS YET EXCELLENT

I saw my Lady weep,
And Sorrow proud to be advancèd so
In those fair eyes where all perfections keep.
    Her face was full of woe;
But such a woe (believe me) as wins more hearts
Than Mirth can do with her enticing parts.

    Sorrow was there made fair,
And Passion wise; Tears a delightful thing;
Silence beyond all speech, a wisdom rare:
    She made her sighs to sing,
And all things with so sweet a sadness move
As made my heart at once both grieve and love.

    O fairer than aught else
The world can show, leave off in time to grieve!
Enough, enough: your joyful look excels:
    Tears kill the heart, believe.
O strive not to be excellent in woe,
Which only breeds your beauty's overthrow.

Anon.

CLXXXV

SWEET MELANCHOLY

Hence, all you vain delights,
As short as are the nights
　　Wherein you spend your folly!
There's naught in this life sweet,
If men were wise to see't,
　　But only melancholy—
　　O sweetest melancholy!
Welcome, folded arms and fixèd eyes,
A sight that piercing mortifies,
A look that's fasten'd to the ground,
A tongue chain'd up without a sound!

Fountain-heads and pathless groves,
Places which pale passion loves!
Moonlight walks, when all the fowls
Are warmly housed, save bats or owls!
　　A midnight bell, a parting groan—
　　These are the sounds we feed upon:
Then stretch our bones in a still gloomy valley,
Nothing's so dainty sweet as lovely melancholy.
J. Fletcher.

CLXXXVI

HER CRUELTY

With how sad steps, O moon, thou climb'st the skies!
How silently, and with how wan a face!
What! may it be that e'en in heavenly place
That busy archer his sharp arrows tries?

Sure, if that long-with-love-acquainted eyes
Can judge of love, thou feel'st a lover's case :
I read it in thy looks; thy languish'd grace
To me, that feel the like, thy state descries.

Then, e'en of fellowship, O Moon, tell me,
Is constant love deem'd there but want of wit ?
Are beauties there as proud as here they be ?
Do they above love to be loved, and yet

Those lovers scorn whom that love doth possess ?
Do they call ' virtue,' there, ungratefulness ?

Sir P. Sidney.

CLXXXVII

DELIA

Fair is my Love and cruel as she's fair ;
Her brow shades frowns, although her eyes are
        sunny,
Her smiles are lightning, though her pride despair,
And her disdains are gall, her favours honey :

A modest maid, deck'd with a blush of honour,
Whose feet do tread green paths of youth and love ;
The wonder of all eyes that look upon her,
Sacred on earth, design'd a Saint above.

Chastity and beauty, which were deadly foes,
Live reconcilèd friends within her brow ;

And had she pity to conjoin with those,
Then who had heard the plaints I utter now?

For had she not been fair, and thus unkind,
My Muse had slept, and none had known my mind.

S. Daniel.

CLXXXVIII

THOU art not fair, for all thy red and white,
    For all those rosy ornaments in thee;
Thou art not sweet, tho' made of mere delight,
    Nor fair, nor sweet—unless thou pity me.
I will not soothe thy fancies: thou shalt prove
That beauty is no beauty without love.

Yet love not me, nor seek not to allure
    My thoughts with beauty, were it more divine:
Thy smiles and kisses I cannot endure,
    I'll not be wrapp'd up in those arms of thine:
Now show it, if thou by a woman right,—
Embrace and kiss and love me in despite.

T. Campion.

CLXXXIX

THE UNWILLING ONE

AH! were she pitiful as she is fair,
Or but as mild as she is seeming so,
Then were my hopes greater than my despair,
Then all the world were heaven, nothing woe.

Ah ! were her heart relenting as her hand,
That seems to melt even with the mildest touch,
Then knew I where to seat me in a land
Under wide heavens, but yet there is none such.

So as she shows she seems the budding rose,
Yet sweeter far than is an earthly flower ;
Sov'ran of beauty, like the spray she grows ;
Compass'd she is with thorns and canker'd bower.

Yet were she willing to be pluck'd and worn,
She would be gathered, though she grew on thorn.

R. Greene.

CXC

Fire that must flame is with apt fuel fed ;
Flowers that will thrive in sunny soil are bred ;
How can a heart feel heat that no hope finds ?
Or can he love on whom no comfort shines ?

Fair ! I confess there 's pleasure in your sight :
Sweet ! you have power, I grant, of all delight :
But what is all to me, if I have none ?
Churl that you are, t' enjoy such wealth alone !

Prayers move the heavens but find no grace with you ;
Yet in your looks a heavenly form I view ;
Then will I pray again, hoping to find,
As well as in your looks, Heaven in your mind.

Saint of my heart, Queen of my life and love,
O let my vows thy loving spirit move !
Let me no longer mourn through thy disdain;
But with one touch of grace cure all my pain !

T. Campion.

CXCI

THE LOVER CURSETH THE TIME WHEN FIRST HE FELL IN LOVE

When first mine eyes did view and mark
  Thy beauty fair for to behold,
And when mine ears 'gan first to hark
  The pleasant words that thou me told;
I would as then I had been free
From ears to hear and eyes to see.

And when my hands did handle oft,
  That might thee keep in memory,
And when my feet had gone so soft
  To find and have thy company;
I would each hand a foot had been,
And eke each foot a hand had seen.

And when in mind I did consent
  To follow thus my fancy's will,
And when my heart did first relent
  To taste such bait myself to spill,
I would my heart had been as thine,
Or else thy heart as soft as mine.

Then should not I such cause have found
    To wish this monstrous sight to see,
Nor thou, alas ! that madest the wound,
    Should not deny me remedy :
Then should one will in both remain,
To ground one heart which now is twain.

                 W. Hunnis (?).

CXCII

O CRUDELIS AMOR

O GENTLE Love, ungentle for thy deed,
      Thou mak'st my heart
      A bloody mark
With piercing shot to bleed.
Shoot soft, sweet Love, for fear thou shoot amiss ;
      For fear too keen
      Thy arrows been,
And hit the heart where my Beloved is.
Too fair that fortune were, nor never I
      Shall be so blest,
      Among the rest,
That Love shall seize on her by sympathy.
Then since with Love my prayers bear no boot,
      This doth remain
      To cease my pain,
I take the wound and die at Venus' foot.

                 Geo. Peele.

CXCIII

VOBISCUM EST OPE, VOBISCUM CANDIDA TYRO

WHEN thou must home to shades of underground,
And there arrived, a new admirèd guest,
The beauteous spirits do engirt thee round,
White Iope, blithe Helen, and the rest,
To hear the stories of thy finish'd love
From that smooth tongue whose music hell can
    move ;

Then wilt thou speak of banqueting delights,
Of masques and revels which sweet youth did make,
Of tourneys and great challenges of knights,
And all these triumphs for thy beauty's sake :
When thou hast told these honours done to thee,
Then tell, O tell, how thou didst murder me !

T. Campion.

CXCIV

A LOVER'S DIRGE

COME away, come away, death,
And in sad cypres [1] let me be laid ;
  Fly away, fly away, breath ;
I am slain by a fair cruel maid.
My shroud of white, stuck all with yew,
    O prepare it !
My part of death, no one so true
    Did share it.

[1] *Cypres,* crape.   Cf. Autolycus' song—
> ' Lawn as white as driven snow,
> Cypres black as e'er was crow.'

and Milton's
> ' Sable stole of cypres-lawn.'—*Il Penseroso.*

Not a flower, not a flower sweet,
On my black coffin let there be strown ;
Not a friend, not a friend greet
My poor corse, where my bones shall be thrown :
A thousand thousand sighs to save
Lay me, O, where
Sad true lover never find my grave
To weep there !

Shakespeare.

CXCV

THE NOBLE FALL

1

My spotless love hovers with purest wings,
About the temple of the proudest frame,
Where blaze those lights, fairest of earthly things,
Which clear our clouded world with brightest flame.

My ambitious thoughts, confinèd in her face,
Affect no honour but what She can give ;
My hopes do rest in limits of her grace ;
I weigh no comfort unless she relieve.

For She, that can my heart imparadise,
Holds in her fairest hand what dearest is ;
My Fortune's wheel's the circle of her eyes,
Whose rolling grace deign once a turn of bliss.

All my life's sweet consists in her alone ;
So much I love the most Unloving one.

S. Daniel.

CXCVI

2

AND yet I cannot reprehend the flight
Or blame th' attempt presuming so to soar ;
The mounting venture for a high delight
Did make the honour of the fall the more :

For who gets wealth, that puts not from the shore ?
Danger hath honour, great designs their fame ;
Glory doth follow, courage goes before ;
And though th' event oft answers not the same—

Suffice that high attempts have never shame.
The mean observer, whom base safety keeps,
Lives without honour, dies without a name,
And in eternal darkness ever sleeps :

And therefore, *Delia*, 'tis to me no blot
To have attempted, tho' attain'd thee not.

S. Daniel.

CXCVII

ICARUS

LOVE wing'd my Hopes and taught me how to fly
Far from base earth, but not to mount too high :
      For true pleasure
      Lives in measure,
      Which if men forsake,
Blind they into folly run and grief for pleasure take.

But my vain Hopes, proud of their new-taught
    flight,
Enamour'd sought to win the sun's fair light,
        Whose rich brightness
        Moved their lightness
        To aspire so high
That all scorch'd and consumed with fire now
    drown'd in woe they lie.

And none but Love their woeful hap did rue,
For Love did know that their desires were true ;
        Though fate frownèd,
        And now drownèd
        They in sorrow dwell,
It was the purest light of heav'n for whose fair love
    they fell.

Anon.

CXCVIII

Arise, my Thoughts, and mount you with the sun !
Call all the winds to make you speedy wings,
And to my fairest Maia see you run
And weep your last while wantonly she sings :
Then if you cannot move her heart to pity,
Let *Oh, alas, ay me !* be all your ditty.

Arise, my Thoughts, beyond the highest star !
And gently rest you in fair Maia's eye,
For that is fairer than the brightest are :
But, if she frown to see you climb so high,
Couch in her lap, and with a moving ditty
Of smiles and love and kisses beg for pity.

Anon.

CXCIX

My Thoughts are wing'd with Hopes, my Hopes
    with Love:
Mount, Love, unto the Moon in clearest night,
And say, As she doth in the heavens move,
In earth so wanes and waxes my delight:
And whisper this, but softly, in her ears,
'Hope oft doth hang the head and Trust shed tears.'
Anon.

CC

TRUE DEVOTION

Follow your saint, follow with accents sweet!
Haste you, sad notes, fall at her flying feet!
There, wrapt in cloud of sorrow, pity move,
And tell the ravisher of my soul I perish for her love:
But if she scorn my never-ceasing pain,
Then burst with sighing in her sight, and ne'er
    return again.

All that I sang still to her praise did tend;
Still she was first, still she my songs did end;
Yet she my love and music both doth fly,
The music that her echo is and beauty's sympathy:
Then let my notes pursue her scornful flight!
It shall suffice that they were breath'd and died for
    her delight.
T. Campion.

M

CCI

THE SHADOW

1

FOLLOW thy fair sun, unhappy shadow !
  Though thou be black as night,
  And she made all of light,
Yet follow thy fair sun, unhappy shadow !

Follow her, whose light thy light depriveth !
  Though here thou liv'st disgraced,
  And she in heaven is placed,
Yet follow her whose light the world reviveth !

Follow those pure beams, whose beauty burneth !
  That so have scorchèd thee
  As thou still black must be,
Till her kind beams thy black to brightness turneth.

Follow her, while yet her glory shineth !
  There comes a luckless night
  That will dim all her light ;
And this the black unhappy shade divineth.

Follow still, since so thy fates ordainèd !
  The sun must have his shade,
  Till both at once do fade,—
The sun still proved, the shadow still disdainèd.

T. Campion.

CCII

2

FOLLOW a shadow, it still flies you;
  Seem to fly it, it will pursue :
So court a mistress, she denies you;
  Let her alone, she will court you.
    Say, are not women truly, then,
    Styled but the shadows of us men?

At morn and even, shades are longest;
  At noon they are or short or none:
So men at weakest, they are strongest,
  But grant us perfect, they're not known.
    Say, are not women truly, then,
    Styled but the shadows of us men?
               B. Jonson.

CCIII

KIND ARE HER ANSWERS

KIND are her answers,
  But her performance keeps no day;
Breaks time, as dancers
  From their own music when they stray.
All her free favours and smooth words
Wing my hopes in vain.
O did ever voice so sweet but only feign?
  Can true love yield such delay,
  Converting joy to pain?

Lost is our freedom
    When we submit to woman so:
Why do we need 'em
    When, in their best, they work our woe?
There is no wisdom
Can alter ends by fate prefixt.
O why is the good of man with evil mixt?
    Never were days yet callèd two
    But one night went betwixt.

T. Campion.

CCIV

THE SCORNER SCORNED

SHALL I, wasting in despair,
Die because a woman's fair?
Or make pale my cheeks with care
'Cause another's rosy are?
Be she fairer than the day,
Or the flowery meads in May—
    If she think not well of me,
    What care I how fair she be?

Shall my silly heart be pined
'Cause I see a woman kind?
Or a well disposèd nature
Joinèd with a lovely feature?

Be she meeker, kinder, than
Turtle-dove or pelican,
  If she be not so to me,
  What care I how kind she be?

Shall a woman's virtues move
Me to perish for her love?
Or her well-deservings known
Make me quite forget my own?
Be she with that goodness blest
Which may merit name of Best;
  If she be not such to me,
  What care I how good she be?

'Cause her fortune seems too high,
Shall I play the fool and die?
She that bears a noble mind,
If not outward helps she find,
Thinks what with them he would do
Who without them dares her woo;
  And unless that mind I see,
  What care I how great she be?

Great, or good, or kind, or fair,
I will ne'er the more despair;
If she love me, this believe,
I will die ere she shall grieve;
If she slight me when I woo,
I can scorn and let her go;
  For if she be not for me,
  What care I for whom she be?

Geo. Wither.

ccv

TO HIS FORSAKEN MISTRESS

I DO confess thou 'rt smooth and fair,
   And I might have gone near to love thee,
Had I not found the slightest prayer
   That lips could move, had power to move thee;
But I can let thee now alone
As worthy to be loved by none.

I do confess thou 'rt sweet; yet find
   Thee such an unthrift of thy sweets,
Thy favours are but like the wind
   That kisseth everything it meets:
And since thou canst with more than one,
Thou 'rt worthy to be kiss'd by none.

The morning rose that untouch'd stands
   Arm'd with her briars, how sweet she smells!
But pluck'd and strain'd through ruder hands,
   Her sweets no longer with her dwells:
But scent and beauty both are gone,
And leaves fall from her, one by one.

Such fate ere long will thee betide
   When thou hast handled been awhile,
With sere flowers to be thrown aside;—
   And I shall sigh, while some will smile,
To see thy love to every one
Hath brought thee to be loved by none.

Sir R. Ayton.

CCVI

FAITHLESS, FICKLE

Can a maid that is well bred,
Hath a blush so lovely red,
Modest looks, wise, mild, discreet,
And a nature passing sweet,

Break her promise, untrue prove,
On a sudden change her love,
Or be won e'er to neglect
Him to whom she vow'd respect?

Such a maid, alas! I know:
O that weeds 'mongst corn should grow!
Or a rose should prickles have,
Wounding where she ought to save!

Reason, wake, and sleep no more!
Land upon some safer shore,
Think on her and be afraid
Of a faithless, fickle maid.

Of a faithless, fickle maid
Thus true love is still betray'd:
Yet it is some ease to sing
That a maid is light of wing.

Anon.

CCVII

TO ŒNONE

WHAT conscience, say, is it in thee
　　When I a heart had one;
To take away that heart from me,
　　And to retain thy own ?

For shame or pity now incline
　　To play a loving part ;
Either to send me kindly thine,
　　Or give me back my heart.

Covet not both ; but if thou dost
　　Resolve to part with neither,
Why, yet to show that thou art just,
　　Take me and mine together.

Herrick.

CCVIII

THE BARGAIN

My true love hath my heart, and I have his,
　　By just exchange one for another given :
I hold his dear, and mine he cannot miss,
　　There never was a better bargain driven :
　　　　My true love hath my heart, and I have his.

is heart in me keeps him and me in one,
My heart in him his thoughts and senses guides:
e loves my heart, for once it was his own,
I cherish his because in me it bides:
> My true love hath my heart, and I have his.
>> *Sir P. Sidney.*

CCIX

THE MESSAGE

Send home my long-stray'd eyes to me,
Which, oh! too long have dwelt on thee;
But if they there have learnt such ill,
> Such forced fashions
> And false passions,
>> That they be
>> Made by thee
Fit for no good sight, keep them still.

Send home my harmless heart again,
Which no unworthy thought could stain;
But if it be taught by thine
> To make jestings
> Of protestings,
>> And break both
>> Word and oath,
Keep it still, 'tis none of mine.

Yet send me back my heart and eyes,
That I may know and see thy lies,

And may laugh and joy when thou
    Art in anguish,
    And dost languish
    For some one
    That will none,
Or prove as false as thou dost now.

J. Donne.

CCX

THE EXCUSE

CALLING to mind, my *eyes* went long about
  To cause my heart for to forsake my breast;
All in a rage I sought to pull them out
  As who had been such traitors to my rest:
    What could they say to win again my grace?—
    Forsooth, that they had seen my Mistress' face.

Another time, my *heart* I call'd to mind,—
  Thinking that he this woe on me had brought,
For he my breast the fort of love, resign'd,[1]
  When of such wars my fancy never thought:
    What could he say when I would have him slain?
    That he was hers, and had forgone my chain.

At last, when I perceived both eyes and heart
  Excuse themselves as guiltless of my ill,
I found *myself* the cause of all my smart,
  And told myself that I myself would kill:
    Yet when I saw myself to you was true,
    I loved myself, because myself loved you.

Sir W. Raleigh.

[1] *v.l.* 'Because that he to love his force resign'd.'

CCXI

AS YE CAME FROM THE HOLY LAND

As ye came from the holy land
  Of Walsinghame,
Met you not with my true love
  By the way as you came?

How should I know your true love,
  That have met many one,
As I came from the holy land,
  That have come, that have gone?

She is neither white nor brown,
  But as the heavens fair;
There is none hath her form divine
  In the earth or the air.

Such a one did I meet, good sir,
  Such an angelic face,
Who like a nymph, like a queen, did appear
  In her gait, in her grace.

She hath left me here alone
  All alone, as unknown,
Who sometime did me lead with herself,
  And me loved as her own.

What's the cause that she leaves you alone
  And a new way doth take,
That sometime did love you as her own,
  And her joy did you make?

I have loved her all my youth,
  But now am old, as you see:
Love likes not the falling fruit,
  Nor the wither'd tree.

Know that Love is a careless child,
  And forgets promise past:
He is blind, he is deaf when he list,
  And in faith never fast.

His desire is a dureless content,
  And a trustless joy;
He is won with a world of despair,
  And is lost with a toy.

Of womenkind such indeed is the love,
  Or the word love abused,
Under which many childish desires
  And conceits are excused.

But true love is a durable fire,
  In the mind ever burning,
Never sick, never old, never dead,
  From itself never turning.

Sir W. Raleigh (?).

CCXII

LOVER BESEECHETH HIS MISTRESS TO FORGET HIS STEADFAST FAITH AND TRUE INTENT

Forget not yet the tried intent
Of such a truth as I have meant;
My great travail so gladly spent,
Forget not yet!

Forget not yet when first began
The weary life ye know, since whan
The suit, the service, none tell can;
Forget not yet!

Forget not yet the great assays,
The cruel wrong, the scornful ways,
The painful patience in delays,
Forget not yet!

Forget not! O, forget not this!—
How long ago hath been, and is
The mind that never meant amiss—
Forget not yet!

Forget not then thine own approved,
The which so long hath thee so loved,
Whose steadfast faith yet never moved:
Forget not this!

Sir Thomas Wyat.

CCXIII

CONSTANCY

O never say that I was false of heart!
Though absence seem'd my flame to qualify.
As easy might I from myself depart,
As from my soul, which in thy breast doth lie:

That is the home of love; if I have ranged,
Like him that travels, I return again,
Just to the time, not with the time exchanged,
So that myself bring water for my stain.

Never believe, though in my nature reign'd
All frailties that besiege all kinds of blood,
That it could so prepost'rously be stain'd,
To leave for nothing all thy sum of good:

For nothing this wide universe I call,
Save thou, my rose ; in it thou art my all.

Shakespeare.

CCXIV

HOW CAN THE HEART FORGET HER?

At her fair hands how have I grace entreated,
With prayers oft repeated !
Yet still my love is thwarted :
Heart, let her go, for she 'll not be converted—
Say, shall she go ?
O no, no, no, no, no !
She is most fair, though she be marble-hearted.

How often have my sighs declared my anguish,
Wherein I daily languish !
Yet still she doth procure it :
Heart, let her go, for I can not endure it—
　　　Say, shall she go ?
　　　O no, no, no, no, no !
She gave the wound, and she alone must cure it.

But shall I still a true affection owe her,
Which prayers, sighs, tears do show her,
And shall she still disdain me ?
Heart, let her go, if they no grace can gain me—
　　　Say, shall she go ?
　　　O no, no, no, no, no !
She made me hers, and hers she will retain me.

But if the love that hath and still doth burn me
No love at length return me,
Out of my thoughts I 'll set her :
Heart, let her go, O heart I pray thee, let her !
　　　Say, shall she go ?
　　　O no, no, no, no, no !
Fix'd in the heart, how can the heart forget her.

F. or W. Davison.

CCXV

SINCE FIRST I SAW YOUR FACE

Since first I saw your face I resolved to honour and
　　renown ye ;
If now I be disdainèd, I wish my heart had never
　　known ye.

What? I that loved and you that liked, shall we
    begin to wrangle?
No, no, no, my heart is fast and cannot disentangle.

If I admire or praise you too much, that fault you
    may forgive me;
Or if my hands had stray'd but a touch, then justly
    might you leave me.
I asked you leave, you bade me love; is't now a
    time to chide me?
No, no, no, I'll love you still what fortune e'er
    betide me.

The sun, whose beams most glorious are, rejecteth
    no beholder,
And your sweet beauty past compare made my poor
    eyes the bolder:
Where beauty moves and wit delights and signs of
    kindness bind me,
There, O there! where'er I go I'll leave my heart
    behind me!

Anon.

CCXVI

FALSE LOVE

When Love on time and measure makes his ground,—
    Time that must end, though Love can never die,—
'Tis Love betwixt a shadow and a sound,
    A love not in the heart but in the eye;
A love that ebbs and flows, now up, now down,
A morning's favour and an evening's frown.

veet looks show love, yet they are but as beams;
Fair words seem true, yet they are but as wind;
res shed their tears, yet are but outward streams;
Sighs paint a shadow in the falsest mind.
ooks, words, tears, sighs, show love when love they
    leave,
lse hearts can weep, sigh, swear, and yet deceive.
                                            Anon.

CCXVII

LOVE UNALTERABLE

T me not to the marriage of true minds
lmit impediments.   Love is not love
hich alters when it alteration finds,
 bends with the remover to remove:

 no! it is an ever-fixèd mark,
lat looks on tempests and is never shaken;
is the star to every wand'ring bark,
hose worth's unknown, although his height be
    taken.

ve's not Time's fool, though rosy lips and cheeks
ithin his bending sickle's compass come;
ve alters not with his brief hours and weeks,
it bears it out even to the edge of doom:—

this be error and upon me proved,
lever writ, nor no man ever loved.
                                       Shakespeare.

N

CCXVIII

FAST FAITH

Dear, if you change, I'll never choose again;
Sweet, if you shrink, I'll never think of love;
Fair, if you fail, I'll judge all beauty vain;
Wise, if too weak, more wits I'll never prove.
Dear, sweet, fair, wise! change, shrink, nor be not
    weak;
And, on my faith, my faith shall never break.

Earth with her flowers shall sooner heaven adorn;
Heaven her bright stars through earth's dim globe
    shall move:
Fire heat shall lose, and frost of flames be born;
Air, made to shine, as black as hell shall prove:
Earth, heaven, fire, air, the world transform'd shall
    view,
Ere I prove false to faith or strange to you.

Anon.

CCXIX

MONTANUS' VOW

First shall the heavens want starry light,
The seas be robbèd of their waves;
The day want sun, the sun want bright,
The night want shade and dead men graves;
    The April, flowers and leaf and tree,
    Before I false my faith to thee.

First shall the tops of highest hills
By humble plains be overpry'd;
And poets scorn the Muses' quills,
And fish forsake the water-glide;
    And Iris lose her colour'd weed
    Before I fail thee at thy need.

First direful Hate shall turn to Peace,
And Love relent in deep disdain;
And Death his fatal stroke shall cease,
And Envy pity every pain;
    And Pleasure mourn, and Sorrow smile,
    Before I talk of any guile.

First Time shall stay his stayless race,
And Winter bless his brows with corn;
And snow bemoisten July's face,
And Winter spring and Summer mourn,
    Before my pen by help of Fame
    Cease to recite thy sacred name.

T. Lodge.

ccxx

LOVE OMNIPRESENT

Turn I my looks unto the skies,
Love with his arrows wounds mine eyes;
If so I gaze upon the ground,
Love then in every flower is found:
Search I the shade to fly my pain,
He meets me in the shade again;

Wend I to walk in secret grove,
Ev'n there I meet with sacred Love;
If so I bain me in the spring,
Ev'n on the bank I hear him sing;
If so I meditate alone,
He will be partner of my moan;
If so I mourn, he weeps with me,
And where I am there he will be.

T. Lodge.

CCXXI

WERE I as base as is the lowly plain,
And you, my Love, as high as heaven above,
Yet should the thoughts of me, your humble swain,
Ascend to heaven in honour of my Love.

Were I as high as heaven above the plain,
And you, my Love, as humble and as low
As are the deepest bottoms of the main,
Whereso'er you were, with you my love should go.

Were you the earth, dear Love, and I the skies,
My love should shine on you like to the Sun,
And look upon you with ten thousand eyes
Till heaven wax'd blind, and till the world were
    done.

Whereso'er I am,—below, or else above you—
Whereso'er you are, my heart shall truly love you.

Joshua Sylvester.

CCXXII

TO ANTHEA, WHO MAY COMMAND HIM ANYTHING

Bɪᴅ me to live, and I will live
　　Thy Protestant to be,
Or bid me love, and I will give
　　A loving heart to thee.

A heart as soft, a heart as kind,
　　A heart as sound and free
As in the whole world thou canst find,
　　That heart I'll give to thee.

Bid that heart stay, and it will stay
　　To honour thy decree :
Or bid it languish quite away,
　　And 't shall do so for thee.

Bid me to weep, and I will weep
　　While I have eyes to see :
And, having none, yet will I keep
　　A heart to weep for thee.

Bid me despair, and I'll despair
　　Under that cypress-tree :
Or bid me die, and I will dare
　　E'en death to die for thee.

Thou art my life, my love, my heart,
　　The very eyes of me :
And hast command of every part
　　To live and die for thee.　　　　*Herrick.*

CCXXIII

Like as a ship, that through the Ocean wide
By conduct of some star doth make her way,
Whenas a storm hath dimm'd her trusty guide,
Out of her course doth wander far astray:

So I—whose star, that wont with her bright ray
Me to direct, with clouds is overcast—
Do wander now in darkness and dismay
Through hidden perils round about me placed.

Yet hope I well that when this storm is past,
My *Helice*, the lodestar of my life,
Will shine again and look on me at last,
With lovely light to clear my cloudy grief.

Till then I wander careful, comfortless,
In secret sorrow and sad pensiveness.

Spenser.

CCXXIV

THE PATIENT LOVER

Though I be scorn'd, yet will I not disdain,
  But bend my thoughts fair beauty to adore;
What though she smile when I sigh and complain?
  It is, I know, to try my faith the more:
      For she is fair, and fairness is regarded;
      And I am firm, firm love will be rewarded.

Suppose I love and languish to my end,
  And she my plaints, my sighs, my tears despise:

O 'tis enough, when Fates for me do send,
If she vouchsafe to close my dying eyes;
    —Which if she do, and chance to drop a tear,
From death to life that balm will me uprear.

Anon.

CCXXV

THE HONEST PEDLAR

Fine knacks for ladies! cheap, choice, brave, and new,
    Good pennyworths,—but money cannot move:
I keep a fair but for the Fair to view,—
    A beggar may be liberal of love.
Though all my wares be trash, the heart is true,
                        The heart is true.

Great gifts are guiles and look for gifts again;
    My trifles come as treasures from my mind:
It is a precious jewel to be plain;
    Sometimes in shell the orient'st pearls we find:—
Of others take a sheaf, of me a grain!
                        Of me a grain!

Anon.

CCXXVI

THE SILENT LOVER

Passions are liken'd best to floods and streams:
    The shallow murmur, but the deep are dumb;
So, when affection yields discourse, it seems
    The bottom is but shallow whence they come.
They that are rich in words, in words discover
That they are poor in that which makes a lover.

Wrong not, sweet empress of my heart,
   The merit of true passion,
With thinking that he feels no smart,
   That sues for no compassion.

Silence in love bewrays more woe
   Than words, though ne'er so witty;
A beggar that is dumb, you know,
   May challenge double pity.

Then wrong not, dearest to my heart,
   My true, though secret passion:
He smarteth most that hides his smart,
   And sues for no compassion.

                              Sir W. Raleigh.

CCXXVII

THE FULL LOVE IS HUSHED

My love is strengthen'd, though more weak in
      seeming;
I love not less, though less the show appear:
That love is merchandised whose rich esteeming
The owner's tongue doth publish everywhere.

Our love was new, and then but in the spring,
When I was wont to greet it with my lays;
As Philomel in summer's front doth sing
And stops her pipe in growth of riper days:

Not that the summer is less pleasant now
Than when her mournful hymns did hush the night,
But that wild music burthens every bough,
And sweets grown common lose their dear delight.

Therefore, like her, I sometimes hold my tongue,
Because I would not dull you with my song.

Shakespeare.

CCXXVIII

ABSENCE

1

How like a winter hath my absence been
From thee, the pleasure of the fleeting year !
What freezings have I felt, what dark days seen,
What old December's bareness everywhere !

And yet this time removed was summer's time ;
The teeming autumn, big with rich increase,
Bearing the wanton burden of the prime
Like widow'd wombs after their lord's decease :

Yet this abundant issue seem'd to me
But hope of orphans and unfather'd fruit ;
For summer and his pleasures wait on thee,
And, thou away, the very birds are mute :

Or if they sing, 'tis with so dull a cheer
The leaves look pale, dreading the winter's near.

Shakespeare.

CCXXIX

2

From you have I been absent in the spring,
When proud-pied April, dress'd in all his trim,
Hath put a spirit of youth in everything,
That heavy Saturn laugh'd and leap'd with him.

Yet nor the lays of birds, nor the sweet smell
Of different flowers in odour and in hue,
Could make me any summer's story tell,
Or from their proud lap pluck them where they
　　grew:

Nor did I wonder at the lily's white,
Nor praise the deep vermilion of the rose;
They were but sweet, but figures of delight,
Drawn after you, you pattern of all those.

Yet seem'd it winter still, and, you away,
As with your shadow I with these did play.
　　　　　　　　　　　　Shakespeare.

CCXXX

3

The forward violet thus did I chide:
Sweet thief, whence didst thou steal thy sweet that
　　smells,
If not from my love's breath?　The purple pride,
Which on thy soft cheek for complexion dwells,

In my love's veins thou hast too grossly dyed.
The lily I condemnèd for thy hand
And buds of marjoram had stolen thy hair ;
The roses fearfully on thorns did stand,
One blushing shame, another white despair ;

A third, nor red nor white, had stolen of both,
And to his robbery had annex'd thy breath ;
But, for his theft, in pride of all his growth
A vengeful canker ate him up to death.

More flowers I noted ; yet I none could see
But sweet or colour it had stolen from thee.

Shakespeare.

CCXXXI

LOVE IN HARBOUR

Sweet, come again !
    Your happy sight, so much desired
    Since you from hence are now retired
I seek in vain :
Still must I mourn
    And pine in longing pain
    Till you, my life's delight, again
Vouchsafe your wish'd return !

If true desire,
    Or faithful vow of endless love,
    Thy heart inflamed may kindly move
With equal fire ;

O then my joys,
  So long distraught, shall rest
  Reposèd soft in thy chaste breast,
Exempt from all annoys.

You had the power
  My wand'ring thoughts first to restrain,
  You first did hear my love speak plain;
A child before,
Now it is grown
  Confirm'd, do you it keep:
  And let 't safe in your bosom sleep,
There ever made your own!
T. Campion.

CCXXXII

That Time and absence proves,
Rather helps than hurts to loves.

ABSENCE, hear thou my protestation,
  Against thy strength,
  Distance and length:
Do what thou can for alteration,
  For hearts of truest mettle
  Absence doth join and time doth settle.

Who loves a mistress of such quality,
  He soon hath found
  Affection's ground
Beyond time, place, and all mortality.
  To hearts that cannot vary
  Absence is present, Time doth tarry.

My senses want their outward motions
    Which now within
    Reason doth win,
Redoubled in her secret notions :
    Like rich men that take pleasure
    In hiding more than handling treasure.

By absence this good means I gain,
    That I can catch her
    Where none doth watch her,
In some close corner of my brain :
    There I embrace and kiss her,
    And so I both enjoy and miss her.

J. Donne.

CCXXXIII

Sweet love, renew thy force : be it not said
Thine edge shall blunter be than appetite,
Which but to-day by feeding is allay'd,
To-morrow sharpen'd in his former might :

So, love, be thou : although to-day thou fill
Thy hungry eyes even till they wink with fulness,
To-morrow see again, and do not kill
The spirit of love with a perpetual dulness.

Let this sad interim like the ocean be
Which parts the shore, where two contracted new
Come daily to the banks, that, when they see
Return of love, more bless'd may be the view :

Or call it winter, which, being full of care,
Makes summer's welcome thrice more wish'd, more
    rare.
                   Shakespeare.

CCXXXIV

BEING your slave, what should I do but tend
Upon the hours and times of your desire ?
I have no precious time at all to spend,
Nor services to do, till you require.

Nor dare I chide the world-without-end hour
Whilst I, my sovereign, watch the clock for you,
Nor think the bitterness of absence sour
When you have bid your servant once adieu :

Nor dare I question with my jealous thought
Where you may be, or your affairs suppose,
But, like a sad slave, stay and think of nought
Save, where you are how happy you make those !

So true a fool is love, that in your will
Though you do any thing, he thinks no ill.
                   Shakespeare.

CCXXXV

COMPLAINT OF THE ABSENCE OF HER LOVER BEING UPON THE SEA

O HAPPY dames ! that may embrace
    The fruit of your delight,
Help to bewail the woful case
    And eke the heavy plight

Of me that wonted to rejoice
The fortune of my pleasant choice :
Good ladies, help to fill my mourning voice.

In ship, freight with rememberance
  Of thoughts and pleasures past,
He sails that hath in governance
  My life while it will last :
With scalding sighs, for lack of gale,
Furthering his hope, that is his sail,
Toward me, the sweet port of his avail.

Alas ! how oft in dreams I see
  Those eyes that were my food ;
Which sometime so delighted me,
  That yet they do me good :
Wherewith I wake with his return
Whose absent flame did make me burn :
But when I find the lack, Lord ! how I mourn !

When other lovers in arms across
  Rejoice their chief delight,
Drownèd in tears, to mourn my loss
  I stand the bitter night
In my window where I may see
Before the winds how the clouds flee :
Lo ! what a mariner love hath made me !

And in green waves when the salt flood
  Doth rise by rage of wind,
A thousand fancies in that mood
  Assail my restless mind.

Alas! now drencheth [1] my sweet foe,
That with the spoil of my heart did go,
And left me; but alas! why did he so?

And when the seas wax calm again
    To chase from me annoy,
My doubtful hope doth cause me plain;
    So dread cuts off my joy.
Thus is my wealth mingled with woe
And of each thought a doubt doth grow;
—Now he comes! Will he come? Alas! no, no.

Earl of Surrey.

CCXXXVI

VALEDICTION, FORBIDDING MOURNING

As virtuous men pass mildly away,
    And whisper to their souls to go;
While some of their sad friends do say,
    Now his breath goes, and some say, No;

So let us melt, and make no noise,
    No tear-floods nor sigh-tempests move;
'Twere profanation of our joys
    To tell the laity our love.

Moving of th' earth brings harms and fears,
    Men reckon what it did and meant;
But trepidations of the spheres,
    Though greater far, are innocent.

[1] *i.e.* is drenched or drowned.

Dull sublunary lovers' love,
　　Whose soul is sense, cannot admit
Absence ; for that it doth remove
　　Those things which elemented it.

But we, by a love so far refined,
　　That ourselves know not what it is,
Inter-assurèd of the mind,
　　Careless, eyes, lips and hands to miss,

—Our two souls therefore, which are one,
　　Though I must go, endure not yet
A breach, but an expansion,
　　Like gold to airy thinness beat.

If they be two, they are two so
　　As stiff twin compasses are two ;
Thy soul, the fixt foot, makes no show
　　To move, but doth if th' other do.

And though it in the centre sit,
　　Yet when the other far doth roam,
It leans and hearkens after it,
　　And grows erect as that comes home.

Such wilt thou be to me, who must,
　　Like th' other foot, obliquely run ;
Thy firmness makes my circles just,
　　And makes me end where I begun.

J. Donne.

o

CCXXXVII

THE GREAT ADVENTURE

As careful merchants do expecting stand,
  After long time and merry gales of wind,
Upon the place where their brave ship must land :
  So wait I for the vessel of my mind.

Upon a great adventure it is bound,
  Whose safe return will valued be at more
Than all the wealthy prizes which have crown'd
  The golden wishes of an age before.

Out of the East jewels of worth she brings;
  Th' unvalued diamond of her sparkling eye
Wants [1] in the treasures of all Europe's kings;
  And were it mine, they nor their crowns should buy.

The sapphires ringèd on her panting breast
  Run as rich veins of ore about the mould,
And are in sickness with a pale possess'd,
  So true, for them I should disvalue gold.

The melting rubies on her cherry lip
  Are of such power to hold, that as one day
Cupid flew thirsty by, he stoop'd to sip,
  And fasten'd there could never get away.

[1] Is lacking.

The sweets of Candy are no sweets to me
  When hers I taste; nor the perfumes of price,
Robb'd from the happy shrubs of Arabye,
  As her sweet breath so powerful to entice.

O hasten then! and if thou be not gone
  Unto that wishèd traffic through the main,
My powerful sighs shall quickly drive thee on,
  And then begin to draw thee back again.

If in the mean rude waves have it oppress'd
It shall suffice I ventured at the best.
Wm. Browne.

CCXXXVIII

AN ECSTASY

E'EN like two little bank-dividing brooks,
  That wash the pebbles with their wanton streams,
And having ranged and search'd a thousand nooks,
  Meet both at length in silver-breasted Thames,
    Where in a greater current they conjoin:
So I my Best-belovèd's am; so He is mine.

E'en so we met; and after long pursuit,
  E'en so we joined; we both became entire;
No need for either to renew a suit,
  For I was flax, and He was flames of fire:
    Our firm-united souls did more than twine;
So I my Best-belovèd's am; so He is mine.

If all those glittering Monarchs, that command
　　The servile quarters of this earthly ball,
Should tender in exchange their shares of land,
　　I would not change my fortunes for them all :
　　　Their wealth is but a counter to my coin :
The world's but theirs ; but my Belovèd's mine.

F. Quarles.

CCXXXIX

THE TRIUMPH

See the Chariot at hand here of Love,
　　Wherein my Lady rideth !
Each that draws is a swan or a dove,
　　And well the car Love guideth.
As she goes, all hearts do duty
　　　　Unto her beauty ;
And enamour'd do wish, so they might
　　　　But enjoy such a sight,
That they still were to run by her side,
Through swords, through seas, whither she would ride.

Do but look on her eyes, they do light
　　All that Love's world compriseth !
Do but look on her hair, it is bright
　　As Love's star when it riseth !
Do but mark—her forehead's smoother
　　　　Than words that soothe her ;

And from her arch'd brows, such a grace
        Sheds itself through the face,
As alone there triumphs to the life
All the gain, all the good, of the elements' strife.

Have you seen but a bright lily grow
    Before rude hands have touch'd it?
Have you marked but the fall of the snow
    Before the soil hath smutch'd it?
Have you felt the wool of the beaver,
        Or swan's down ever?
Or have smelt o' the bud o' the brier,
        Or the nard in the fire?
Or have tasted the bag of the bee?
O so white, O so soft, O so sweet is she!

                    B. Jonson.

CCXL

BRIDAL SONG

Roses, their sharp spines being gone,
Not royal in their smells alone,
    But in their hue;
Maiden pinks, of odour faint,
Daisies smell-less, yet most quaint,
    And sweet thyme true;

Primrose, firstborn child of Ver;
Merry springtime's harbinger,
    With her bells dim;

Oxlips in their cradles growing,
Marigolds on deathbeds blowing,
   Larks'-heels trim.

All dear Nature's children sweet
Lie 'fore bride and bridegroom's feet,
   Blessing their sense !
Not an angel of the air,
Bird melodious or bird fair,
   Be absent hence !

The crow, the slanderous cuckoo, nor
The boding raven, nor chough hoar,
   Nor chattering pye,
May on our bridehouse perch or sing,
Or with them any discord bring,
   But from it fly !

Shakespeare (?).

CCXLI

BRIDAL SONG

Now hath Flora robb'd her bowers
To befriend this place with flowers :
   Strow about, strow about !
The sky rain'd never kindlier showers.
Flowers with bridals well agree,
Fresh as brides and bridegrooms be :
   Strow about, strow about,

And mix them with fit melody!
Earth hath no princelier flowers
Than roses white and roses red,
But they must still be mingled:
And as a rose new pluckt from Venus' thorn,
So doth a bride her bridegroom's bed adorn.

Divers divers flowers affect
For some private dear respect:
    Strow about, strow about!
Let every one his own protect;
But he's none of Flora's friend
That will not the rose commend:
    Strow about, strow about!
Let princes princely flowers defend:
Roses, the garden's pride,
Are flowers for love and flowers for kings,
In courts desirèd and weddings:
And as a rose in Venus' bosom worn,
So doth a bridegroom his bride's bed adorn.
                    T. Campion.

CCXLII

FAR ABOVE RUBIES

WHAT is it all that men possess, among themselves
    conversing?
Wealth, or fame, or some such boast, scarce worthy
    the rehearsing:
Women only are men's good, with them in love con-
    versing.

If weary, they prepare us rest; if sick, their hand
    attends us;
When with grief our hearts are press'd, their com-
    fort best befriends us;
Sweet or sour, they willing go to share what fortune
    sends us.

What pretty babes with pains they bear, our name
    and form presenting!
What we get how wise they keep, by sparing wants
    preventing!
Sorting all their household cares to our observed
    contenting!

All this, of whose large use I sing, in two words is
    expressèd:
Good Wife is the good I praise, if by good men
    possessèd.
Bad with bad in ill suit well, but good with good
    live blessèd.

T. Campion.

CCXLIII

A LULLABY

Upon my lap my sovereign sits
And sucks upon my breast;
Meantime his love maintains my life
And gives my sense her rest.
    Sing lullaby, my little boy,
    Sing lullaby, mine only joy!

When thou hast taken thy repast,
Repose, my babe, on me ;
So may thy mother and thy nurse
Thy cradle also be.
    Sing lullaby, my little boy,
    Sing lullaby, mine only joy !

I grieve that duty doth not work
All that my wishing would ;
Because I would not be to thee
But in the best I should.
    Sing lullaby, my little boy,
    Sing lullaby, mine only joy !

Yet as I am, and as I may,
I must and will be thine,
Though all too little for thyself
Vouchsafing to be mine.
    Sing lullaby, my little boy,
    Sing lullaby, mine only joy !

Anon.

CCXLIV

SEPHESTIA'S SONG TO HER CHILD

WEEP not, my wanton, smile upon my knee ;
When thou art old there 's grief enough for thee.
    Mother's wag, pretty boy,
    Father's sorrow, father's joy ;

When thy father first did see
Such a boy by him and me,
He was glad, I was woe;
Fortune changèd made him so,
When he left his pretty boy,
Last his sorrow, first his joy.

Weep not, my wanton, smile upon my knee;
When thou art old there's grief enough for thee.
Streaming tears that never stint,
Like pearl-drops from a flint,
Fell by course from his eyes,
That one another's place supplies;
Thus he griev'd in every part,
Tears of blood fell from his heart,
When he left his pretty boy,
Father's sorrow, father's joy.

Weep not, my wanton, smile upon my knee;
When thou art old there's grief enough for thee.
The wanton smiled, father wept,
Mother cried, baby leapt;
More he crow'd, more we cried,
Nature could not sorrow hide:
He must go, he must kiss
Child and mother, baby bless,
For he left his pretty boy,
Father's sorrow, father's joy.
Weep not, my wanton, smile upon my knee,
When thou art old there's grief enough for thee.

R. Greene.

CCXLV

A CRADLE SONG

Come little babe, come silly soul,
Thy father's shame, thy mother's grief,
Born as I doubt to all our dole,
And to thyself unhappy chief:
    Sing lullaby, and lap it warm,
    Poor soul that thinks no creature harm.

Thou little think'st and less dost know
The cause of this thy mother's moan;
Thou want'st the wit to wail her woe,
And I myself am all alone:
    Why dost thou weep? why dost thou wail?
    And knowest not yet what thou dost ail.

Come little wretch—ah, silly heart!
Mine only joy, what can I more?
If there be any wrong thy smart,
That may the destinies implore:
    'Twas I, I say, against my will,
    I wail the time, but be thou still.

And dost thou smile? O, thy sweet face!
Would God Himself He might thee see!—
No doubt thou wouldst soon purchase grace,
I know right well, for thee and me:
    But come to mother, babe, and play,
    For father false is fled away.

Sweet boy, if it by fortune chance
Thy father home again to send,
If death do strike me with his lance,
Yet mayst thou me to him commend :
    If any ask thy mother's name,
    Tell how by love she purchased blame.

Then will his gentle heart soon yield :
I know him of a gentle mind :
Although a lion in the field,
A lamb in town thou shalt him find :
    Ask blessing, babe, be not afraid,
    His sugar'd words hath me betray'd.

Then mayst thou joy and be right glad ;
Although in woe I seem to moan,
Thy father is no rascal lad,
A noble youth of blood and bone :
    His glancing looks, if he once smile,
    Right honest women may beguile.

Come little boy and rock asleep,
Sing lullaby and be thou still ;
I, that can do naught else but weep,
Will sit by thee and wail my fill :
    God bless my babe, and lullaby
    From this thy father's quality.

N. Breton.

CCXLVI

WALY WALY, LOVE BE BONNY

O WALY waly up the bank,
　And waly waly down the brae,
And waly waly yon burnside
　Where I and my Love wont to gae !
I leant my back unto an aik,
　I thought it was a trusty tree;
But first it bow'd and syne it brak,
　Sae my true Love did lightly me.

O waly waly, gin love be bonny
　A little time while it is new;
But when 'tis auld, it waxeth cauld,
　And fades awa' like morning dew.
O wherefore should I busk my head?
　Or wherefore should I kame my hair?
For my true Love has me forsook,
　And says he 'll never love me mair.

Now Arthur Seat sall be my bed;
　The sheets shall ne'er be 'filed[1] by me:
Saint Anton's Well sall be my drink,
　Since my true Love has forsaken me.
Marti'mas wind, when wilt thou blaw
　And shake the green leaves aff the tree?
O gentle Death, when wilt thou come?
　For of my life I am wearie.

[1] Defiled. ·

'Tis not the frost, that freezes fell,
   Nor blawing snaw's inclemencie;
'Tis not sic cauld that makes me cry,
   But my Love's heart grown cauld to me.
When we came in by Glasgow town
   We were a comely sight to see;
My love was clad in the black velvèt,
   And I mysell in cramasie.[1]

But had I wist, before I kist,
   That love had been sae ill tae win;
I had lockt my heart in a case of gowd,
   And pinn'd it with a siller pin.
And O! if my young babe were born,
   And set upon the nurse's knee,
And I myself were dead and gane,
   And the green grass growing over me!

Anon.

CCXLVII

OPHELIA SINGS

How should I your true love know
   From another one?
By his cockle hat and staff,
   And his sandal shoon.

[1] Crimson.

He is dead and gone, lady,
  He is dead and gone ;
At his head a grass-green turf,
  At his heels a stone.

White his shroud as the mountain snow,
  Larded with sweet flowers,
Which bewept to the grave did go
  With true-love showers.

Shakespeare.

CCXLVIII

ASPATIA'S SONG

Lay a garland on my hearse
  Of the dismal yew ;
Maidens, willow branches bear ;
  Say, I died true.

My love was false, but I was firm
  From my hour of birth.
Upon my buried body lie
  Lightly, gentle earth !

J. Fletcher.

CCXLIX

THE MAD MAID'S SONG

Good-morrow to the day so fair,
  Good-morrow, sir, to you ;
Good-morrow to mine own torn hair
  Bedabbled with the dew.

Good-morning to this primrose too,
　Good-morrow to each maid
That will with flowers the tomb bestrew
　Wherein my love is laid.

Ah ! woe is me, woe, woe is me,
　Alack and well-a-day !
For pity, sir, find out that bee
　Which bore my love away.

I 'll seek him in your bonnet brave,
　I 'll seek him in your eyes ;
Nay, now I think they 've made his grave
　I' th' bed of strawberries.

I 'll seek him there ; I know ere this
　The cold, cold earth doth shake him ;
But I will go or send a kiss
　By you, sir, to awake him.

Pray hurt him not ; though he be dead,
　He knows well who do love him,
And who with green turfs rear his head,
　And who do rudely move him.

He 's soft and tender (pray take heed) ;
　With bands of cowslips bind him,
And bring him home ; but 'tis decreed
　That I shall never find him.

Herrick.

CCL

SIGH NO MORE, LADIES

Sigh no more, ladies, sigh no more;
　Men were deceivers ever;
One foot in sea, and one on shore,
　To one thing constant never.
　　　Then sigh not so,
　　　But let them go,
　And be you blithe and bonny,
Converting all your sounds of woe
　Into Hey nonny, nonny.

Sing no more ditties, sing no moe,
　Of dumps so dull and heavy;
The fraud of men was ever so,
　Since summer first was leafy.
　　　Then sigh not so,
　　　But let them go,
　And be you blithe and bonny,
Converting all your sounds of woe
　Into Hey nonny, nonny.

Shakespeare.

P

CCLI

TAKE, O TAKE THOSE LIPS AWAY

TAKE, O take those lips away,
　　That so sweetly were forsworn;
And those eyes, the break of day,
　　Lights that do mislead the morn:
But my kisses bring again,
　　　　　Bring again;
Seals of love, but seal'd in vain,
　　　　　Seal'd in vain!

Shakespeare.

CCLII

A LEAVE-TAKING

HARDEN now thy tirèd heart with more than flinty
　　rage!
Ne'er let her false tears henceforth thy constant
　　grief assuage!
Once true happy days thou saw'st when she stood
　　firm and kind,
Both as one then lived and held one ear, one tongue,
　　one mind:
But now those bright hours be fled, and never may
　　return;
What then remains but her untruths to mourn?

Silly traitress, who shall now thy careless tresses
　　place?
Who thy pretty talk supply, whose ear thy music
　　grace?

Who shall thy bright eyes admire? What lips
　　triumph with thine?
Day by day who 'll visit thee and say 'Th' art only
　　mine'?
Such a time there was, God wot; but such can
　　never be:
Too oft, I fear, thou wilt remember me.

T. Campion.

CCLIII

FAREWELL, FALSE LOVE!

Away, delights ! go seek some other dwelling,
　　　　For I must die.
Farewell, false love ! thy tongue is ever telling
　　　　Lie after lie.
For ever let me rest now from thy smarts ;
　　　　Alas, for pity go
　　　　And fire their hearts
That have been hard to thee ! Mine was not so.

Never again deluding love shall know me,
　　　　For I will die ;
And all those griefs, that think to overgrow me,
　　　　Shall be as I :
For ever will I sleep, while poor maids cry—
　　　　' Alas, for pity stay,
　　　　And let us die
With thee ! Men cannot mock us in the clay.'

J. Fletcher.

CCLIV

AN EARNEST SUIT TO HIS UNKIND MISTRESS, NOT TO FORSAKE HIM

AND wilt thou leave me thus?
Say nay, say nay, for shame!
—To save thee from the blame
Of all my grief and grame.[1]
And wilt thou leave me thus?
    Say nay! say nay !

And wilt thou leave me thus,
That hath loved thee so long
In wealth and woe among:
And is thy heart so strong
As for to leave me thus?
    Say nay! say nay!

And wilt thou leave me thus,
That hath given thee my heart
Never for to depart
Neither for pain nor smart:
And wilt thou leave me thus?
    Say nay! say nay!

And wilt thou leave me thus,
And have no more pitye
Of him that loveth thee?
Alas, thy cruelty!
And wilt thou leave me thus?
    Say nay! say nay!

Sir Thomas Wyat.

[1] Sorrow.

CCLV

THE RECALL OF LOVE

FAREWELL ! thou art too dear for my possessing,
And like enough thou know'st thy estimate :
The charter of thy worth gives thee releasing ;
My bonds in thee are all determinate.

For how do I hold thee but by thy granting ?
And for that riches where is my deserving ?
The cause of this fair gift in me is wanting,
And so my patent back again is swerving.

Thyself thou gav'st, thy own worth then not knowing,
Or me, to whom thou gav'st it, else mistaking ;
So thy great gift, upon misprision growing,
Comes home again, on better judgment making.

Thus have I had thee as a dream doth flatter,
In sleep a king ; but waking, no such matter.

Shakespeare.

CCLVI

THE PARTING

SINCE there 's no help, come let us kiss and part—
Nay, I have done, you get no more of me ;
And I am glad, yea, glad with all my heart,
That thus so cleanly I myself can free ;

Shake hands for ever, cancel all our vows,
And when we meet at any time again,
Be it not seen in either of our brows
That we one jot of former love retain.

Now at the last gasp of Love's latest breath,
When, his pulse failing, Passion speechless lies,
When Faith is kneeling by his bed of death,
And Innocence is closing up her eyes,

—Now if thou wouldst, when all have given him
    over,
From death to life thou mightst him yet recover.
                                        M. Drayton.

CCLVII

THEN hate me when thou wilt; if ever, now;
Now, while the world is bent my deeds to cross,
Join with the spite of fortune, make me bow,
And do not drop in for an after-loss:

Ah! do not, when my heart hath 'scaped this sorrow,
Come in the rearward of a conquer'd woe;
Give not a windy night a rainy morrow,
To linger out a purposed overthrow.

If thou wilt leave me, do not leave me last,
When other petty griefs have done their spite,
But in the onset come: so shall I taste
At first the very worst of fortune's might;

And other strains of woe, which now seem woe,
Compared with loss of thee will not seem so!
                                        Shakespeare.

CCLVIII

FORGET

No longer mourn for me when I am dead
Than you shall hear the surly sullen bell
Give warning to the world that I am fled
From this vile world, with vilest worms to dwell:

Nay, if you read this line, remember not
The hand that writ it; for I love you so,
That I in your sweet thoughts would be forgot
If thinking on me then should make you woe.

O if, I say, you look upon this verse,
When I perhaps compounded am with clay,
Do not so much as my poor name rehearse,
But let your love even with my life decay;

Lest the wise world should look into your moan,
And mock you with me after I am gone.

Shakespeare.

CCLIX

THE FUNERAL

Whoever comes to shroud me, do not harm
    Nor question much
That subtle wreath of hair about mine arm;
The mystery, the sign you must not touch,
    For 'tis my outward soul,
Viceroy to that which, unto heav'n being gone,
    Will leave this to control
And keep these limbs, her provinces, from dissolution.

For if the sinewy thread my brain lets fall
      Through every part
Can tie those parts, and make me one of all;
Those hairs, which upward grow, and strength and art
      Have from a better brain,
Can better do't: except she meant that I
      By this should know my pain,
As prisoners then are manacled, when they're com-
    demn'd to die.

Whate'er she meant by't, bury it with me,
      For since I am
Love's martyr, it might breed idolatry
If into other hands these reliques came.
      As 'twas humility
T' afford to it all that a soul can do,
      So 'tis some bravery
That, since you would have none of me, I bury some
    of you.

J. Donne.

CCLX

DAPHNAIDA

AN ELEGY

How happy was I when I saw her lead
The shepherd's daughters dancing in a round!
How trimly would she trace and softly tread
The tender grass, with rosy garland crown'd!
And when she list advance her heavenly voice,
Both Nymphs and Muses nigh she made astown'd
And flocks and shepherds caused to rejoice.

But now, ye shepherd lasses, who shall lead
Your wandering troops, or sing your virelays?
Or who shall dight your bow'rs, sith she is dead
That was the Lady of your holy days?
Let now your bliss be turnèd into bale,
And into plaints convert your joyous plays,
And with the same fill every hill and dale.

But I will walk this wandering pilgrimage
Throughout the world from one to other end,
And in affliction waste my better age:
My bread shall be the anguish of my mind,
My drink the tears which fro' mine eyes do rain,
My bed the ground that hardest I may find;
So will I wilfully increase my pain.

Ne sleep (the harbinger of weary wights)
Shall ever lodge upon mine eye-lids more;
Ne shall with rest refresh my fainting sprights,
Nor failing force to former strength restore:
But I will wake and sorrow all the night
With Philomene, my fortune to deplore,
—With Philomene, the partner of my plight.

And ever as I see the star to fall,
And underground to go to give them light
Which dwell in darkness, I to mind will call
How my fair star, that shined on me so bright,
Fell suddenly and faded underground;
Since whose departure day is turn'd to night,
And night without a Venus star is found.

And she,—my Love that was, my Saint that is,—
When she beholds from her celestial throne,
In which she joyeth in eternal bliss,
My bitter penance, will my case bemoan,
And pity me that living thus do die;
For heavenly spirits have compassion
On mortal men, and rue their misery.

So when I have with sorrow satisfied
Th' importune Fates, which vengeance on me seek,
And th' Heavens with long languor pacified,
She, for pure pity of my sufferance meek,
Will send for me: for which I daily long:
And will till then my painful penance eke.
Weep, shepherd, weepe, to make my undersong?

Spenser.

CCLXI

GONE IS THE FLOWER OF FLOWERS

When thou from earth didst pass,
Sweet nymph, perfection's mirror broken was,
And this of late so glorious world of ours,
   Like meadow without flowers,
Or ring of a rich gem made blind, appear'd;
Or night, by star nor Cynthia neither cleared.
   Love when he saw thee die
Entomb'd him in the lid of either eye,
And left his torch within thy sacred urn,
   There for a lamp to burn.
Worth, honour, pleasure, with thy life expired,
Death since, grown sweet, begins to be desired.

That zephyr every year
So soon was heard to sigh in forests here,
It was for her: that wrapp'd in gowns of green
   Meads were so early seen,
That in the saddest months oft sung the merles,
It was for her; for her trees dropp'd forth pearls.
   That proud and stately courts
Did envy those our shades and calm resorts,
It was for her; and she is gone, O woe!
   Woods cut again do grow,
Bud doth the rose and daisy, winter done;
But we, once dead, no more do see the sun.

Drummond of Hawthornden.

CCLXII

SPRING DESOLATE

Sweet Spring, thou turn'st with all thy goodly train,
Thy head with flames, thy mantle bright with
      flow'rs:
The zephyrs curl the green locks of the plain,
The clouds for joy in pearls weep down their
      show'rs.

Thou turn'st, sweet youth, but ah! my pleasant
      hours
And happy days with thee come not again;
The sad memorials only of my pain
Do with thee turn, which turn my sweets in sours.

Thou art the same which still thou wast before,
Delicious, wanton, amiable, fair;
But she, whose breath embalm'd thy wholesome air,
Is gone—nor gold nor gems her can restore.

Neglected virtue, seasons go and come,
While thine forgot lie closèd in a tomb.

Drummond of Hawthornden.

CCLXIII

TO HIS LUTE

My lute, be as thou wast when thou didst grow
With thy green mother in some shady grove,
When immelodious winds but made thee move,
And birds on thee their ramage[1] did bestow.

Sith that dear voice which did thy sounds approve,
Which wont in such harmonious strains to flow,
Is reft from earth to tune those spheres above,
What art thou but an harbinger of woe?

Thy pleasing notes be pleasing notes no more,
But orphan wailings to the fainting ear;
Each stop a sigh, each sound draws forth a tear;
Be therefore silent as in woods before:

Or if that any hand to touch thee deign,
Like widow'd turtle, still her loss complain.

Drummond of Hawthornden.

---

[1] Music of the bough, woodland song.

CCLXIV

FIDELE

FEAR no more the heat o' the sun,
    Nor the furious winter's rages;
Thou thy worldly task hast done,
    Home art gone, and ta'en thy wages:
Golden lads and girls all must,
As chimney-sweepers, come to dust.

Fear no more the frown o' the great,
    Thou art past the tyrant's stroke;
Care no more to clothe and eat;
    To thee the reed is as the oak:
The sceptre, learning, physic, must
All follow this, and come to dust.

Fear no more the lightning-flash,
    Nor the all-dreaded thunder-stone;
Fear not slander, censure rash;
    Thou hast finish'd joy and moan:
All lovers young, all lovers must
Consign to thee, and come to dust.

No exorciser harm thee!
Nor no witchcraft charm thee!
Ghost unlaid forbear thee!
Nothing ill come near thee!
Quiet consummation have;
And renownèd be thy grave!

Shakespeare.

CCLXV

IDLE TEARS

WEEP no more, nor sigh, nor groan
Sorrow calls no time that 's gone:
Violets pluck'd, the sweetest rain
Makes not fresh nor grow again;
Trim thy locks, look cheerfully;
Fate's hid ends eyes cannot see;
Joy as wingèd dreams fly past,
Why should sadness longer last?
Grief is but a wound to woe;
Gentlest fair, mourn, mourn no moe.

J. Fletcher

CCLXVI

MARINA 's gone, and now sit I
   As Philomela—on a thorn,
Turn'd out of nature's livery—
   Mirthless, alone, and all forlorn:
Only she sings not, while my sorrows can
Breathe forth such notes as fit a dying swan

So shuts the marigold her leaves
   At the departure of the sun;
So from the honeysuckle sheaves
   The bee goes when the day is done;
So sits the turtle when she is but one,
And so all woe, as I, now she is gone.

To some few birds kind Nature hath
  Made all the summer as one day ;
Which once enjoy'd, cold winter's wrath,
  As night, they sleeping pass away.
Those happy creatures are, that know not yet
The pain to be deprived or to forget.

Wm. Browne.

CCLXVII

COMFORT TO A YOUTH THAT HAD LOST HIS LOVE

WHAT needs complaints,
When she a place
Has with the race
  Of saints ?

In endless mirth
She thinks not on
What's said or done
  In Earth.

She sees no tears,
Or any tone
Of thy deep groan
  She hears :

Nor does she mind
Or think on 't now
That ever thou
  Wast kind ;

But changed above,
She likes not there,
As she did here,
Thy love.

Forbear therefore,
And lull asleep
Thy woes, and weep
No more.

Herrick.

CCLXVIII

LET NO BIRD SING!

GLIDE soft, ye silver floods,
And every spring:
Within the shady woods
Let no bird sing!
Nor from the grove a turtle-dove
Be seen to couple with her love;
But silence on each dale and mountain dwell,
Whilst Willy bids his friend and joy farewell.

But of great Thetis' train,
Ye mermaids fair,
That on the shores do plain [1]
Your sea-green hair,
As ye in trammels knit your locks,
Weep ye; and so enforce the rocks
In heavy murmurs through the broad shores tell
How Willy bade his friend and joy farewell.

[1] Smooth.

Cease, cease, ye murdering winds,
    To move a wave ;
But if with troubled minds
    You seek his grave,
Know 'tis as various as yourselves,
Now in the deep, then on the shelves,
His coffin toss'd by fish and surges fell,
Whilst Willy weeps and bids all joy farewell.

Had he Arion-like
    Been judged to drown,
He on his lute could strike
    So rare a sown,
A thousand dolphins would have come
And jointly strove to bring him home.
But he on shipboard died, by sickness fell,
Since when his Willy bade all joy farewell.

Great Neptune, hear a swain !
    His coffin take,
And with a golden chain
    For pity make
It fast unto a rock near land !
Where every calmy morn I 'll stand,
And ere one sheep out of my fold I tell,
Sad Willy's pipe shall bid his friend farewell.

Wm. Browne.

CCLXIX

THE NOBLE BALM

HIGH-SPIRITED friend,
I send nor balms nor cor'sives to your wound:
Your fate hath found
A gentler and more agile hand to tend
The cure of that which is but corporal;
And doubtful days, which were named critical,
Have made their fairest flight
And now are out of sight.
Yet doth some wholesome physic for the mind
Wrapped in this paper lie,
Which in the taking if you misapply,
You are unkind.

Your covetous hand,
Happy in that fair honour it hath gain'd,
Must now be rein'd.
True valour doth her own renown command
In one full action; nor have you now more
To do, than be a husband of that store.
Think but how dear you bought
This same which you have caught—
Such thoughts will make you more in love with truth.
'Tis wisdom, and that high,
For men to use their fortune reverently,
Even in youth.

B. Jonson.

CCLXX

A LOVER'S LULLABY

Sɪɴɢ lullaby, as women do,
   Wherewith they bring their babes to rest;
And lullaby can I sing too,
   As womanly as can the best.
With lullaby they still the child;
And if I be not much beguiled,
Full many a wanton babe have I,
Which must be still'd with lullaby.

First lullaby my youthful years,
   It is now time to go to bed:
For crookèd age and hoary hairs
   Have won the haven within my head.
With lullaby, then, youth be still;
With lullaby content thy will;
Since courage quails and comes behind,
Go sleep, and so beguile thy mind!

Next lullaby my gazing eyes,
   Which wonted were to glance apace;
For every glass may now suffice
   To show the furrows in thy face.
With lullaby then wink awhile;
With lullaby your looks beguile;
Let no fair face, nor beauty bright,
Entice you eft with vain delight.

And lullaby my wanton will;
　　Let reason's rule now reign thy thought;
Since all too late I find by skill
　　How dear I have thy fancies bought;
With lullaby now take thine ease,
With lullaby thy doubts appease;
For trust to this, if thou be still,
My body shall obey thy will.

Thus lullaby my youth, mine eyes,
　　My will, my ware, and all that was:
I can no more delays devise;
　　But welcome pain, let pleasure pass.
With lullaby now take your leave;
With lullaby your dreams deceive;
And when you rise with waking eye,
Remember then this lullaby.

Geo. Gascoigne.

CCLXXI

LINES WRITTEN ON A GARDEN SEAT

If thou sit here to view this pleasant garden place,
Think thus—At last will come a frost and all these
　　flowers deface:
But if thou sit at ease to rest thy weary bones,
Remember death brings final rest to all our grievous
　　groans;
So whether for delight, or here thou sit for ease,
Think still upon the latter day: so shalt thou God
　　best please.

Geo. Gascoigne.

CCLXXII

VIXI PUELLIS NUPER IDONEUS . . .

They flee from me that sometime did me seek,
   With naked foot stalking within my chamber:
Once have I seen them gentle, tame, and meek,
   That now are wild, and do not once remember
That sometime they have put themselves in danger
To take bread at my hand; and now they range,
   Busily seeking in continual change.

Thanked be fortune, it hath been otherwise
   Twenty times better; but once especial.—
In thin array: after a pleasant guise,
   When her long gown did from her shoulders fall,
And she me caught in her arms long and small,
And therewithal so sweetly did me kiss,
   And softly said, '*Dear heart, how like you this?*'

It was no dream; for I lay broad awaking:
   But all is turn'd now, through my gentleness,
Into a bitter fashion of forsaking;
   And I have leave to go of her goodness;
And she also to use new-fangleness.
But since that I unkindly so am servèd,
'*How like you this?*'—what hath she now deservèd?
Sir Thomas Wyat.

CHIDIOCK TICHBORNE'S LAMENT

My prime of youth is but a frost of cares ;
　My feast of joy is but a dish of pain ;
My crop of corn is but a field of tares ;
　And all my good is but vain hope of gain ;
The day is fled, and yet I saw no sun ;
And now I live, and now my life is done !

The spring is past, and yet it hath not sprung ;
　The fruit is dead, and yet the leaves be green ;
My youth is gone, and yet I am but young ;
　I saw the world, and yet I was not seen ;
My thread is cut, and yet it is not spun ;
And now I live, and now my life is done !

I sought my death, and found it in my womb ;
　I look'd for life, and saw it was a shade ;
I trod the earth, and knew it was my tomb ;
　And now I die, and now I am but made ;
The glass is full, and now my glass is run ;
And now I live, and now my life is done.

Chidiock Tichborne.

HER AUTUMN

1

When I do count the clock that tells the time,
And see the brave day sunk in hideous night ;
When I behold the violet past prime,
And sable curls all silver'd o'er with white ;

When lofty trees I see barren of leaves,
Which erst from heat did canopy the herd,
And summer's green, all girded up in sheaves,
Borne on the bier with white and bristly beard;

Then of thy beauty do I question make,
That thou among the wastes of time must go,
Since sweets and beauties do themselves forsake
And die as fast as they see others grow;

And nothing 'gainst Time's scythe can make defence
Save breed, to brave him when he takes thee hence.
Shakespeare.

CCLXXV

2

To me, fair friend, you never can be old;
For as you were when first your eye I eyed,
Such seems your beauty still.   Three winters cold
Have from the forests shook three summers' pride;

Three beauteous springs to yellow autumn turn'd
In process of the seasons have I seen,
Three April perfumes in three hot Junes burn'd,
Since first I saw you fresh, which yet are green.

Ah! yet doth beauty, like a dial-hand,
Steal from his figure, and no pace perceived;
So your sweet hue, which methinks still doth stand,
Hath motion, and mine eye may be deceived:

For fear of which, hear this, thou age unbred:
Ere you were born was beauty's summer dead.
Shakespeare.

CCLXXVI

TO MEADOWS

Yᴇ have been fresh and green,
  Ye have been fill'd with flowers,
And ye the walks have been
  Where maids have spent their hours.

You have beheld how they
  With wicker arks did come
To kiss and bear away
  The richer cowslips home.

You've heard them sweetly sing,
  And seen them in a round:
Each virgin like a spring,
  With honeysuckles crown'd.

But now we see none here
  Whose silvery feet did tread
And with dishevell'd hair
  Adorn'd this smoother mead.

Like unthrifts, having spent
  Your stock and needy grown,
You're left here to lament
  Your poor estates, alone.

Herrick.

CCLXXVII

BRIGHT SOUL OF THE SAD YEAR

Fair summer droops, droop men and beasts therefore,
So fair a summer look for never more:
All good things vanish less than in a day,
Peace, plenty, pleasure suddenly decay.
    Go not yet away, bright soul of the sad year,
    The earth is hell when thou leav'st to appear.

What, shall those flowers, that deck'd thy garland
    erst,
Upon thy grave be wastefully dispersed?
O trees, consume your sap in sorrow's source,
Streams, turn to tears your tributary course.
    Go not yet hence, bright soul of the sad year,
    The earth is hell when thou leav'st to appear.
T. Nashe.

CCLXXVIII

IN TIME OF PLAGUE

Adieu, farewell earth's bliss,
This world uncertain is:
Fond are life's lustful joys,
Death proves them all but toys.
None from his darts can fly:
I am sick, I must die—
    Lord have mercy on us !

Rich men, trust not in wealth,
Gold cannot buy you health ;
Physic himself must fade ;
All things to end are made ;
The plague full swift goes by ;
I am sick, I must die—
        Lord have mercy on us !

Beauty is but a flower
Which wrinkles will devour :
Brightness falls from the air ;
Queens have died young and fair ;
Dust hath closed Helen's eye :
I am sick, I must die—
        Lord have mercy on us !

Strength stoops unto the grave,
Worms feed on Hector brave :
Swords may not fight with fate :
Earth still holds ope her gate.
Come, come ! the bells do cry :
I am sick, I must die—
        Lord have mercy on us !

Wit with his wantonness
Tasteth death's bitterness :
Hell's executioner
Hath no ears for to hear
What vain art can reply ;
I am sick, I must die—
        Lord have mercy on us !

Haste therefore each degree
To welcome destiny :
Heaven is our heritage,
Earth but a player's stage.
Mount we unto the sky :
I am sick, I must die—
    Lord have mercy on us !
              T. Nashe.

CCLXXIX

EMBERS

That time of year thou may'st in me behold
When yellow leaves, or none, or few, do hang
Upon those boughs which shake against the cold,—
Bare ruin'd choirs where late the sweet birds sang.

In me thou see'st the twilight of such day
As after sunset fadeth in the west,
Which by and by black night doth take away,
Death's second self, that seals up all in rest.

In me thou see'st the glowing of such fire
That on the ashes of his youth doth lie,
As the death-bed whereon it must expire,
Consumed with that which it was nourish'd by.

This thou perceiv'st, which makes thy love more
    strong,
To love that well which thou must leave ere long.
              Shakespeare.

CCLXXX

A FAREWELL TO ARMS

(TO QUEEN ELIZABETH)

His golden locks time hath to silver turn'd;
  O time too swift, O swiftness never ceasing!
His youth 'gainst time and age hath ever spurn'd,
  But spurn'd in vain; youth waneth by increasing:
Beauty, strength, youth are flowers but fading
    seen;
Duty, faith, love are roots, and ever green.

His helmet now shall make a hive for bees;
  And, lovers' sonnets turn'd to holy psalms,
A man-at-arms must now serve on his knees,
  And feed on prayers, which are age his alms:
But though from court to cottage he depart,
His Saint is sure of his unspotted heart.

And when he saddest sits in homely cell,
  He'll teach his swains this carol for a song,—
'Blest be the hearts that wish my sovereign well,
  Curst be the souls that think her any wrong.'
Goddess, allow this aged man his right
To be your beadsman now that was your knight.

Geo. Peele.

CCLXXXI

WHEN THAT I WAS AND A LITTLE TINY BOY

WHEN that I was and a little tiny boy,
   With hey, ho, the wind and the rain;
A foolish thing was but a toy,
   For the rain it raineth every day.

But when I came to man's estate,
   With hey, ho, the wind and the rain;
'Gainst knaves and thieves men shut their gate,
   For the rain it raineth every day.

But when I came, alas! to wive,
   With hey, ho, the wind and the rain;
By swaggering could I never thrive,
   For the rain it raineth every day.

But when I came unto my beds,
   With hey, ho, the wind and the rain;
With toss-pots still had drunken heads,
   For the rain it raineth every day.

A great while ago the world begun,
   With hey, ho, the wind and the rain;
But that's all one, our play is done,
   And we'll strive to please you every day.

Shakespeare.

CCLXXXII

TIMES GO BY TURNS

THE loppèd tree in time may grow again,
Most naked plants renew both fruit and flower;
The sorest wight may find release of pain,
The driest soil suck in some moist'ning shower;
Times go by turns and chances change by course,
From foul to fair, from better hap to worse.

The sea of Fortune doth not ever flow,
She draws her favours to the lowest ebb;
Her time hath equal times to come and go,
Her loom doth weave the fine and coarsest web;
No joy so great but runneth to an end,
No hap so hard but may in fine amend.

Not always fall of leaf nor ever spring,
No endless night yet not eternal day;
The saddest birds a season find to sing,
The roughest storm a calm may soon allay:
Thus with succeeding turns God tempereth all,
That man may hope to rise, yet fear to fall.

A chance may win that by mischance was lost;
The well that holds no great, takes little fish;
In some things all, in all things none are cross'd,
Few all they need, but none have all they wish;
Unmeddled[1] joys here to no man befall:
Who least, hath some; who most, hath never all.

R. Southwell.

[1] Unmixed. Cf. p. 51, line 1.

CCLXXXIII

THE MERRY HEART

Jog on, jog on, the footpath way,
  And merrily hent the stile-a:
A merry heart goes all the day,
  Your sad tires in a mile-a.
Shakespeare.

CCLXXXIV

Laugh ! laugh ! laugh ! laugh !
  Wide, loud, and vary !
A smile is for a simpering novice,
  One that ne'er tasted caviare
Nor knows the smack of dear anchovies.
J. Fletcher.

CCLXXXV

ANACREONTIC

1

Come, thou monarch of the vine,
Plumpy Bacchus with pink eyne
In thy vats our cares be drown'd,
With thy grapes our hair be crown'd:
  Cup us till the world go round,
  Cup us till the world go round !
Shakespeare.

CCLXXXVI

2

God Lyaeus, ever young,
Ever honour'd, ever sung,
Stain'd with blood of lusty grapes,
In a thousand lusty shapes
Dance upon the mazer's[1] brim,
In the crimson liquor swim;
From thy plenteous hand divine
Let a river run with wine:
 God of youth, let this day here
 Enter neither care nor fear.

J. Fletcher.

CCLXXXVII

3

Born was I to be old
 And for to die here:
After that, in the mould
 Long for to lie here.
But before that day comes
 Still I be bouzing,
For I know in the tombs
 There 's no carousing.

Herrick.

[1] A bowl of maple-wood.

CCLXXXVIII

TROLL THE BOWL!

Cold's the wind, and wet's the rain,
Saint Hugh be our good speed !
Ill is the weather that bringeth no gain,
Nor helps good hearts in need.

Troll the bowl, the jolly nut-brown bowl,
And here's, kind mate, to thee !
Let's sing a dirge for Saint Hugh's soul,
And down it merrily.

T. Dekker.

CCLXXXIX

A RELIGIOUS USE OF TAKING TOBACCO

The Indian weed witherèd quite ;
Green at morn, cut down at night ;
Shows thy decay ; all flesh is hay :
    Thus think, then drink tobacco.

And when the smoke ascends on high,
Think thou beholds the vanity
Of worldly stuff ; gone with a puff :
    Thus think, then drink tobacco.

But when the pipe grows foul within,
Think of thy soul defiled with sin,
And that the fire doth it require :
    Thus think, then drink tobacco.

R

The ashes that are left behind,
May serve to put thee still in mind,
That unto dust return thou must :
Thus think, then drink tobacco.

Robert Wisdome.

CCXC

AMANTIUM IRAE

In going to my naked bed as one that would have slept,
I heard a wife sing to her child, that long before
     had wept ;
She sighèd sore and sang full sweet, to bring the
     babe to rest,
That would not cease but crièd still, in sucking at
     her breast.
She was full weary of her watch, and grievèd with
     her child,
She rockèd it and rated it, till that on her it smiled.
Then did she say, Now have I found this proverb
     true to prove,
The falling out of faithful friends renewing is of love.

Then took I paper, pen, and ink, this proverb for to
     write,
In register for to remain, of such a worthy wight :
As she proceeded thus in song unto her little brat,
Much matter utter'd she of weight, in place whereas
     she sat :
And provèd plain there was no beast, nor creature
     bearing life,
Could well be known to live in love without discord
     and strife :

Then kissèd she her little babe, and sware by God
    above,
The falling out of faithful friends renewing is of love.

She said that neither king nor prince nor lord could
    live aright,
Until their puissance they did prove, their manhood
    and their might.
When manhood shall be matchèd so that fear can
    take no place,
Then weary works make warriors each other to
    embrace,
And left their force that failèd them, which did
    consume the rout,
That might before have lived their time, their
    strength and nature out:
Then did she sing as one that thought no man
    could her reprove,
The falling out of faithful friends renewing is of love.

She said she saw no fish nor fowl, no beast within
    her haunt,
That met a stranger in their kind, but could give it
    a taunt:
Since flesh might not endure, but rest must wrath
    succeed,
And force the fight to fall to play in pasture where
    they feed,
So noble nature can well end the work she hath
    begun,
And bridle well that will not cease her tragedy in
    some:

Thus in song she oft rehearsed, as did her well behove,
The falling out of faithful friends renewing is of love.

I marvel much pardy (quoth she) for to behold the
    rout,
To see man, woman, boy, and beast, to toss the
    world about:
Some kneel, some crouch, some beck, some check,
    and some can smoothly smile,
And some embrace others in arm, and there think
    many awile,
Some stand aloof at cap and knee, some humble and
    some stout,
Yet are they never friends in deed until they once
    fall out;
Thus ended she her song and said, before she did
    remove,
The falling out of faithful friends renewing is of love.

Anon.

CCXCI

MYRA

I, with whose colours Myra dress'd her head,
    I, that wore posies of her own hand-making,
I, that mine own name in the chimneys[1] read
    By Myra finely wrought ere I was waking:
Must I look on, in hope time coming may
With change bring back my turn again to play?

---

[1] *Cheminées*, chimney-screens of tapestry work.

I, that on Sunday at the church-stile found
  A garland sweet with true-love-knots in flowers,
Which I to wear about mine arms was bound
  That each of us might know that all was ours:
Must I lead now an idle life in wishes,
And follow Cupid for his waves and fishes?

I, that did wear the ring her mother left,
  I, for whose love she gloried to be blamed,
I, with whose eyes her eyes committed theft,
  I, who did make her blush when I was named:
Must I lose ring, flowers, blush, theft, and go naked,
Watching with sighs till dead love be awakèd?

Was it for this that I might Myra see
  Washing the water with her beauties white?
Yet would she never write her love to me.
  Thinks wit of change when thoughts are in delight!
Mad girls may safely love as they may leave;
No man can *print* a kiss: lines may deceive.[1]

               Fulke Greville, Lord Brooke.

CCXCII

A NOSEGAY

SAY, crimson Rose and dainty Daffodil,
  With Violet blue;
Since you have seen the beauty of my saint,
  And eke her view;

[1] Betray.

Did not her sight (fair sight !) you lonely fill,
     With sweet delight
Of goddess' grace and angels' sacred teint [1]
     In fine, most bright ?

Say, golden Primrose, sanguine Cowslip fair,
     With Pink most fine ;
Since you beheld the visage of my dear,
     And eyes divine ;
Did not her globy front, and glistening hair,
     With cheeks most sweet,
So gloriously like damask flowers appear,
     The gods to greet ?

Say, snow-white Lily, speckled Gilly-flower,
     With Daisy gay ;
Since you have viewed the Queen of my desire,
     In her array ;
Did not her ivory paps, fair Venus' bower,
     With heavenly glee,
A Juno's grace, conjure you to require
     Her face to see ?

Say Rose, say Daffodil, and Violet blue,
     With Primrose fair,
Since ye have seen my nymph's sweet dainty face,
     And gesture rare,
Did not (bright Cowslip, blooming Pink) her view
     (White Lily) shine—
(Ah, Gilly-flower, ah Daisy !) with a grace
     Like stars divine ?

John Reynolds.

Tint, hue.

CCXCIII

MY LADY GREENSLEEVES

Alas! my love, you do me wrong
　　To cast me off discourteously;
And I have lovèd you so long,
　　Delighting in your company.
For oh, Greensleeves was all my joy!
And oh, Greensleeves was my delight!
And oh, Greensleeves was my heart of gold!
　　And who but my Lady Greensleeves!

I bought thee petticoats of the best,
　　The cloth as fine as might be;
I gave thee jewels for thy chest,
　　And all this cost I spent on thee.
　　　　　　For oh, Greensleeves . . .

Thy smock of silk, both fair and white,
　　With gold embroider'd gorgeously:
Thy petticoat of sendal right:
　　And these I bought thee gladly.
　　　　　　For oh, Greensleeves . . .

Greensleeves now farewell! adieu!
　　God I pray to prosper thee!
For I am still thy lover true:
　　Come once again and love me!
　　　　　　For oh, Greensleeves . . .

Anon.

CCXCIV

A NOBLE SUIT

THOUGH beauty be the mark of praise,
   And yours of whom I sing be such
   As not the world can praise too much,
Yet 'tis your Virtue now I raise.

A virtue, like allay [1] so gone
   Throughout your form as, though that move
   And draw and conquer all men's love,
This subjects you to love of one.

Wherein you triumph yet,—because
   'Tis of your flesh, and that you use
   The noblest freedom, not to choose
Against or faith or honour's laws.

But who should less expect from you?—
   In whom alone Love lives again:
   By whom he is restored to men,
And kept and bred and brought up true.

His falling temples you have rear'd,
   The wither'd garlands ta'en away;
   His altars kept from that decay
That envy wish'd, and nature fear'd:

[1] Alloy.

And on them burn so chaste a flame,
  With so much loyalty's expense,
  As Love to acquit such excellence
Is gone himself into your name.—

And you are he,—the deity
  To whom all lovers are design'd
  That would their better objects find;
Among which faithful troop am I

—Who as an off'ring [1] at your shrine
  Have sung this hymn, and here entreat
  One spark of your diviner heat
To light upon a love of mine.

Which if it kindle not, but scant
  Appear, and that to shortest view,
  Yet give me leave to adore in you
What I in her am grieved to want!

B. Jonson.

CCXCV

BEYOND

O no, Belov'd : I am most sure
  These virtuous habits we acquire
  As being with the soul entire
Must with it evermore endure.

---

[1] Old editions—' off-spring.'

Else should our souls in vain elect;
   And vainer yet were Heaven's laws,
   When to an everlasting cause
They give a perishing effect.

These eyes again thine eyes shall see,
   These hands again thine hand enfold,
   And all chaste blessings can be told
Shall with us everlasting be.

For if no use of sense remain
   When bodies once this life forsake,
   Or they could no delight partake,
Why should they ever rise again?

And if ev'ry imperfect mind
   Make love the end of knowledge here,
   How perfect will our love be where
All imperfection is refined!

So when from hence we shall be gone,
   And be no more nor you or I;
   As one another's mystery
Each shall be both, yet both but one.

            Edward, Lord Herbert of Cherbury.

CCXCVI

FOR SOLDIERS

YE buds of Brutus' land,[1] courageous youths, now
   play your parts;
Unto your tackle stand, abide the brunt with valiant
   hearts.

---

[1] 'Scions of England' held of mythical descent from Brute, or
Brutus.

For news is carried to and fro, that we must forth to
    warfare go :
Men muster now in every place, and soldiers are
    prest forth apace.
Faint not, spend blood, to do your Queen and
    country good ;
Fair words, good pay, will make men cast all care
    away.

The time of war is come, prepare your corslet,
    spear and shield ;
Methinks I hear the drum strike doleful marches to
    the field ;
Tantara, tantara, ye trumpets sound, which makes
    our hearts with joy abound.
The roaring guns are heard afar, and everything
    denounceth war.
Serve God ; stand stout ; bold courage brings this
    gear about ;
Fear not ; fate run ; faint heart fair lady never won.

Ye curious [1] carpet-knights, that spend the time in
    sport and play ;
Abroad and see new sights, your country's cause calls
    you away ;
Do not to make your ladies' game, bring blemish to
    your worthy name.
Away to field and win renown, with courage beat
    your enemies down.

[1] Dainty.

Stout hearts gain praise, when dastards sail in
　　Slander's seas:
Hap what hap shall, we sure shall die but once for
　　all.

Alarm methinks they cry, Be packing, mates; begone
　　with speed ;
Our foes are very nigh ; shame have that man that
　　shrinks at need,
Unto it boldly let us stand, God will give Right the
　　upper hand.
Our cause is good, we need not doubt, in sign of
　　coming give a shout.
March forth, be strong, good hap will come ere it
　　be long.
Shrink not, fight well, for lusty lads must bear the
　　bell.

All you that will shun evil, must dwell in warfare
　　every day ;
The world, the flesh, and devil, always do seek our
　　soul's decay.
Strive with these foes with all your might, so shall
　　you fight a worthy fight.
That conquest doth deserve most praise, where vice
　　do yield to virtue's ways.
Beat down foul sin, a worthy crown then shall ye
　　win ;
If ye live well, in heaven with Christ our souls shall
　　dwell.

Humfrey Gifford.

CCXCVII

A SONG FOR PRIESTS

O WEARISOME condition of humanity!
  Born under one law, to another bound;
Vainly begot, and yet forbidden vanity;
  Created sick, commanded to be sound:
    —What meaneth Nature by these diverse laws?
    Passion and Reason self-division cause.

Is it the mark or majesty of power
  To make offences that it may forgive?
Nature herself doth her own self deflower,
  To hate those errors she herself doth give.
    But how should Man think that he may not do,
    If Nature did not fail and punish too?

Tyrant to others, to herself unjust,
  Only commands things difficult and hard.
Forbids us all things which it knows we lust;
  Makes easy pains, impossible reward.
    If Nature did not take delight in blood,
    She would have made more easy ways to good.

We that are bound by vows, and by promotion,
  With pomp of holy sacrifice and rites,
To lead belief in good and 'stil[1] devotion.
  To preach of Heaven's wonders and delights;
    Yet when each of us in his own heart looks,
    He finds the God there far unlike his books
              Fulke Greville, Lord Brooke.

[1] Instil.

CCXCVIII

THE LIFE OF MAN

1

LIKE to the falling of a star,
Or as the flights of eagles are,
Or like the fresh spring's gaudy hue,
Or silver drops of morning dew,
Or like the wind that chafes the flood,
Or bubbles which on water stood:
Even such is Man, whose borrow'd light
Is straight call'd in and paid to night.

The wind blows out; the bubble dies;
The spring entomb'd in autumn lies;
The dew 's dry'd up; the star is shot;
The flight is past; and man forgot.
Henry King.

CCXCIX

2

THE World 's a bubble; and the life of Man
    Less than a span:
In his conception wretched—from the womb
    So to the tomb;
Curst from his cradle, and brought up to years
    With cares and fears.
Who then to frail mortality shall trust
But limns on water, or but writes in dust.

Yet whilst with sorrow here we live opprest,
    What life is best?
Courts are but only superficial schools
    To dandle fools;
The rural part is turn'd into a den
    Of savage men;
And where's the city from foul vice so free
But may be term'd the worst of all the three?

Domestic cares afflict the husband's bed,
    Or pains his head:
Those that live single take it for a curse,
    Or do things worse:
These would have children; those that have them
    moan,
    Or wish them gone:
What is it then, to have, or have no wife,
But single thraldom, or a double strife?

Our own affections still at home to please,
    Is a disease;
To cross the seas to any foreign soil,
    Peril and toil;
Wars with their noise affright us: when they
    cease,
    We're worse in peace:
—What then remains, but that we still should
    cry
For being born, or, being born, to die?

                        Francis, Lord Bacon.

CCC

3

This life, which seems so fair,
Is like a bubble blown up in the air
By sporting children's breath,
Who chase it everywhere
And strive who can most motion it bequeath.
And though it sometime seem of its own might
Like to an eye of gold to be fix'd there,
And firm to hover in that empty height,
That only is because it is so light.
—But in that pomp it doth not long appear;
For e'en when most admired, it in a thought,
As swell'd from nothing, doth dissolve in naught.

Drummond of Hawthornden.

CCCI

INEXORABLE DEATH

My thoughts hold mortal strife;
I do detest my life,
And with lamenting cries
Peace to my soul to bring
Oft call that prince which here doth monarchise:
—But he, grim-grinning King,
Who caitiffs scorns, and doth the blest surprise,
Late having deck'd with beauty's rose his tomb,
Disdains to crop a weed, and will not come.

Drummond of Hawthornden.

CCCII

OF MISERY

Corpse,[1] clad with carefulness;
Heart, heap'd with heaviness;
Purse, poor and penniless;
Back bare in bitterness;
O get my grave in readiness;
Fain would I die to end this stress.

Thomas Howell.

CCCIII

A PASSION

Happy were he could finish forth his fate
In some unhaunted desert, where, obscure
From all society, from love and hate
Of worldly folk, there might he sleep secure;

Then wake again, and ever give God praise;
Content with hips, with haws, with bramble-berry;
In contemplation spending still his days,
And change of holy thoughts to make him merry:

Where, when he dies, his tomb may be a bush,
Where harmless robin dwells with gentle thrush:
    —Happy were he!

R. Devereux, Earl of Essex.

[1] Body.

CCCIV

THE CHARACTER OF A HAPPY LIFE

How happy is he born and taught
That serveth not another's will;
Whose armour is his honest thought,
And simple truth his utmost skill!

Whose passions not his masters are;
Whose soul is still prepared for death,
Untied unto the world by care
Of public fame or private breath;

Who envies none that chance doth raise,
Nor vice; who never understood
How deepest wounds are given by praise;
Nor rules of state, but rules of good;

Who hath his life from rumours freed;
Whose conscience is his strong retreat;
Whose state can neither flatterers feed,
Nor ruin make oppressors great;

Who God doth late and early pray
More of His grace than gifts to lend;
And entertains the harmless day
With a religious book or friend;

—This man is freed from servile bands
Of hope to rise or fear to fall:
Lord of himself, though not of lands,
And having nothing, yet hath all.

Sir H. Wotton.

cccv

MY MIND A KINGDOM

My mind to me a kingdom is;
 Such present joys therein I find,
That it excels all other bliss
 That earth affords or grows by kind :
Though much I want that most would have,
Yet still my mind forbids to crave.

No princely pomp, no wealthy store,
 No force to win the victory,
No wily wit to salve a sore,
 No shape to feed a loving eye ;
To none of these I yield as thrall ;
For why? my mind doth serve for all.

I see how plenty surfeits oft,
 And hasty climbers soon do fall ;
I see that those which are aloft
 Mishap doth threaten most of all :
They get with toil, they keep with fear :
Such cares my mind could never bear.

Content I live, this is my stay ;
 I seek no more than may suffice ;
I press to bear no haughty sway ;
 Look, what I lack my mind supplies.
Lo, thus I triumph like a king,
· Content with that my mind doth bring.

Some have too much, yet still do crave;
    I little have, and seek no more.
They are but poor, though much they have,
    And I am rich with little store;
They poor, I rich; they beg, I give;
They lack, I leave; they pine, I live.

I laugh not at another's loss,
    I grudge not at another's gain;
No worldly waves my mind can toss;
    My state at one doth still remain:
I fear no foe, I fawn no friend;
I loathe not life, nor dread my end.

Some weigh their pleasure by their lust,
    Their wisdom by their rage of will;
Their treasure is their only trust,
    A cloakèd craft their store of skill:
But all the pleasure that I find
Is to maintain a quiet mind.

My wealth is health and perfect ease,
    My conscience clear my chief defence;
I neither seek by bribes to please,
    Nor by deceit to breed offence:
Thus do I live; thus will I die;
Would all did so as well as I!

Sir E. Dyer.

CCCVI

It is not growing like a tree,
  In bulk, doth make man better be;
Or standing long an oak, three hundred year,
To fall a log at last, dry, bald and sere:
    A lily of a day
    Is fairer far in May:
Although it fall and die that night,
  It was the plant and flower of light.
In small proportions we just beauties see;
And in short measures life may perfect be.

B. Jonson.

CCCVII

THE GENTLE MAN

Wise men patience never want,
  Good men pity cannot hide;
Feeble spirits only vaunt
  Of revenge, the poorest pride:
He alone, forgive that can,
Bears the true soul of a man.

Deeds from love, and words, that flow,
  Foster like kind April showers;
In the warm sun all things grow,
  Wholesome fruits and pleasant flowers:
All so thrives his gentle rays
Whereon human love displays.

T. Campion.

CCCVIII

INTEGER VITAE

THE man of life upright,
  Whose guiltless heart is free
From all dishonest deeds,
  Or thought of vanity;

The man whose silent days
  In harmless joys are spent,
Whom hopes cannot delude,
  Nor sorrow discontent;

That man needs neither towers
  Nor armour for defence,
Nor secret vaults to fly
  From thunder's violence:

He only can behold
  With unaffrighted eyes
The horrors of the deep
  And terrors of the skies.

Thus, scorning all the cares
  That fate or fortune brings,
He makes the heaven his book,
  His wisdom heavenly things;

Good thoughts his only friends,
  His wealth a well-spent age,
The earth his sober inn
  And quiet pilgrimage.

T. Campion.

MAN'S SERVICE

THE chief use then in Man of that he knows
　Is his pains-taking for the good of all;
Not fleshly weeping for our own made woes,
　Not laughing from a melancholy gall,
Not hating from a soul that overflows
　　With bitterness, breath'd out from inward thrall:
　　But sweetly rather to ease, loose, or bind,
　　As need requires, this frail, fall'n humankind.
Fulke Greville, Lord Brooke.

A WISH

ALL I can
My worldly strife shall be
They one day say of me
　' He died a good old man ':
On his sad soul a heavy burden lies
Who, known to all, unknown to himself dies.
Anon.

HIS WINDING-SHEET

COME thou, who art the wine and wit
　Of all I 've writ:
The grace, the glory, and the best
　Piece of the rest.

Thou art of what I did intend
    The all and end;
And what was made, was made to meet
    Thee, thee, my sheet.
Come then and be to my chaste side
    Both bed and bride:
We two, as reliques left, will have
    One rest, one grave:
And hugging close, we will not fear
    Lust entering here:
Where all desires are dead and cold
    As is the mould;
And all affections are forgot,
    Or trouble not.
Here, here, the slaves and prisoners be
    From shackles free:
And weeping widows long oppress'd
    Do here find rest.
The wrongèd client ends his laws
    Here, and his cause.
Here those long suits of Chancery lie
    Quiet, or die:
And all Star-Chamber bills do cease
    Or hold their peace.
Here needs no Court for our Request
    Where all are best,
All wise, all equal, and all just
    Alike i' th' dust.
Nor need we here to fear the frown
    Of court or crown:
Where fortune bears no sway o'er things,
    There all are kings.

In this securer place we 'll keep
As lull'd asleep;
Or for a little time we 'll lie
As robes laid by;
To be another day reworn,
Turn'd, but not torn;
Or like old testaments engross'd,
Lock'd up, not lost.
And for a while lie here conceal'd,
To be reveal'd
Next at the great Platonick year,[1]
And then meet here.

Herrick.

CCCXII

A SEA DIRGE

Full fathom five thy father lies;
Of his bones are coral made;
Those are pearls that were his eyes:
Nothing of him that doth fade,
But doth suffer a sea-change
Into something rich and strange.
Sea-nymphs hourly ring his knell:
Ding-dong.
Hark now I hear them,—
Ding-dong, bell!

Shakespeare.

[1] The 36,000th year, when all creation returns upon itself, and
begins a new cycle.

CCCXIII

A LAND DIRGE

CALL for the robin-redbreast and the wren,
Since o'er shady groves they hover,
And with leaves and flowers do cover
The friendless bodies of unburied men.
Call unto his funeral dole [1]
The ant, the field-mouse, and the mole,
To rear him hillocks that shall keep him warm,
And (when gay tombs are robb'd) sustain no harm;
But keep the wolf far hence, that's foe to men,
For with his nails he'll dig them up again.

J. Webster.

CCCXIV

THE SHROUDING OF THE DUCHESS OF MALFI

HARK!   Now everything is still,
The screech-owl and the whistler shrill,
Call upon our dame aloud,
And bid her quickly don her shroud!

Much you had of land and rent;
Your length in clay's now competent:
A long war disturb'd your mind;
Here your perfect peace is sign'd.

[1] Lamentation.

Of what is 't fools make such vain keeping ?—
Sin their conception, their birth weeping,
Their life a general mist of error,
Their death a hideous storm of terror.
Strew your hair with powders sweet,
Don clean linen, bathe your feet,
And—the foul fiend more to check—
A crucifix let bless your neck :
'Tis now full tide 'tween night and day ;
End your groan and come away.

J. Webster.

CCCXV

URNS AND ODOURS BRING AWAY !

Urns and odours bring away !
Vapours, sighs, darken the day !
Our dole[1] more deadly looks than dying ;
Balms and gums and heavy cheers,
Sacred vials filled with tears,
And clamours through the wild air flying !

Come, all sad and solemn shows,
That are quick-eyed Pleasure's foes !
We convent naught else but woes.

Shakespeare or *Fletcher.*

[1] See note opposite.

CCCXVI

VANITAS VANITATUM

ALL the flowers of the spring
Meet to perfume our burying;
These have but their growing prime,
And man does flourish but his time:
Survey our progress from our birth—
We are set, we grow, we turn to earth.
Courts adieu, and all delights,
All bewitching appetites!
Sweetest breath and clearest eye
Like perfumes go out and die;
And consequently this is done
As shadows wait upon the sun.
Vain the ambition of kings
Who seek by trophies and dead things
To leave a living name behind,
And weave but nets to catch the wind.

J. Webster.

CCCXVII

IN WESTMINSTER ABBEY

MORTALITY, behold and fear!
What a change of flesh is here!
Think how many royal bones
Sleep beneath this heap of stones!

Here they lie had realms and lands,
Who now want strength to stir their hands:
Here from their pulpits seal'd with dust
They preach, 'In greatness is no trust.'
Here is an acre sown indeed
With the richest, royall'st seed
That the earth did e'er suck in
Since the first man died for sin:
Here the bones of birth have cried,
'Though gods they were, as men they died!'
Here are sands, ignoble things,
Dropt from the ruin'd sides of kings;
Here 's a world of pomp and state,
Buried in dust, once dead by fate.

Francis Beaumont.

CCCXVIII

DEATH'S EMISSARIES

Victorious men of earth, no more
  Proclaim how wide your empires are;
Though you bind on every shore
  And your triumphs reach as far
      As night or day,
  Yet you, proud monarchs, must obey
And mingle with forgotten ashes, when
Death calls ye to the crowd of common men.

Devouring Famine, Plague, and War,
　Each able to undo mankind,
Death's servile emissaries are ;
　Nor to these alone confined,
　　He hath at will
　More quaint and subtle ways to kill ;
A smile or kiss, as he will use the art,
Shall have the cunning skill to break a heart.

James Shirley.

CCCXIX

DEATH THE LEVELLER

THE glories of our blood and state
　Are shadows, not substantial things ;
There is no armour against Fate ;
　Death lays his icy hand on kings :
　　　Sceptre and Crown
　　　Must tumble down,
And in the dust be equal made
With the poor crookèd scythe and spade.

Some men with swords may reap the field,
　And plant fresh laurels where they kill :
But their strong nerves at last must yield ;
　They tame but one another still :
　　　Early or late
　　　They stoop to fate,
And must give up their murmuring breath
When they, pale captives, creep to death.

The garlands wither on your brow ;
  Then boast no more your mighty deeds ;
Upon Death's purple altar now
  See where the victor-victim bleeds.
      Your heads must come
      To the cold tomb :
Only the actions of the just
Smell sweet and blossom in the dust.

James Shirley.

CCCXX

THE WIDOW

How near me came the hand of Death,
When at my side he struck my Dear,
And took away the precious breath
What quicken'd my belovèd peer[1] !
    How helpless am I thereby made !
    By day how grieved, by night how sad !
And now my life's delight is gone,
—Alas ! how I am left alone !

The voice which I did more esteem
Than music in her sweetest key,
Those eyes which unto me did seem
More comfortable than the day ;
    Those now by me, as they have been
    Shall never more be heard or seen ;
But what I once enjoy'd in them
Shall seem hereafter as a dream.

[1] Companion.

Lord ! keep me faithful to the trust
Which my dear spouse reposed in me :
To him now dead preserve me just
In all that should performèd be !
　　For though our being man and wife
　　Extendeth only to this life,
Yet neither life nor death shall end
The being of a faithful friend.

Geo. Wither.

CCCXXI

THE MOURNING DOVE

LIKE as the Culver[1] on the barèd bough
　Sits mourning for the absence of her mate ;
And in her song sends many a wishful vow
　For his return that seems to linger late.

So I alone now left disconsolate
　Mourn to myself the absence of my love :
And wand'ring here and there all desolate
　Seek with my plaints to match that mournful dove

Ne joy of aught that under heaven doth hove
　Can comfort me, but her own joyous sight
Whose sweet aspect both God and man can move
　In her unspotted pleasance to delight.

Dark is my day whiles her fair light I miss,
And dead my life that wants such lively bliss.

Spenser.

[1] Dove.

CCCXXII

THE PHŒNIX AND THE TURTLE

LET the bird of loudest lay
  On the sole Arabian tree,
  Herald sad and trumpet be
To whose sound chaste wings obey.

But thou shrieking harbinger,
  Foul precurrer of the fiend,
  Augur of the fever's end,
To this troop come thou not near.

From this session interdict
  Every fowl of tyrant wing
  Save the eagle, feathered king:
Keep the obsequy so strict.

Let the priest in surplice white
  That defunctive music can,[1]
  Be the death divining swan,
Lest the requiem lack his right.

And thou, treble-dated crow,
  That thy sable gender mak'st
  With the breath thou giv'st and tak'st,
'Mongst our mourners shalt thou go.

[1] Knows.

T

Here the anthem doth commence :—
　　Love and constancy is dead ;
　　Phœnix and the turtle fled
In a mutual flame from hence.

So they loved, as love in twain
　　Had the essence but in one ;
　　Two distincts, division none ;
Number there in love was slain.

Hearts remote, yet not asunder ;
　　Distance, and no space was seen
　　'Twixt the turtle and his queen :
But in them it were a wonder.

So beween them love did shine,
　　That the turtle saw his right
　　Flaming in the phœnix sight ;
Either was the other's mine.

Property was thus appall'd,
　　That the self was not the same ;
　　Single nature's double name
Neither two nor one was call'd.

Reason, in itself confounded,
　　Saw division grow together ;
　　To themselves yet either neither,
Simple were so well compounded.

That it cried, ' How true a twain
  Seemeth this concordant one !
  Love hath reason, reason none
If what parts can so remain.'

Whereupon it made this threne
  To the phœnix and the dove,
  Co-supremes and stars of love
As chorus to their tragic scene.

THRENOS

Beauty, truth, and rarity,
Grace in all simplicity,
Here enclosed in cinders lie.

Death is now the phœnix' nest ;
And the turtle's loyal breast
To eternity doth rest.

Leaving no posterity :
'Twas not their infirmity,
It was married chastity.

Truth may seem, but cannot be ;
Beauty brag, but 'tis not she ;
Truth and beauty buried be.

To this urn let those repair
That are either true or fair ;
For these dead birds sigh a prayer.

                    Shakespeare.

CCCXXIII

ON THE DEATH OF SIR PHILIP SIDNEY

Give pardon, blessèd soul, to my bold cries,
If they, importunate, interrupt the song
Which now, with joyful notes, thou sing'st among
The angel-choristers of heavenly skies.

Give pardon eke, sweet soul, to my slow eyes,
That since I saw thee now it is so long,
And yet the tears that unto thee belong
To thee as yet they did not sacrifice.

I did not know that thou wert dead before;
I did not feel the grief I did sustain;
The greater stroke astonisheth the more;
Astonishment takes from us sense of pain;

I stood amazed when others' tears begun,
And now begin to weep when they have done.

H. Constable.

CCCXXIV

UPON THE DEATH OF SIR ALBERTUS MORTON'S WIFE

He first deceased; she for a little tried
To live without him, liked it not, and died.

Sir H. Wotton.

CCCXXV

IN OBITUM M S, X° MAIJ, 1614

May!   Be thou never graced with birds that sing,
      Nor Flora's pride!
In thee all flowers and roses spring,
      Mine only died.

Wm. Browne.

CCCXXVI

AN EPITAPH ON THE COUNTESS DOWAGER OF PEMBROKE

Underneath this sable herse
Lies the subject of all verse :
Sidney's sister, Pembroke's mother :
Death, ere thou hast slain another
Fair and learn'd and good as she,
Time shall throw a dart at thee.

B. Jonson or *Wm. Browne.*

CCCXXVII

ON SALATHIEL PAVY

A CHILD OF QUEEN ELIZABETH'S CHAPEL

Weep with me, all you that read
      This little story ;
And know, for whom a tear you shed
      Death's self is sorry.

'Twas a child that so did thrive
　　In grace and feature,
As Heaven and Nature seem'd to strive
　　Which own'd the creature.
Years he number'd scarce thirteen
　　When Fates turn'd cruel,
Yet three fill'd zodiacs had he been
　　The stage's jewel;
And did act (what now we moan)
　　Old men so duly,
As sooth the Parcae thought him one,
　　He played so truly.
So, by error, to his fate
　　They all consented;
But, viewing him since, alas, too late!
　　They have repented;
And have sought, to give new birth,
　　In baths to steep him;
But, being so much too good for earth,
　　Heaven vows to keep him.

B. Jonson.

CCCXXVIII

ON THE LADY MARY VILLIERS

THE Lady *Mary Villiers* lies
Under this stone; with weeping eyes
The parents that first gave her birth,
And their sad friends, laid her in earth.

If any of them, Reader, were
Known unto thee, shed a tear ;
Or if thyself possess a gem
As dear to thee, as this to them,
Though a stranger to this place,
Bewail in theirs thine own hard case :
  For thou perhaps at thy return
  May'st find thy Darling in an urn.
T. Carew.

CCCXXIX

UPON A CHILD THAT DIED

Here she lies, a pretty bud,
Lately made of flesh and blood :
Who as soon fell fast asleep
As her little eyes did peep.
Give her strewings, but not stir
The earth that lightly covers her.
Herrick.

CCCXXX

ANOTHER

Here a pretty baby lies
Sung asleep with lullabies :
Pray be silent and not stir
Th' easy earth that covers her.
Herrick.

CCCXXXI

THE BURNING BABE

As I in hoary winter's night
  Stood shivering in the snow,
Surprised was I with sudden heat
  Which made my heart to glow;
And lifting up a fearful eye
  To view what fire was near,
A pretty babe all burning bright
  Did in the air appear;
Who, scorchèd with excessive heat,
  Such floods of tears did shed
As though His floods should quench His
      flames,
  Which with His tears were fed:
'Alas!' quoth He, 'but newly born
  In fiery heats I fry,
Yet none approach to warm their hearts
  Or feel my fire but I!

'My faultless breast the furnace is;
  The fuel, wounding thorns;
Love is the fire, and sighs the smoke;
  The ashes, shames and scorns;
The fuel Justice layeth on,
  And Mercy blows the coals,
The metal in this furnace wrought
  Are men's defilèd souls:

For which, as now on fire I am
  To work them to their good,
So will I melt into a bath,
  To wash them in my blood.'
With this He vanish'd out of sight
  And swiftly shrunk away,
And straight I callèd unto mind
  That it was Christmas Day.

R. Southwell.

CCCXXXII

A HYMN ON THE NATIVITY OF MY SAVIOUR

I sing the Birth was born to-night,
The Author both of life and light;
  The angels so did sound it,
And like the ravish'd shepherds said,
Who saw the light, and were afraid,
  Yet search'd, and true they found it.

The Son of God, th' eternal King,
That did us all salvation bring,
  And freed the soul from danger;
He whom the whole world could not take,
The Word, which heaven and earth did make,
  Was now laid in a manger.

The Father's wisdom will'd it so,
The Son's obedience knew no No,
    Both wills were in one stature;
And as that wisdom hath decreed,
The Word was now made flesh indeed,
    And took on him our nature.

What comfort by him do we win,
Who made himself the price of sin,
    To make us heirs of glory!
To see this Babe, all innocence;
A martyr born in our defence;
    Can man forget this story?

B. Jonson.

CCCXXXIII

A CHRISTMAS CAROL

Chorus

WHAT sweeter music can we bring
Than a carol for to sing
The birth of this our Heavenly King?
Awake the voice! awake the string!
Heart, ear, and eye, and everything
Awake! the while the active finger
Runs division with the singer.

From the Flourish they came to the Song.

1. Dark and dull night fly hence away!
   And give the honour to this day
   That sees December turn'd to May.

2. If we may ask the reason, say
The why and wherefore all things here
Seem like the spring-time of the year.

3. Why does the chilling winter's morn
Smile like a field beset with corn ?
Or smell like to a mead new shorn,
Thus on a sudden ?

4.   Come and see
The cause why things thus fragrant be :
'Tis He is born, whose quick'ning birth
Gives life and lustre, public mirth,
To heaven and the under-earth.

Chorus

We see Him come, and know him ours,
Who with his sunshine and his showers
Turns all the patient ground to flowers.

1. The darling of the world is come,
And fit it is we find a room
To welcome Him.

2.   The nobler part
Of all the house here is the heart,

Chorus

Which we will give Him ; and bequeath
This holly and this ivy wreath
To do Him honour, who's our King
And Lord of all this revelling.

Herrick.

CCCXXXIV

VERSES FROM THE SHEPHERDS' HYMN

WE saw Thee in Thy balmy nest,
  Young dawn of our eternal day;
We saw Thine eyes break from the East,
  And chase the trembling shades away:
We saw Thee, and we blest the sight,
We saw Thee by Thine own sweet light.

Poor world, said I, what wilt thou do
  To entertain this starry stranger?
Is this the best thou canst bestow—
  A cold and not too cleanly manger?
Contend, the powers of heaven and earth,
To fit a bed for this huge birth.

Proud world, said I, cease your contest,
  And let the mighty babe alone,
The phœnix builds the phœnix' nest,
  Love's architecture is His own.
The babe, whose birth embraves this morn,
Made His own bed ere He was born.

I saw the curl'd drops, soft and slow,
  Come hovering o'er the place's head,
Off'ring their whitest sheets of snow,
  To furnish the fair infant's bed.
Forbear, said I, be not too bold,
  Your fleece is white, but 'tis too cold.

I saw th' obsequious seraphim
   Their rosy fleece of fire bestow,
For well they now can spare their wings,
   Since Heaven itself lies here below.
Well done, said I ; but are you sure
Your down, so warm, will pass for pure ?

No, no, your King's not yet to seek
   Where to repose His royal head ;
See, see how soon His new-bloom'd cheek
   'Twixt mother's breasts is gone to bed.
Sweet choice, said we, no way but so,
Not to lie cold, yet sleep in snow !

She sings Thy tears asleep, and dips
   Her kisses in Thy weeping eye ;
She spreads the red leaves of Thy lips,
   That in their buds yet blushing lie.
She 'gainst those mother diamonds tries
The points of her young eagle's eyes.

Welcome—tho' not to those gay flies,
   Gilded i' th' beams of earthly beings,
Slippery souls in smiling eyes—
   But to poor shepherds, homespun things,
Whose wealth 's their flocks, whose wit 's to be
Well read in their simplicity.

Yet, when young April's husband show'rs
   Shall bless the fruitful Maia's bed,
We'll bring the first-born of her flowers,
   To kiss Thy feet and crown Thy head.

To Thee, dread Lamb! whose love must keep
The shepherds while they feed their sheep.

To Thee, meek Majesty, soft King
    Of simple graces and sweet loves!
Each of us his lamb will bring,
    Each his pair of silver doves!
At last, in fire of Thy fair eyes,
Ourselves become our own best sacrifice!

R. Crashaw.

CCCXXXV

TO HIS SAVIOUR, A CHILD: A PRESENT BY A CHILD

Go, pretty child, and bear this flower
Unto thy little Saviour;
And tell Him, by that bud now blown,
He is the Rose of Sharon known.
When thou hast said so, stick it there
Upon His bib or stomacher;
And tell Him for good handsel,[1] too,
That thou hast brought a whistle new,
Made of a clean straight oaten reed,
To charm His cries at time of need.
Tell Him, for coral, thou hast none,
But if thou hadst, He should have one;
And poor thou art, and known to be
Even as moneyless as He.

[1] Earnest money.

Lastly, if thou canst win a kiss
From those mellifluous lips of His ;
Then never take a second one,
To spoil the first impression.

Herrick.

CCCXXXVI

THE NEW YEAR'S GIFT

Let others look for pearl and gold,
Tissues or tabbies [1] manifold :
One only lock of that sweet hay
Whereon the blessèd baby lay,
Or one poor swaddling-clout, shall be
The richest New Year's gift for me.

Herrick.

CCCXXXVII

A CHILD'S GRACE

Here a little child I stand
Heaving up my either hand ;
Cold as paddocks [2] though they be,
Yet I lift them up to Thee,
For a benison to fall
On our meat and on us all.   Amen.

Herrick.

[1] Shot silks.   [2] Frogs.

CCCXXXVIII

THY KING COMETH

YET if His Majesty, our sovereign lord,
Should of his own accord
Friendly himself invite,
And say 'I 'll be your guest to-morrow night,'
How should we stir ourselves, call and command
All hands to work!   'Let no man idle stand.
Set me fine Spanish tables in the hall ;
See they be fitted all ;
Let there be room to eat
And order taken that there want no meat.
See every sconce and candlestick made bright,
That without tapers they may give a light.
Look to the presence : are the carpets spread,
The dazie o'er the head,
The cushions in the chairs,
And all the candles lighted on the stairs ?
Perfume the chambers, and, in any case,
Let each man give attendance in his place !'

Thus if a king were coming would we do ;
And 'twere good reason too ;
For 'tis a duteous thing
To show all honour to an earthly king,
And after all our travail and our cost,
So he be pleased, to think no labour lost.

But at the coming of the King of Heaven
All's set at six and seven ;
We wallow in our sin,
Christ cannot find a chamber in the inn.
We entertain Him always like a stranger,
And, as at first, still lodge Him in a manger.

Anon.

CCCXXXIX

CEREMONIES FOR CHRISTMAS

Come, bring with a noise,
   My merry, merry boys,
The Christmas log to the firing ;
   While my good dame, she
   Bids ye all be free
And drink to your heart's desiring.

With the last year's brand
   Light the new block, and
For good success in his spending
   On your psaltries play,
   That sweet luck may
Come while the log is a-teending.[1]

Drink now the strong beer,
   Cut the white loaf here ;
The while the meat is a-shredding
   For the rare mince-pie,
   And the plumes stand by
To fill the paste that's a-kneading.

Herrick.

---

[1] Kindling.

U

CCCXL

WINTER

WHEN icicles hang by the wall,
  And Dick the shepherd blows his nail,
And Tom bears logs into the hall,
  And milk comes frozen home in pail,
When blood is nipped, and ways be foul,
Then nightly sings the staring owl,
        To-whit;
To-who, a merry note,
While greasy Joan doth keel[1] the pot.

When all around the wind doth blow,
  And coughing drowns the parson's saw,
And birds sit brooding in the snow,
  And Marian's nose looks red and raw,
When roasted crabs hiss in the bowl,
Then nightly sings the staring owl
        To-whit;
To-who, a merry note,
While greasy Joan doth keel the pot.

Shakespeare.

CCCXLI

WINTER'S GAIETY

Now winter nights enlarge
The number of their hours,
And clouds their storms discharge
Upon the airy towers.

[1] Skim.

Let now the chimneys blaze
And cups o'erflow with wine ;
Let well-tuned words amaze
With harmony divine.
Now yellow waxen lights
Shall wait on honey love,
While youthful revels, masques, and courtly
        sights
Sleep's leaden spells remove.

This time doth well dispense
With lovers' long discourse ;
Much speech hath some defence
Though beauty no remorse.
All do not all things well ;
Some measures comely tread,
Some knotted riddles tell,
Some poems smoothly read.
The summer hath his joys,
And winter his delights ;
Though love and all his pleasures are but
        toys,
They shorten tedious nights.

T. Campion.

CCCXLII

TO HIS DELAYING SOUL

New doth the sun appear,
The mountain snows decay,
Crown'd with frail flowers forth comes the baby year.
My soul, time posts away ;

And thou yet in that frost
Which flower and fruit hath lost,
As if all here immortal were, dost stay.
For shame! thy powers awake,
Look to that Heaven which never night makes black,
And there at that immortal sun's bright rays,
Deck thee with flowers which fear not rage of days.

Drummond of Hawthornden.

CCCXLIII

THE FLOWER

How fresh, O Lord, how sweet and clean
Are thy returns!   Ev'n as the flowers in Spring,
　To which, besides their own demean,[1]
The late-past frosts tributes of pleasure bring ;
　　　Grief melts away
　　　Like snow in May,
　　As if there were no such cold thing.

Who would have thought my shrivell'd heart
Could have recover'd greenness?   It was gone
　Quite under ground ; as flowers depart
To see their mother-root, when they have blown,
　　　Where they together
　　　All the hard weather,
　　Dead to the world, keep house unknown.

[1] Demesne, domain ; "which, as coming after a season of
frost, have a pleasantness over and above their own proper
charm."

These are Thy wonders, Lord of power,
Killing and quick'ning, bringing down to Hell
And up to Heaven in an hour;
Making a chiming of a passing bell.
We say amiss
This or that is;
Thy word is all, if we could spell.[1]

O that I once past changing were,
Fast in thy Paradise where no flower can wither!
Many a Spring I shoot up fair,
Off'ring at Heaven, growing and groaning thither;
Nor doth my flower
Want a Spring shower,
My sins and I joining together.

But while I grow in a straight line,
Still upwards bent, as if Heaven were mine own,
Thy anger comes, and I decline;
What frost to that? What pole is not the zone
Where all things burn,
When Thou dost turn,
And the least frown of Thine is shown?

And now in age I bud again,
After so many deaths I live and write;
I once more smell the dew and rain,
And relish versing: O my only Light!
—It cannot be
That I am he
On whom Thy tempests fell all night.

[1] Interpret.

These are thy wonders, Lord of love,
To make us see we are but flowers that glide;
  Which when we once can find and prove,
Thou hast a garden for us where to bide.
            Who would be more,
            Swelling through store,
  Forfeit their Paradise by their pride.
                              Geo. Herbert.

CCCXLIV

SELF-TRIAL

LET not the sluggish sleep
    Close up thy waking eye,
Until with judgment deep
    Thy daily deeds thou try:
He that one sin in conscience keeps
    When he to quiet goes,
More vent'rous is than he that sleeps
    With twenty mortal foes.
                              Anon.

CCCXLV

THE BOOK

OF this fair volume which we World do name
If we the sheets and leaves could turn with care,
Of Him who it corrects and did it frame
We clear might read the art and wisdom rare:

Find out His power which wildest powers doth tame,
His providence extending everywhere,
His justice which proud rebels doth not spare,
In every page, no period of the same.

But silly we, like foolish children, rest
Well pleased with colour'd vellum, leaves of gold,
Fair dangling ribands, leaving what is best,
On the great Writer's sense ne'er taking hold;

Or, if by chance we stay our minds on aught,
It is some picture on the margin wrought.

Drummond of Hawthornden.

CCCXLVI

O COME QUICKLY !

NEVER weather-beaten sail more willing bent to shore,
Never tirèd pilgrim's limbs affected slumber more,
Than my wearied sprite now longs to fly out of my
    troubled breast:
O come quickly, sweetest Lord, and take my soul
    to rest!

Ever blooming are the joys of heaven's high Paradise,
Cold age deafs not there our ears nor vapour dims
    our eyes:
Glory there the sun outshines; whose beams the
    Blessèd only see:
O come quickly, glorious Lord, and raise my sprite
    to Thee!

T. Campion.

CCCXLVII

TO HIS EVER-LOVING GOD

Can I not come to Thee, my God, for these
So very-many-meeting hindrances,
That slack my pace, but yet not make me stay?
Who slowly goes, rids, in the end, his way.
Clear Thou my paths, or shorten Thou my miles,
Remove the bars, or lift me o'er the stiles;
Since rough the way is, help me when I call,
And take me up; or else prevent the fall.
I ken my home, and it affords some ease
To see far off the smoking villages.
Fain would I rest, yet covet not to die
For fear of future biting penury:
No, no, my God,—Thou know'st my wishes be
To leave this life not loving it, but Thee.

Herrick.

CCCXLVIII

THE PULLEY

When God at first made Man,
Having a glass of blessings standing by,—
Let us (said He) pour on him all we can;
Let the world's riches which dispersèd lie
Contract into a span.

So strength first made a way,
Then beauty flow'd, then wisdom, honour, pleasure:
When almost all was out, God made a stay,
Perceiving that, alone of all his treasure,
    Rest in the bottom lay.

    For if I should (said He)
Bestow this jewel also on My creature,
He would adore My gifts instead of Me,
And rest in Nature, not the God of Nature:
    So both should losers be.

    Yet let him keep the rest,
But keep them with repining restlessness;
Let him be rich and weary, that at least,
If goodness lead him not, yet weariness
    May toss him to My breast.

Geo. Herbert.

CCCXLIX

THE COLLAR

I struck the board and cried, No more;
    I will abroad.
What, shall I ever sigh and pine?
My lines and life are free, free as the road,
Loose as the wind, as large as store.

Shall I be still in suit ?
Have I no harvest but a thorn
To let me blood, and not restore
What I have lost with cordial fruit ?
        Sure there was wine
Before my sighs did dry it ; there was corn
Before my tears did drown it.
Is the year only lost to me ?
Have I no bays to crown it ?
No flowers, no garlands gay ?   All blasted ?
        All wasted ?
Not so, my heart ; but there is fruit,
        And thou hast hands.
Recover all thy sigh-blown age
On double pleasure : leave thy cold dispute
Of what is fit and not ; forsake thy cage,
        Thy rope of sands
Which petty thoughts have made, and made to thee
Good cable to enforce and draw
        And be thy law,
While thou dost wink and would'st not see.
        Away : take heed,
        I will abroad.
Call in thy death's-head there : tie up thy fears.
        He that forbears
        To suit and serve his need
        Deserves his load.
But as I raved and grew more fierce and wild
        At every word,
Methought I heard one calling ' *Child !* '
        And I replied ' *My Lord.*'

Geo. Herbert.

CCCL

THE WHITE ISLAND

In this world, the Isle of Dreams,
While we sit by sorrow's streams,
Tears and terror are our themes
       Reciting :

But when once from hence we fly,
More and more approaching nigh
Unto young Eternity
       Uniting :

In that whiter island, where
Things are evermore sincere ;
Candour here, and lustre there
       Delighting :

—There no monstrous fancies shall
Out of Hell an horror call,
To create (or cause at all)
       Affrighting.

There in calm and cooling sleep
We our eyes shall never steep ;
But eternal watch shall keep
       Attending

Pleasures such as shall pursue
Me immortalised, and you ;
And fresh joys, as never too
Have ending.

Herrick.

CCCLI

GOOD FRIDAY

Most glorious Lord of Life, that on this day
Didst make Thy triumph over death and sin,
And having harrow'd hell, didst bring away
Captivity thence captive, us to win :

This joyous day, dear Lord, with joy begin,
And grant that we, for whom thou diddest die,
Being with Thy dear blood clean wash'd from sin,
May live for ever in felicity :

And that Thy love we weighing worthily,
May likewise love Thee for the same again ;
And for Thy sake, that all like dear didst buy,
With love may one another entertain.

So let us love, dear Love, like as we ought,
—Love is the lesson which the Lord us taught.

Spenser.

CCCLII

THE WEEPER

MARY MAGDALENE

THE dew no more will weep
  The primrose's pale cheek to deck:
The dew no more will sleep
  Nuzzled in the lily's neck:
Much rather would it tremble here
And leave them both to be thy tear.

Not the soft gold which
  Steals from the amber-weeping tree,
Makes Sorrow half so rich
  As the drops distill'd from thee:
Sorrow's best jewels lie in these
Caskets of which Heaven keeps the keys.

When Sorrow would be seen
  In her brightest majesty,
—For she is a Queen—
  Then is she drest by none but thee:
Then, and only then, she wears
Her richest pearls—I mean thy tears.

Not in the evening's eyes,
  When they red with weeping are
For the sun that dies,
  Sits Sorrow with a face so fair:
Nowhere but here doth meet
Sweetness so sad, sadness so sweet.

When some new bright guest
  Takes up among the stars a room,
And Heaven will make a feast,
  Angels with their bottles come,
And draw from these full eyes of thine
Their Master's water, their own wine.

Does the night arise?
  Still thy tears do fall and fall.
Does night lose her eyes?
  Still the fountain weeps for all.
Let night or day do what they will,
Thou hast thy task, thou weepest still.

R. Crashaw.

CCCLIII

DISCIPLINE

Throw away Thy rod,
Throw away Thy wrath :
    O my God,
Take the gentle path.

For my heart's desire
Unto Thine is bent :
    I aspire
To a full consent.

Not a word or look
I affect to own,
    But by book
And Thy book alone.

Though I fail, I weep;
Though I halt in pace,
        Yet I creep
To the throne of grace.

Then let wrath remove;
Love will do the deed;
        For with love
Stony hearts will bleed.

Love is swift of foot;
Love's a man of war,
        And can shoot,
And can hit from far.

Who can 'scape his bow?
That which wrought on Thee,
        Brought Thee low,
Needs must work on me.

Throw away Thy rod;
Though man frailties hath,
        Thou art God:
Throw away Thy wrath.

Geo. Herbert.

CCCLIV

SAINT JOHN BAPTIST

THE last and greatest Herald of Heaven's King,
Girt with rough skins, hies to the deserts wild,
Among that savage brood the woods forth bring,
Which he than man more harmless found and mild.

His food was locusts, and what young doth spring
With honey that from virgin hives distill'd ;
Parch'd body, hollow eyes, some uncouth thing,
Made him appear, long since from earth exiled.

Then burst he forth : ' All ye, whose hopes rely
On God, with me amidst these deserts mourn ;
Repent, repent, and from old errors turn !'
—Who listen'd to his voice, obey'd his cry?

Only the echoes, which he made relent,
Rung from their flinty[1] caves 'Repent ! Repent !'
                    Drummond of Hawthornden.

CCCLV

LITANY TO THE HOLY SPIRIT

In the hour of my distress,
When temptations me oppress,
And when I my sins confess,
        Sweet Spirit, comfort me !

When I lie within my bed,
Sick in heart and sick in head,
And with doubts discomforted,
        Sweet Spirit, comfort me !

When the house doth sigh and weep,
And the world is drown'd in sleep,
Yet mine eyes the watch do keep,
        Sweet Spirit, comfort me !

[1] *v.l.* ' marble.'

When the passing bell doth toll,
And the furies in a shoal
Come to fright a parting soul,
          Sweet Spirit, comfort me !

When the tapers now burn blue,
And the comforters are few,
And that number more than true,
          Sweet Spirit, comfort me !

When the priest his last hath pray'd,
And I nod to what is said,
'Cause my speech is now decay'd,
          Sweet Spirit, comfort me !

When, God knows, I 'm toss'd about
Either with despair or doubt ;
Yet before the glass be out,
          Sweet Spirit, comfort me !

When the tempter me pursu'th
With the sins of all my youth,
And half-damns me with untruth,
          Sweet Spirit, comfort me !

When the flames and hellish cries
Fright mine ears and fright mine eyes,
And all terrors me surprise,
          Sweet Spirit, comfort me !

When the judgment is reveal'd,
And that open'd which was seal'd,
When to Thee I have appeal'd,
          Sweet Spirit, comfort me !

Herrick.

x

A LITANY

Drop, drop, slow tears,
   And bathe those beauteous feet
Which brought from Heaven
   The news and Prince of Peace:
Cease not, wet eyes,
   His mercy to entreat:
To cry for vengeance
   Sin doth never cease.
In your deep floods
   Drown all my faults and fears;
Nor let His eye
   See sin, but through my tears.

Phineas Fletcher.

EASTER SONG

I got me flowers to strew Thy way,
   I got me boughs off many a tree;
But Thou wast up by break of day,
   And brought'st Thy sweets along with Thee.

The sun arising in the East,
   Though he give light and th' East perfume,
If they should offer to contest
   With Thy arising, they presume.

Can there be any day but this,
  Though many suns to shine endeavour?
We count three hundred, but we miss:
  There is but one, and that one ever.

Geo. Herbert.

CCCLVIII

A HYMN TO GOD THE FATHER

WILT Thou forgive that sin, where I begun,
  Which was my sin, though it were done before?
Wilt Thou forgive that sin through which I run,
  And do run still, though still I do deplore?
When Thou hast done, Thou hast not done;
      For I have more.

Wilt Thou forgive that sin which I have won
  Others to sin, and made my sins their door?
Wilt Thou forgive that sin which I did shun
  A year or two, but wallow'd in a score?
When Thou hast done, Thou hast not done;
      For I have more.

I have a sin of fear, that when I've spun
  My last thread, I shall perish on the shore;
But swear by Thyself that at my death Thy Son
  Shall shine as He shines now and heretofore:
And having done that, Thou hast done;
      I fear no more.

J. Donne.

CCCLIX

LOVE

Love bade me welcome ; yet my soul drew back,
    Guilty of dust and sin.
But quick-eyed Love, observing me grow slack
    From my first entrance in,
Drew nearer to me, sweetly questioning
    If I lack'd anything.

' A guest,' I answer'd, ' worthy to be here ' :
    Love said, ' You shall be he.'
' I, the unkind, ungrateful ?   Ah, my dear,
    I cannot look on Thee.'
Love took my hand and smiling did reply,
    ' Who made the eyes but I ? '

' Truth, Lord ; but I have marr'd them : let my
    shame
    Go where it doth deserve.'
' And know you not,' says Love, ' Who bore the
    blame ? '
    ' My dear, then I will serve.'
' You must sit down,' says Love, ' and taste my
    meat.'
    So I did sit and eat.

Geo. Herbert.

CCCLX

SIR WALTER RALEIGH'S PILGRIMAGE

GIVE me my scallop-shell of quiet,
  My staff of faith to walk upon,
My scrip of joy, immortal diet,
  My bottle of salvation,
My gown of glory, hope's true gage;
And thus I 'll take my pilgrimage.

Blood must be my body's balmer;
  No other balm will there be given;
Whilst my soul, like quiet palmer,
  Travelleth towards the land of heaven;
Over the silver mountains,
Where spring the nectar fountains:
    There will I kiss
    The bowl of bliss;
And drink mine everlasting fill
Upon every milken hill.
My soul will be a-dry before;
But after it will thirst no more.

Sir W. Raleigh.

CCCLXI

THE CONCLUSION

EVEN such is Time, that takes in trust
   Our youth, our joys, our all we have,
And pays us but with earth and dust;
   Who in the dark and silent grave,
When we have wander'd all our ways,
Shuts up the story of our days;
But from this earth, this grave, this dust,
My God shall raise me up, I trust.

Sir W. Raleigh.

NOTES

I

Page 1, line 1—'*Hark, hark! the lark at heaven's gate sings.*
Compare with the opening line Lyly's verse on p. 44:

> ' Who is 't now we hear?
> None but the lark so shrill and clear;
> Now at heaven's gates she claps her wings,
> The morn not waking till she sings.'

and Davenant's

> ' The lark now leaves his watery nest
> And climbing shakes his dewy wings . . .'

IV

Page 3, line 1—' Phœbus, arise ! ' The text (except in the three concluding lines) is that of the Maitland Club reprint (1832) of the 1616 edition, the last published during Drummond's lifetime. The ending there given, however,

> ' The clouds bespangle with bright gold their blue :
> Here is the pleasant place,
> And everything, save her, who all should grace.'

seems comparatively weak.

Page 3, line 4—*Memnon's mother* is Aurora.

Page 4, line 9—*by Penéus' streams.* It was by Penéus, in the vale of Tempe, that Phœbus met and loved Daphne, daughter of the river-god.—Ovid's *Metaph.*, Lib. I.

Page 4, line 12—*When two thou did to Rome appear.* Cf. Livy, xxviii. 11 (of the second Punic War, B.C. 206) : ' In civitate tanto discrimine belli sollicita . . . multa prodigia nuntiabantur . . . et Albae duos soles visos referebant.' A like phenomenon is mentioned again in xxxix. 14 (B.C. 204).

Cf. also Pliny, *Natural History*, ii. 31. Thus translated by Philemon Holland : ' Over and besides, many Sunnes are seen at once, neither above nor beneath the bodie of the true Sunne indeed, but crosswise and overthwart : never neere, nor directly against the earthe, neither in the night season, but when the Sunne either riseth or setteth. Once they are reported to have been seene

327

at noone day in Bosphorus, and continued from morne to even.'
(This is from Aristotle, *Meteor.* iii. 2, 6.) 'Three Sunnes together
our Auncitors in old time have often beheld, as namely, when
Sp. Posthumius with Q. Mutius, Q. Martius with M. Porcius,
M. Antonius with P. Dolabella, and Mar. Lepidus with L. Plancus
were consuls. Yea, and we in our daies have seene the like, in
the time of Cl. Cæsar of famous memorie, his consulship, together
with Cornelius Orsitus his colleague. More than three we never to
this day find to have been seene together.'

Drummond's reference is perhaps to the famous instance itali-
cised.

Page 4, line 19—*These purple ports of death.* Elsewhere
Drummond speaks of the lips as 'those coral ports of bliss.'
'Lips, double port of love.' Ports = gates.

Page 4, line 24—*Night like a drunkard reels.* Professor
Masson compares *Romeo and Juliet,* Act ii. Sc. iii. l. 4 :

> 'And fleckèd darkness like a drunkard reels
> From forth day's path and Titan's fiery wheels.'

V

Page 5—'Corydon, arise, my Corydon.' This artless and
beautiful song is from *England's Helicon*, where it is signed
Ignoto. Like most pieces thus subscribed it has been attributed
to Sir Walter Raleigh, but with no good reason.

VI

Page 7—'Get up, get up for shame! The blooming morn' :
line 2, *the god unshorn* : Imberbis Apollo. For a full account
of the May-day customs alluded to in this glowing pastoral, con-
sult Brand's *Popular Antiquities*, vol. i. pp. 212 *sqq.*

VII

Page 10—'Is not thilke the merry month of May.' From
The Shepherd's Calendar: May. This is one of the few instances
in which I have ventured to make a short extract from a long
poem and present it as a separate lyric.

IX

Page 11—'See where my Love a-maying goes.' From Francis
Pilkington's *First Set of Madrigals*, 1614.

XV

Page 15—'Gather ye rosebuds while ye may.' The advice
is of course a commonplace of the poets ; but Herrick's opening
lines seem to be taken direct from Ausonius, 361, ll. 49 50 :

> 'Collige, virgo, rosas, dum flos novus et nova pubes,
> Et memor esto aevum sic properare tuum.'

and again—

> 'Quam longa una dies, aetas tam longa rosarum.

which in turn reminds us of—

> 'Et Rose, elle a vécu ce que vivent les roses
> L'espace d'un matin.'

Compare this number with XVII., 'Love in thy youth, fair maid, be wise . . .' and the sonnets of Shakespeare and Daniel that follow (XXI.-XXIV.), where the same note is sounded with deeper thought and feeling.

XVI

Page 15—'Shun delays, they breed remorse.' Southwell added four stanzas to the three here given : they convey the same advice in a variety of forms, and conclude—

> 'Happy man, that soon doth knock
> Babel's babes against the rock !'

XX

Page 18—'Come, my Celia, let us prove.' Imitated from Catullus'

> 'Vivamus, mea Lesbia, atque amemus.'

For another rendering of the same see the first song in Campion and Rosseter's first *Book of Airs*, the verses being undoubtedly Campion's :—

> 'My sweetest Lesbia, let us live and love ;
> And though the sager sort our deeds reprove,
> Let us not weigh them : heaven's great lamps do dive
> Into the west, and straight again revive :
> But soon as once is set our little light,
> Then must we sleep in ever-during night.
>
> If all would lead their lives in love like me,
> Then bloody swords and armour should not be ;
> No drum or trumpet peaceful sleeps should move,
> Unless alarm came from the camp of Love :
> But fools do live, and waste their little light,
> And seek with pain their ever-during night.
>
> When timely death my life and fortune ends,
> Let not my heart be vext with mourning friends ;
> But let all lovers, rich in triumph, come
> And with sweet pastimes grace my happy tomb :
> And, Lesbia, close thou up my little light,
> And crown with love my ever-during night.'

XXVII

Page 23—'The ousel-cock, so black of hue' : line 6, *The plain-song cuckoo gray :* In 'plain-song' the descant rested with the will of the singer ; in ' prick-song,' on the other hand, the harmony,

being more elaborate, was pricked or written down. Thus the
rich and involved music of the nightingale is often called 'prick-
song.' *E.g.:*

> ' What bird so sings, yet so does wail?
> O, 'tis the ravish'd nightingale.
> *Jug, jug, jug, jug, tereu!* she cries,
> And still her woes at midnight rise.
> Brave prick-song ! . . .'
>
> *Lyly.*

XXVIII

Page 23—'Spring, the sweet Spring, is the year's pleasant
king.' Nashe's *Summer's Last Will and Testament*, from which
this is taken, was acted in the autumn of 1593, while London
was being devastated by the plague. It is pathetic to contrast
these gay spring lines with numbers CCLXXVII. and CCLXXVIII.,
extracts from the same play.

> ' Autumn hath all the summer's fruitful treasure;
> Gone is our sport, fled is our Croydon's pleasure !
> Short days, sharp days, long nights come on apace :
> Ah, who shall hide us from the winter's face?
> Cold doth increase, the sickness will not cease,
> And here we lie, God knows, with little ease.
> From winter, plague, and pestilence, good Lord deliver us !'

XXXI

Page 25—This rapturous little catch we owe to Mr. A. H. Bullen,
who disinterred it from the collection of early MS. music-books preserved in the library of Christ Church, Oxford. In the MS. the lines
are subscribed 'Mr. Gyles.' Nathaniel Giles was a chorister at
Magdalen, and successively organist and master of the choristers at
St. George's, Windsor, and master of the Children of the Chapel
Royal. He died January 24th, 1633, and was buried at Windsor.

XXXII

Page 25—From Thomas Morley's *Madrigals to Four Voices*,
1600.

XXXIV

Page 27, line 1—*The Golden Pomp is come* is Ovid's 'Aurea
pompa venit,' and *Now reigns the rose* Martial's 'nunc regnat
rosa.' 'My retorted hairs' seems to be Martial again, vi. 39, 6,
'retorto crine Maurus.' 'My uncontrolled brow' may be 'soluta,
libera, explicita frons.' But Herrick used his classics so freely that
it would be a mistake to seek to identify all that looks like direct
translation.

XXXVI

Page 30—'Sweet day, so cool, so calm, so bright' is from
The Temple: Sacred Poems and Private Ejaculations, 1632-33.

But it is hard now to dissociate it from its exquisite context in the *Compleat Angler* :—

Piscator. 'And now, scholar, my direction for fly-fishing is ended with this shower, for it has done raining ; and now look about you, and see how pleasantly that meadow looks ; nay, and the earth smells as sweetly too. Come, let me tell you what holy Mr. Herbert says of such days and flowers as these ; and then we will thank God that we enjoy them, and walk to the river and sit down quietly and try to catch the other brace of trouts. . . .'

Here follow the verses.

Venator. 'I thank you, good master, for your good direction for fly-fishing, and for the sweet enjoyment of the pleasant day, which is so far spent without offence to God or man : and I thank you for the sweet close of your discourse with Mr. Herbert's verses, who, I have heard, loved angling ; and I do the rather believe it, because he had a spirit suitable to anglers, and to those primitive Christians that you love and have so much commended.'

Compare also Walton's *Life of Herbert* :—'The Sunday before his death he rose suddenly from his bed or couch, called for one of his instruments, took it into his hand, and said—

> 'My God, my God,
> My musick shall find Thee
>   And every string
> Shall have his attribute to sing';

and having tuned it, he played and sung :

> 'The Sundaies of man's life
> Thredded together on Time's string,
> Make bracelets to adorn the wife
> Of the eternall glorious King :
> On Sunday, Heaven's dore stands ope,
> Blessings are plentiful and rife,
>   More plentiful then hope.'

Thus he sang on earth such hymns and anthems as the angels and he and Mr. Farrar [Nicholas Ferrar of Little Gidding] now sing in heaven.'

XXXIX

Page 33—In the merry month of May.' This song of Breton's first appeared, under the title of 'The ploughman's Song,' in *The Honourable Entertainment given to the Queen's Majesty at Elvetham in Hampshire, by the Right Honourable the Earl of Hertford*; printed in 1591. It was set to music in Michael Este's *Madrigals*, 1604, and again in Henry Youll's *Canzonets*, 1608 ; and is included in *England's Helicon*.

XLVI

Page 38—'Hark, all you ladies that do sleep!' From Campion and Rosseter's *A Book of Airs*, 1601.

XLVIII, XLIX

Pages 40, 41—'Come live with me and be my love.' Marlowe's song (minus the fourth and sixth verses and without the author's name) was first published in *The Passionate Pilgrim*, 1599, followed by the first verse of the 'Reply.' The next year it was printed complete, with Marlowe's name attached, in *England's Helicon*.

The 'Reply' in *England's Helicon* is signed 'Ignoto'; and the evidence that Raleigh wrote it is confined to a famous passage in the *Compleat Angler*: 'As I left this place, and entered into the next field, a second pleasure entertained me. 'Twas a handsome milkmaid, that had not yet attained so much age and wisdom as to load her mind with any fears of many things that will never be, as too many men too often do: but she cast away all care, and sung like a nightingale: her voice was good, and the ditty fitted for it: it was that smooth song which was made by Kit Marlowe, now at least fifty years ago: and the milkmaid's mother sung an answer to it, which was made by Sir Walter Raleigh in his younger days.'

In the second edition of the *Angler* Walton inserted—probably from a broad-sheet—an extra penultimate stanza in both Song and Reply:

> *Marlowe.*—'Thy silver dishes for thy meat,
> As precious as the gods do eat,
> Shall on an ivory table be
> Prepared each day for thee and me.'

> *Raleigh.*—'What should we talk of dainties, then,—
> Of better meat than's fit for men?
> These are but vain: that's only good
> Which God hath blest, and sent for food.'

We may conclude with a modest conjecture of the late Professor Henry Morley's. 'Sharing,' he says, 'the spell upon the mind that is in every familiar word of this old song, I feel like a dunce when suggesting that there may be two original misprints in it, of "cup" for "cap," and of "fair-lined" for "fur-lined."'—*English Writers*, vol. x. p. 135, note.

LII

Page 44—'What bird so sings, yet so does wail.' For '*pricksong*' see note on No. XXVII.

LIII

Page 44—'This day Dame Nature seem'd in love': *Reliquiæ Wottonianæ*. Quoted in Walton's *Angler*: 'And I do easily believe, that peace and patience and a calm content did cohabit in the cheerful heart of Sir Henry Wotton; because I know that when he was beyond seventy years of age, he made this description of a part of the present pleasure that possessed him, as he sat quietly, in a summer's evening, on a bank a-fishing. It is a description of the spring; which because it glided as soft and sweetly from his pen, as that river does at this time, by which it was then made, I shall repeat unto you.'

LVII

Page 48—'Quivering fears, heart-tearing cares': *Rel. Wotton.* with the signature 'Ignoto.' Also described in Walton's *Angler* as 'a copy printed among some of Sir Henry Wotton's, and doubtless made either by him or by a lover of angling.' It has been claimed (*vide* note on No. v.) for Sir Walter Raleigh, but on no evidence.

LIX

Page 53—'The damask meadows and the crawling streams.' From 'A Country Life: To his brother, Mr. Tho. Herrick.' —*Hesperides*, 106. The poem is usually attributed to Bishop Corbet (1582-1635), but every line seems to claim Herrick for its author.

It is based on Horace, *Ep.* i. 10, and is full of classical reminiscences. *E.g.*, 'With holy meal and crackling salt' is Horace's 'farre pio et saliente mica.'

The Thomas Herrick, to whom it is dedicated, was an elder brother of the poet's, born May 7, 1588, and apprenticed by his uncle, Sir William Herrick, to a London merchant, Mr. Massam. In 1610, however, Thomas quitted London and returned to the country, where he cultivated a small farm.

LX

Page 53—'Heigho! chill go to plough no more.' From John Mundy's *Songs and Psalms*, 1594.

LXI

Page 54—'My Love is neither hot nor cold.' From Robert Jones's *Second Book of Songs and Airs*, 1601.

LXIII

Page 55—'Diaphenia like the daffadowndilly.' Signed 'H. C.' in *England's Helicon*. It is set to music in Francis Pilkington's *First Book of Songs or Airs*, 1605.

Henry Constable was born about 1555, of a staunch Roman Catholic family: was educated at St. John's College, Cambridge, where he took his degree in 1579. In 1595 falling (as a Roman Catholic) under suspicion of treasonable correspondence with France, he had to fly the country. About 1601 he ventured to return; but was detected and committed to the Tower, where he languished until the close of 1604. The exact date of his death is uncertain, but it happened before 1616.

LXIV

Page 56—'Like to Diana in her summer weed.' From Greene's romance of *Menaphon*, 1589. 'What manner of woman is she?' quoth Melicertus. 'As well as I can, answered Doron, 'I will make description of her:

Like to Diana, etc.'

'Thou hast,' quoth Melicertus, 'made such a description as if Priamus' young boy should paint out the perfection of his Greekish paramour.'

LXV

Page 57—'See where she sits upon the grassy green.' An extract from *The Shepherd's Calendar: April.* The same being 'purposely intended to the honour and prayse of our most gratious soveraigne, queene Elizabeth . . . whom abruptly he termeth Eliza.' The original ditty extends to fourteen stanzas. The opulence of Spenser's muse will always be the despair of the anthologist, and I commend my extracts to the reader with much diffidence. But it was a question between curtailment and omitting altogether.

LXVII

Page 66—'It fell upon a holy eve.' From *The Shepherd's Calendar: August.*

LXVIII

Page 66—'Tell me, thou skilful shepherd swain.' From Drayton's *Pastorals: The Ninth Eclogue.* It is included, under the title here given, in *England's Helicon.*

LXIX

Page 67—'Fair and fair and twice so fair.' From Peele's *Arraignment of Paris*, 1584. For light-hearted melody I believe this little duet can hardly be matched in the whole range of our poetry. Its charm is impossible to analyse as that of Shakespeare's 'It was a lover and his lass'—mere spontaneous gaiety and the perfection of writing.

LXX

Page 68—'Like the Idalian queen.' *Paramours*—sing. *paramour* (of course without the offensive modern connotation). Compare Chaucer, *Troilus and Criseyde*, v. 157:

'I lovede never womman herebiforn
As paramours, ne never shall no mo.'

Page 68, line 6—*Which of her blood were born.* See Bion's first Idyll ; also the *Pervigilium Veneris*, l. 23 ; and compare Drummond's little poem, ' The Rose ':

> ' Flower, which of Adon's blood
> Sprang, when of that clear flood
> Which Venus wept another white was born. . . .'

Which is a translation of Tasso :

> ' O del sangue d' Adone
> Nata fior, quando un altro del' acque
> Lacrimose di Venere ne nacque.'

Bion's story was that the red rose sprang from the blood of Adonis, and the anemone from the tears shed by Venus over him. But there is a variant, that the rose sprang from the blood of Venus herself as she passed barefoot through the briars in her grief at Adonis's death.

LXXI

Page 69—' Beauty sat bathing by a spring.' From *England's Helicon* where, with six other pieces, it is signed ' Shepherd Tony.' It is also found in Antony Munday's *Primaleon*, 1619 ; and though Antony Munday (' our best plotter ' according to Meres, and elsewhere, less reverently, ' the Grub Street Patriarch ') could write poorly enough as a rule, the evidence is sufficient that he was the ' Shepherd Tony ' and author of this graceful lyric. Others have identified the shepherd with one Antony Copley, author of *A Fig for Fortune*, 1596, and *Wits, Fits, and Fancies*, 1614.

LXXII

Page 70—' Open the door ! ' From Martin Peerson's *Private Music*, 1620 : Bodleian Library, Douce Collection.

LXXIII

Page 70—' On a time the amorous Silvy.' From John Attye's *First Book of Airs*, 1622. Mr. Bullen points out that this is a graceful rendering from the French of Pierre Guedron :

> ' Un jour l'amoureuse Silvie
> Disoit, baise moy, je te prie,
> Au berger qui seul est sa vie
> Et son amour ;
> Baise moy, pasteur, je te prie,
> Et te lève, car il est jour.' . . .

LXXVI

Page 73—' Art thou gone in haste ? ' From *The Thracian Wonder*, which was published by Francis Kirkman in 1661 and assigned on the title-page to Webster and Rowley. It is as certain as can be that Webster took no hand in it. William Rowley, 'once a rare Schollar of learned Pembroke Hall of Cambridge,' colaborated with Middleton in *The Spanish Gipsy* (published in 1652, though written quite thirty years earlier), and probably also in *More Dissemblers besides Women* written at least as early as 1623 and published in 1657). The dates of his birth and death are alike uncertain.

LXXIX

Page 76—'Shepherd, what's Love, I pray thee tell.' Originally subscribed 'S. W. R.' in *England's Helicon*, 1600 ; but in extant copies this has been obliterated by a label on which is printed 'Ignoto.' Signed 'S. W. Rawly,' in Davison's list, Harl. MS. 280, fol. 99, but anonymous in *The Phoenix Nest*, 1593, and Davison's *Poetical Rhapsody*, 1602, where it is headed 'The Anatomy of Love.' In the two last the first line runs 'Now what is Love, I pray thee tell?' There is an early MS. copy in Harl. MS. 6910, and an imperfect copy of the first and last stanzas form the 'third song' in T. Heywood's *The Rape of Lucrece*, 1608. The song was also set to music in Robert Jones's *Second Book of Songs and Airs*, 1601.

LXXXII

Page 79—'Hey, down a down! did Dian sing.' From *England's Helicon*. The signature again is 'Ignoto.'

LXXXIII

Page 80—'Never love unless you can.' From Thomas Campion's *Third Book of Airs*, not dated, but certainly not earlier than 1617.

LXXXIV

Page 81—'Thus saith my Chloris bright.' From John Wilbye's *Madrigals*, 1598 : a rendering of an Italian madrigal by Luca Marenzio. Another version is found in *Musica Transalpina. The Second Book of Madrigals*, 1597 :

> 'So saith my fair and beautiful Lycoris,
> When now and then she talketh
> With me of love :
> "Love is a spirit that walketh,
> That soars and flies,
> And none alive can hold him,
> Nor touch him, nor behold him."
> Yet when her eye she turneth,
> I spy where he sojourneth :
> In her eyes there he flies,
> But none can catch him
> Till from her lips he fetch him.'

LXXXV

Page 81—'Come hither, shepherd's swain.' Found entire in Deloney's *Garland of Goodwill* (whence Percy obtained the version in his *Reliques*) and in Breton's *Bower of Delights,* 1597. A shorter copy is found in Puttenham's *Art of Poesy,* 1589, where it is attributed to 'Edward, Earl of Oxford, a most noble and learned gentleman.'

Edward Vere, seventeenth earl of Oxford, was born not earlier than 1540: travelled in Italy in early youth, and returned with very foppish manners and a pair of gloves which so pleased Elizabeth, to whom he presented them, that she was drawn with them on her hands. In 1585 he took part in the Earl of Leicester's expedition for the relief of the states of Holland and Zealand. In the following year he sat as Lord Great Chamberlain of England at the trial of Mary, Queen of Scots. In 1588 he fitted out ships at his own charges against the Spanish Armada. In 1589 he helped to try Philip Howard, Earl of Arundel; and in 1601, the Earls of Essex and Southampton. In private life he appears to have been something of a ruffian. He died in the summer of 1604.

Page 81, line 6—*Prime of May: v.l.* 'pride of May.'

Page 82, line 2—*Unfeigned lovers' tears: v.l.* 'unsavoury lovers' tears.'

Page 82, line 20—*A thousand times a day: v.l.* 'ten thousand times a day.'

LXXXVI

Page 83—'The sea hath many thousand sands.' From Robert Jones's *The Muses Garden of Delights,* 1610—a book which (says Mr. Bullen) 'I have sought early and late without success. In 1812 a copy was in the library of the Marquis of Stafford; and in that year Beloe printed six songs from it in the sixth volume of his *Anecdotes*'—the song under notice is one of that half-dozen. 'These six songs . . . are so delightful that I am consumed with a desire to see the rest of the contents of the song-book.'

LXXXVII

Page 83—'If thou long'st so much to learn,' etc. This and the following song, so similar in subject and treatment, are both from Campion's *Third Book of Songs and Airs* (circ. 1617).

LXXXIX

Page 86—'Love guards the roses of thy lips.' From Lodge's *Phillis.* The old editions have 'Love guides the roses'—'evidently (says Mr. Bullen), a misprint for "guildes."' But the reading here adopted seems even more obvious.

XC

Page 87—'Sweet Love, if thou wilt gain a monarch's glory.'
From John Wilbye's *Madrigals*, 1598.

XCI

Page 87—'Cupid and my Campaspe played.' This little
poem, so easy and yet inimitable, so artless apparently and yet
unapproachable, is from Lyly's *Alexander and Campaspe*, probably acted at Court in the year 1581. Lyly's songs, however, were
not included in the early editions of his plays, but appear for the
first time in the collected edition of 1597.

XCIV

Page 89—'Come, you pretty false-eyed wanton.' From the
second book of *Two Books of Airs*. The first containing *Divine
and Moral Songs*: the second, *Light Conceits of Lovers*' (circ.
1613), where a third stanza is given :

> 'Would it were dumb midnight now,
>   When all the world lies sleeping !
> Would this place some desert were,
>   Which no man hath in keeping !
> My desires should then be safe,
>   And when you cried, then would I laugh :
> But if aught might breed offence,
>   Love only should be blamèd :
> I would live your servant still,
>   And you my saint unnamèd.'

XCVI

Page 90—'Turn back, you wanton flyer.' From Campion
and Rosseter's *A Book of Airs*, 1601.
Page 91, line 8—'*times*' or *seasons*' *swerving*.' Old ed. 'changing.' 'Swerving' is Mr. Bullen's correction.
Page 91, lines 10, 11—The original reads :

> 'Then what we sow with our lips,
>   Let us reap, love's gains dividing.'

And it is so printed in Mr. Bullen's edition of Campion (1889).
The arrangement in the text, however, gives us two even stanzas,
and has the further advantage of making sense.

XCVII

Page 91—'Steer, hither steer your wingèd pines.' The
opening song of *The Inner Temple Masque*, 'presented by the
gentlemen there,' in January 1614, but not printed until 1772,
when Thomas Davies included it in his edition of Browne, his
authority being a MS. in the library of Emmanuel College, Cambridge.

XCVIII

Page 92—'Come, worthy Greek! Ulysses, come.' Homer, *Odyssey* xii. 184.

Δεῦρ' ἄγ' ἰὼν πολύαιν' Ὀδυσεῦ, μέγα κῦδος Ἀχαιῶν . . .

It is to be observed particularly with what ease this song of 'well-languaged Daniel' runs upon the tongue. Such ease would be remarkable in a lyric of mere emotion or ecstasy: it is wonderful in lines that discuss a question of high morality. *E.g.*:

> 'But natures of the noblest frame
>   These toils and dangers please;
> And they take comfort in the same
>   As much as you in ease;
> And with the thought of actions past
>   Are recreated still:
> When Pleasure leaves a touch at last
>   To show that it was ill.'

CIII

Page 104—'The Nightingale, as soon as April bringeth.' From the poems appended to Sidney's *Arcadia*, ed. 1598. Also in *England's Helicon*.

Philomela. The legends differ, making now Philomela, now Procne (the swallow), to suffer Tereus' violence.

CIV

Page 105—'As it fell upon a day.' For an extended and weaker form of this little poem see the *Sonnets to Sundry Notes of Music*, appended to *The Passionate Pilgrim*, 1599, 'by W. Shakespeare. At London: Printed for W. Jaggard, and are to be sold by W. Leake, at the Greyhound in Paule's Churchyard.' But in this little book of thirty leaves, 16mo, even Marlowe's 'Come live with me and be my love' is audaciously claimed for Shakespeare. In the third edition of *The Passionate Pilgrim*, Shakespeare's name was cut out of the title-page, possibly at his own request.

The present poem was 'conveyed' out of *Poems in divers Humours*, appended to *The Encomion of Lady Pecunia: or the praise of Money*, the last book of verses written by R. Barnefield, or Barnfield, who was born in 1574, the eldest son of a Shropshire country gentleman; was educated at B. N. C., Oxford; and died at Dorlestone, Staffordshire, in 1627. On leaving Oxford he came to London, consorted with the poets there, and himself published at least one immortal lyric; but his Muse was silent after his twenty-fifth year, when he went back to live the life of a country gentleman and no doubt to remember Clements Inn and 'the chimes at midnight,' in his Staffordshire home. 'As it fell upon a day' was also included in *England's Helicon*.

Page 105, line 14—*Tereu, Tereu!* For the meaning of this cry see the poem preceding. *Pandion* was Philomela's father.

CV

Page 106—'While that the sun with his beams hot.' The author of these delicate and simple-hearted lines cannot be discovered. They appeared first in *Songs of Sundry Natures*, 1589, where they were set to music by William Byrd, a gentleman of the Chapel Royal, previously (1563-69) organist of Lincoln Cathedral, and one of the earliest of Elizabethan composers. It was copied 'Out of M. Bird's Set Songs' into *England's Helicon*.

CVII

Page 108—'The earth, late choked with showers.' From *Scylla's Metamorphosis*, 1589. Imitated from a poem of Philippe Desportes:

> ' La terre naguère glacée
> Est ores de vert tapissée,
> Son sein est embelli de fleurs,
> L'air est encore amoureux d'elle,
> Le ciel rit de la voir si belle,
> Et moi j'en augmente mes pleurs.
>
> Les bois sont couverts de feuillage,
> De vert se pare le bocage,
> Ses rameaux sont tous verdissants ;
> Et moi, las ! privé de ma gloire,
> Je m'habille de couleur noire,
> Signe des ennuis que je sens.
>
> Des oiseaux la troupe légère
> Chantant d'une voix ramagère
> S'égaye aux bois à qui mieux mieux :
> Et moi tout rempli de furie
> Je sanglotte, soupire et crie
> Par les plus solitaires lieux.
>
> Les oiseaux cherchent la verdure :
> Moi, je cherche une sépulture,
> Pour voir mon malheur limité.
> Vers le ciel ils ont leur volée :
> Et mon âme trop désolée
> N'aime rien que l'obscurité.'

Lodge was an admirer and imitator of Desportes, of whose poems he speaks, in 1589, as 'being for the most part Englished and ordinarily in every man's hands.' Cf. note on number CCXX., 'First shall the heavens want starry light.'

CIX

Page 109—' Little think'st thou, poor flower.' Having omitted

the three concluding stanzas of Donne's poem, I now repent
and add them in the notes :

> ' But thou, which lov'st to be
>   Subtle to plague thyself, wilt say—
> " Alas ! if you must go, what 's that to me ?
>   Here lies my business, and here will I stay :
> You go to friends, whose love and means present
>   Various content
> To your eyes, ears, and taste, and every part :
> If then your body go, what need your heart ?"
>
> Well, then, stay here : but know
>   When thou hast said and done thy most,
> A naked thinking heart, that makes no show,
>   Is to a woman but a kind of ghost ;
> How shall she know my heart ? Or, having none,
>   Know thee for one ?
> Practice may make her know some other part,
> But take my word, she doth not know a heart.
>
> Meet me in London, then,
>   Twenty days hence, and thou shalt see
> Me fresher and more fat, by being with men,
>   Than if I had stay'd still with her and thee.
> For God's sake, if you can, be you so too :
>   I will give you
> There to another friend, whom you shall find
> As glad to have my body as my mind.

CXIV

Page 113—'Clear had the day been from the dawn.' From
The Muses' Elysium, Nymphal vi.

CXV

Page 114—' Like to the clear in highest sphere.' Written
by Lodge on a voyage 'to the islands of Terceras and the
Canaries.' This little poem—the gorgeous imagery of the Song
of Songs set in finest Renaissance work—may be taken as a
beautiful and striking illustration of the influence of Italian art
upon English literature : an influence which began with Surrey
and Wyatt, and was not finally superseded by French models
until the Restoration of King Charles II.
Page 114, line 1—*the clear*. The extreme, surrounding crystalline
æther of the old cosmography.

CXVIII

Page 117—'One day I wrote her name upon the strand.'
The lady of this sonnet—the Elizabeth whom Spenser married in
Ireland on St. Barnabas' Day, 1594, and for whom he wrote his
magnificent *Epithalamion*—was almost certainly Elizabeth Boyle,
of Kilcoran by the Bay of Youghal, a kinswoman of the Great

Earl of Cork. Dr. Grosart (*Complete Works in Verse and Prose of Edmund Spenser*, vol. i.) has discovered a grant, made in 1606 by Sir Richard Boyle to Elizabeth Boyle, *alias* Seckerstone, widow, of her house at Kilcoran for half-a-crown a year.   Now it is known that Spenser's widow married one Roger Seckerstone in 1603 ; and it is, to say the least, unlikely that there were two Elizabeth Seckerstones (unusual name !) in the neighbourhood at the same time.

Page 117, line 1—*upon the Strand.*   The strand of Kilcoran—three miles long—is famous.

CXXI

Page 119—'There is none, O, none but you.'   From *Light Conceits of Lovers*: being the second part of Campion's *Two Books of Airs* (circ. 1613).   But the lines are given by Dr. Hannah to Robert, Earl of Essex (Elizabeth's luckless favourite, and writer of CCCIII.), on the testimony of Aubrey's MSS., whence they were printed by Dr. Bliss, editor of Wood's ' Fasti.'

CXXII

Page 120—'Give place, you ladies, and begone !' appears among poems by 'Uncertain Authors' in *Tottel's Miscellany*, 1557 —the first English Anthology, where it bears the title given in our text.   Ascribed to John Heywood (with title ' A Description of a Most Noble Lady') in a copy in the Harl. MSS., where two execrable stanzas are tagged on to adapt the poem to Queen Mary.

CXXIII

Page 122—'You meaner beauties of the night.'   From *Rel. Wotton.*   Written upon the 'Queen of Hearts,' Elizabeth, daughter of James I. and wife of the Elector Palatine, who was unhappily chosen King of Bohemia, Sept. 19th, 1619.   Sir Henry Wotton in that and the following year was employed on several embassies in Germany on behalf of this unhappy lady, whose reign in Prague lasted but one winter.

The poem first appeared (with music), in 1624, in Michael Este's *Sixt Set of Bookes*, etc.: was afterwards printed in *Wit's Recreations*, 1640, in *Wit's Interpreter*, 1671, and in *Songs and Fancies to Severall Musicall parts, both apt for Voices and Viols*, Aberdeen, 1682.   It also found its way, with variations, among Montrose's *Poems*; and Robert Chambers (ignorant of Wotton's claim to the authorship) printed it in his *Scottish Songs* as ' written by Darnley in praise of the beauty of Queen Mary before their marriage.'

It has been a favourite mark for the second-rate imitator ; and ' additional verses ' are common.

CXXIV

Page 123—'There is a Lady sweet and kind.' From Thomas Ford's *Music of Sundry Kinds*, 1607, three stanzas being omitted.

CXXXII

Page 129—'There is a garden in her face.' From Campion's *Fourth Book of Airs*, (circ. 1617); but the poem occurs in Alison's *Hour's Recreation*, 1606, and Robert Jones's *Ultimum Vale*, 1608.

CXXXIII

Page 130—'My Love in her attire doth show her wit.' From Davison's *Poetical Rhapsody*, 1602.

CXXXIV

Page 130—'Still to be neat, still to be drest.' Imitated from the *Basia* of Johannes Bonefonius. See note on CXLVII. : this number should be compared with the three following, all by Herrick.

CXXXVIII

Page 133—'For her gait, if she be walking.' First printed in Mr. Gordon Goodwin's edition of Browne's *Poems* in 'The Muses Library' (London : Lawrence & Bullen, 1894), from the MS. in the library of Salisbury Cathedral.

CXXXIX

Page 133—'Love not me for comely grace.' From John Wilbye's *Second Set of Madrigals*, 1609.

CXLII

Page 136—'Lady, when I behold the roses sprouting.' From John Wilbye's *Madrigals*, 1598. It is paraphrased from an Italian madrigal—

> ' Quand' io miro le rose
> Ch' in voi natura pose
> E quelle che v'ha l'arte
> Nel vago seno sparte
> Non so conoscer poi
> Se voi le rose, o sian le rose in voi.'

CXLIII

Page 136—'Rose-cheek'd Laura, come.' From Campion's 'Observations in the Art of English Poesie. Wherein it is demonstratively prooued, and by example confirmed, that the English toong will receiue eight seuerall kinds of numbers, proper to it selfe, which are all in this booke set forth, and were neuer before this time by any man attempted,' 1602. These verses to Laura are given as an example of one of these new kinds of numbers—a lyrical variation on the Sapphic.

CXLIV

Page 137—'I saw fair Chloris walk alone.' Ashmole MS. 38, Art. 11. It is given in *Wit's Recreations*, 1645, and *Wit's Interpreter*, 1655, 1671. Purcell set it to music (Henry Playford's *Theater of Musick*, Pt. 3, 1686).

CXLVII

Page 138—'Drink to me only with thine eyes.' It is one of Ben Jonson's distinctions among English poets that he contrives to be most spontaneous when most imitative. This immortally careless rapture is meticulously pieced together from scraps of the Love Letters of Philostratus, a Greek rhetorician of the second century A.D. Cf. Herrick, *Hesp.* 144, *Upon a Virgin Kissing a Rose*:

> ' 'Twas but a single rose
> Till you on it did breathe ;
> But since, methinks, it shows
> Not so much rose as wreath.'

CXLIX

Page 139—'Sweet Love, mine only treasure.' One of the 'A. W.' poems in Davison's *Poetical Rhapsody*. Also found in Robert Jones's *Ultimum Vale*, 1608. Nobody knows who was 'A. W.'

CL

Page 140—'So sweet is thy discourse to me.' From Campion's *Fourth Book of Airs* (circ. 1617).

CLI

Page 141—'Fain would I change that note.' This is one of the many lovely lyrics restored to their right place in English poetry by the labours and taste of Mr. A. H. Bullen. It was found in a certain Captain Tobias Hume's *First Part of Airs, French, Polish, and others together*, 1605.

CLII

Page 142—'O Love, sweet Love, O high and heavenly Love!' From the once famous 'Mirror of Knighthood,' a translation of the Spanish romance 'Espeio de Principes y Cavalleros.' The translation appeared in nine volumes between 1583 and 1601. The two stanzas here given as a complete lyric are taken from a poem of eight stanzas, to be found in Mr. Bullen's *Poems from Elizabethan Romances*. (Nimmo: 1890.)

CLVII

Page 145—'Though others may her brow adore.' These two stanzas are taken from one of J. Danyel's *Songs for the Lute, Viol, and Voice*, 1606.

CLX

Page 147—'Maid, will you love me, yea or no?' From *A Handful of Pleasant Delights*, a miscellany edited by one Clement Robinson in 1584. The full title of the ditty is 'A Proper Wooing-Song, intituled "Maid, will ye love me, yea or no?" To the tune of "The Merchant's Daughter went over the field."' I I have omitted four stanzas which conclude the original.

CLXI

Page 148—'Ask me why I send you here.' Printed as No. 582 in Herrick's *Hesperides*, 1648, and generally believed to be Herrick's. But the Song was included in the 1640 edition of Carew. I have given Carew's text, which appears to me superior at almost every point. In the *Hesperides* the first stanza runs :

> ' Ask me why I send you here
> This sweet Infanta of the year?
> Ask me why I send to you
> This primrose, thus bepearl'd with dew?
> I will whisper to your ears
> The sweets of love are mixed with tears.'

CLXIV

Page 150—'Fain would I have a pretty thing.' This again (cf. CLX.) is 'a proper song,' from *A Handful of Pleasant Delights*, 1584, where it is directed to be sung 'To the tune of "Lusty Gallant."' A couple of stanzas are here omitted.

CLXV

Page 152—'Happy ye leaves whenas those lily hands.' The opening sonnet of the *Amoretti*, 1595. The line 'Of *Helicon* whence she derivèd is,' was obscure until Dr. Grosart suggested that it might be an allusion to the name of Mistress Elizabeth Boyle, Spenser's wife (see note on No. CXVIII.). In the twenty-fourth sonnet, given by me on p. 198, we have a similar allusion :

> ' Yet hope I well, that when this storm is past,
> My *Helice*, the lodestar of my life,
> Will shine again, and look on me at last,
> With lovely light to clear my cloudy grief.'

Helice = Elisè?

CLXX

Page 155—'O Night, O jealous Night, repugnant to my measures!' From *The Phœnix' Nest*, a miscellany edited in 1593 by 'R. S. of the Inner Temple, gentleman.'

Mr. Bullen has pointed out that the first verse of this poem is clearly taken from Desportes' :—

> ' O Nuit, jalouse Nuit, contre moi conjurée,
> Qui renflammes le ciel de nouvelle clairté,
> T'ai-je donc aujourd'hui tant de fois désirée
> Pour être si contraire à ma félicité?'

CLXXI

Page 156—'Sleep, angry beauty, sleep and fear not me.' From Campion's *Third Book of Airs* (circ. 1617).

CLXXIII

Page 158—'Care-charming Sleep, thou easer of all woes.' William Cartwright's *The Siege, or Love's Convert*, published in 1651, contains an echo of this beautiful invocation :

> 'Seal up her eyes, O Sleep, but flow
> Mild as her manners, to and fro ;
> *Slide soft into her, that yet she*
> *May receive no wound from thee.*
> *And ye present her thoughts, O dreams,*
> *With hushing winds and purling streams,*
> Whiles hovering silence sits without,
> Careful to keep disturbance out.
> Thus seize her, Sleep, thus her again resign ;
> So what was Heaven's gift we 'll reckon thine.'

CLXXIV

Page 158—'Care-charmer Sleep, son of the sable Night.' 'Bartholomew Griffin, gent,' in his *Fidessa, more chaste than kind*, published in 1596, has a sonnet reminiscent of this and of the two preceding numbers : the opening is worth quotation :

> 'Care-charmer Sleep, sweet ease in restless misery,
> The captive's liberty, and his freedom's song,
> Balm of the bruisèd heart, man's chief felicity,
> Brother of quiet death, when life is too too long. . . .'

CLXXVII

Page 160—'Good Muse, rock me asleep.'   From *England's Helicon*.

CLXXXI

Page 164—'Weep you no more, sad fountains.'   From John Dowland's *Third and Last Book of Songs or Airs*, 1603.

CLXXXIV

Page 166—'I saw my Lady weep.'   From the same.

CLXXXVIII

Page 169—'Thou art not fair, for all thy red and white.'
From Campion and Rosseter's *A Book of Airs*, 1601. It has been
attributed to Donne and to Joshua Sylvester.

CXC

Page 170—'Fire that must flame is with apt fuel fed.' From
Campion's *Third Book of Airs* (circ. 1617).

CXCI

Page 171—'When first mine eyes did view and mark.' From
The Paradise of Dainty Devices (first ed., 1576). William Hun-
nis was a gentleman of the Chapel Royal under Edward VI.,
and afterwards master of the singing-boys in Queen Elizabeth's
Chapel. But *Tottel's Miscellany*, 1557, had already given a version
as written by Wyatt.

CXCIII

Page 173—'When thou must home to shades of underground.'
Another number from Campion and Rosseter's *A Book of Airs*,
1601. Mr. Bullen notes that the mention of 'white Iope' must
have been suggested by Propertius (ii. 28):

> 'Sunt apud inferos tot millia formosarum;
> Pulchra sit in superis, si licet, una locis.
> Vobiscum est Iope, vobiscum candida Tyro,
> Vobiscum Europe, nec proba Pasiphae.'

CXCVII

Page 175—'Love wing'd my Hopes and taught me how
to fly.' From Robert Jones's *Second Book of Songs and Airs*,
1601.

CXCVIII

Page 176—'Arise, my Thoughts, and mount you with the sun!'
From the same, where the song has three stanzas. I have omitted
the middle one, but restore it here:

> 'Arise, my Thoughts, no more, if you return
> Denied of grace which only you desire,
> But let the sun your wings to ashes burn
> And melt your passions in his quenchless fire;
> Yet, if you move fair Maia's heart to pity,
> Let smiles and love and kisses be your ditty.'

CXCIX

Page 177—'My Thoughts are wing'd with Hopes, my Hopes
with Love.' The first of three stanzas of a song in John Dowland's
First Book of Songs or Airs, 1597; also given in *England's
Helicon*.

CC

Page 177—'Follow your Saint, follow with accents sweet!' From Campion and Rosseter's *Book of Airs*, 1601.

CCI

Page 178—'Follow thy fair sun, unhappy shadow!' From the same.

CCIII

Page 179—'Kind are her answers.' From Campion's *Third Book of Airs* (circ. 1617).

CCIV

Page 180—'Shall I, wasting in despair.' A well-known imitation of this song is attributed, but on next to no evidence, to Sir Walter Raleigh. It begins :

> 'Shall I like a hermit dwell
> On a rock or in a cell?
> Calling home the smallest part
> That is missing of my heart,
> To bestow it where I may
> Meet a rival every day?
> If she undervalue me,
> What care I how fair she be?'

CCVI

Page 183—'Can a maid that is well bred.' From Martin Peerson's *Private Music*, 1620.

CCVII

Page 184—'What conscience, say, is it in thee.' Compare with the following verse, very popular in commonplace books of the period :

> 'When first I saw thee, thou did'st sweetly play
> The gentle Thief, and stolest my heart away.
> Render me mine again, or leave thine own,
> Two are too much for thee, since I have none.
> And if thou wilt not, I will swear thou art
> A sweet-faced creature with a double heart.'

CCVIII

Page 184—'My true love hath my heart, and I have his.' Printed, as here given, in Puttenham's *Art of English Poesy*, 1589, as an example of a 'linking verse.' The Greeks 'called such linking verse *Epimone*, the Latins *versus intercalaris*, and we may term him the Love-burden, following the original, or, if it please

you, the long repeat.'   A longer version appears in the *Arcadia*
(1590).   The additional lines are vastly inferior:

> ' His heart his wound receivèd from my sight ;
>   My heart was wounded with his wounded heart :
> For as from me on him his heart did light,
>   So still methought in me his hurt did smart.
> Both equal hurt, in this change sought our bliss :
> My true love hath my heart, and I have his.'

CCX

Page 186—'Calling to mind, my eyes went long about.'
The text is that taken by Hannah from Oldys' *Life of Raleigh*,
after 'the copy of a celebrated lady, Lady Isabella Thynne, who
probably had it out of the family.'   Puttenham gave it (1589) as
' a most excellent ditty, written by Sir Walter Raleigh.'   In *The
Phœnix' Nest*, 1593, it is anonymous.   The versions differ con-
siderably.

CCXI

Page 187—'As ye came from the holy land.'   The shrine
of the Blessed Virgin at Walsingham in Norfolk was famous
throughout Europe : and in Norfolk the Milky Way, being supposed to point the pilgrim to this shrine, was called the 'Walsingham way,' just as it was called 'St. Jago's way' in Italy, and
' Jacobstrasse' in Germany, as pointing to Compostella.   In 1538,
at the dissolution of the monasteries, the great image of the Virgin
was carried off to Chelsea, and there burnt.   It had been perhaps
a more famous shrine of pilgrimage than even the tomb of St.
Thomas of Canterbury.   Cf. Erasmus. Colloq. *Peregrinatio re-
ligionis ergo.*   Ascham, visiting Cologne in 1550, says : ' The
Three Kings be not so rich, I believe, as was the Lady of Walsingham ' : the wealth of the shrine at Cologne being then valued
at about six millions of francs (£240,000).
   A copy of this song was given by Shenstone to Bishop Percy
' as corrected by him from an ancient copy, and supplied with a
concluding stanza.'   Shenstone's ' corrections' are not improve-
ments ; but the concluding stanza is fine, of its kind :

> ' But true love is a lasting fire
>   Which viewless vestals tend,
> That burns for ever in the soul,
>   And knows nor change nor end.'

A copy in the Bodleian is signed ' W. R.' ; and on the strength
of this it has been claimed for Raleigh.

CCXIV

Page 190—'At her fair hands how have I grace entreated.'
From Davison's *Poetical Rhapsody*, 1602 ; also Robert Jones's
Ultimum Vale, 1608.

CCXVI

Page 192—'When Love on time and measure makes his ground.' From Robert Jones's *First Book of Songs and Airs*, 1601.

CCXVII

Page 194—'Dear, if you change, I'll never choose again.' From John Dowland's *First Book of Songs or Airs*, 1597.

CCXIX

Page 194—'First shall the heavens want starry light.' Imitated from a sonnet of Philippe Desportes:

> 'On verra défaillir tous les astres aux cieux,
> Les poissons à la mer, le sable à son rivage,' etc.

CCXX

Page 195—'Turn I my looks unto the skies.' Also from Desportes:

> 'Si je me siez à l'ombre, aussi soudainement
> Amour, laissant son arc, s'assied et se repose ;
> Si je pense à des vers, je le voy qui compose ;
> Si je plains mes douleurs, il se plaint hautement.
>
> Si je me plains au mal, il accroist mon tourment ;
> Si je respans des pleurs, son visage il arrose ;
> Si je monstre mon playe en ma poitrine enclose,
> Il defait son bandeau, l'essuyant doucement.
>
> Si je vais par les bois, aux bois il m'accompagne ;
> Si je me suis cruel, dans mon sang il se bagne ;
> Si je vais à la guerre, il devient mon soldart.
>
> Si je passe la mer, il conduit ma nacelle ;
> Bref, jamais l'importun de moy ne se départ,
> Pour rendre mon désir et ma peine éternelle.

Lodge gave also a literal rendering of this sonnet in *Scylla's Metamorphosis*, 1589.

CCXXI

Page 196—'Were I as base as is the lowly plain.' With the third quatrain compare Plato's lovely conceit:

> 'ἀστέρας εἰσαθρεῖς, ἀστὴρ ἐμός. αἴθε γενοίμαν
> οὐρανός, ὡς πολλοῖς ὄμμασιν εἴς σε βλέπω.

CCXXIII

Page 198—'Like as a ship that through the Ocean wide.' For the allusion to *Helice*, see note on No. CLXV. For the simile cf. Carew:

> 'You're the bright Pole-star, which in the dark
> Of this long absence, guides my wandering bark,' etc.

CCXXIV

Page 198—'Though I be scorn'd, yet will I not disdain.' From *The Mirror of Knighthood*, Part vi., 1598.

CCXXVI

Page 199—'Fine knacks for ladies. . . .' From John Dowland's *Second Book of Songs or Airs*, 1600.

CCXXXI

Page 203—'Sweet, come again!' From Campion and Rosseter's *Book of Airs*, 1601.

CCXXXII

Page 204—'Absence, hear thou my protestation.' The circumstances of Donne's life give these verses a peculiar interest. Being secretary to the Lord Chancellor Ellesmere, he 'passionately fell in love with, and privately married, a niece of the Lady Elsemere's, the daughter of Sir George Moor, Chancellor of the Garter and Lieutenant of the Tower; which so much enraged Sir George, that he not only procured Mr. Donne's dismission from his employment under the Lord Chancellor, but never rested till he had caused him likewise to be imprisoned. Though it was not long before he was enlarged from his confinement, yet his troubles still encreased upon him; for his Wife being detained from him, he was constrained to claim her by a troublesome and expensive lawsuit, which, together with travel, books, and a too liberal disposition, contributed to reduce his fortune to a very narrow compass.

'Adversity has its peculiar Virtues to exercise and work upon, as well as the most flourishing condition of life; and Mr. Donne had now an opportunity of showing his patience and submission, which, together with the general approbation he everywhere met with of Mr. Donne's good qualities, with an irresistible kind of persuasion so won upon Sir George, that he began now not wholly to disapprove of his daughter's choice; and was at length so far reconciled as not to deny them his blessing.' The death of his wife broke Donne's heart.

With these verses of his compare Carew's *To his Mistress in Absence*.

CCXXXVI

Page 208—'As virtuous men pass mildly away.' For the concluding image of the compasses compare Ben Jonson's *Epistle to Master John Selden*:

> 'You that have been
> Ever at home, yet have all countries seen;
> And like a compass, keeping one foot still
> Upon your centre, do your circle fill
> Of general knowledge.'

Dr. Grosart notes that the *impresa* of John Haywood, Donne's maternal grandfather, was a compass with a sound foot in centre and the other broken : the motto, 'Deest quod ducerit orbem.' This may well have suggested the image, which was a favourite one with Donne.

CCXXXVII

Page 210—'As careful merchants do expecting stand.' Compare this song of Browne's with the sonnet (Amoretti, xv.) of his master, Spenser, which begins :

> 'Ye tradeful Merchants that with weary toil,
> Do seek most precious things to make your gain
> And both the Indias of their treasures spoil ;
> What needeth you to seek so far in vain ?
> For lo ! my love doth in herself contain
> All this world's riches. . . .'

CCXXXIX

Page 212—'See the Chariot at hand here of Love.' This magnificent song is taken for the 'Celebration of Charis' in *Underwoods*; but two stanzas were inserted by Jonson in his *The Devil is an Ass*, ii. 6, acted in 1616.

I am not aware if any critic has noted how constantly and curiously Jonson, especially in the *Underwoods*, seems to anticipate the best, and something more than the best, manner of Browning. The difficult rapture of Charis' *Triumph*, here, is a striking instance.   Of the lines

> 'Do but mark, her forehead's smoother
>   Than words that soothe her ;
> And from her arched brows such a grace
>   Sheds itself through the face,
> As alone there triumphs to the life
> All the gain, all the good of the elements' strife.'

it may fairly be said that England has taken two and a half centuries to produce another poet who could conceivably have written them.

Suckling wrote a weak imitation of the last stanza, beginning

> 'Hast thou seen the down in the air,
> When wanton blasts have toss'd it ?'

And T. Carew—

> 'Would you know what's soft?   I dare
> Not bring to you the down, or air ;
>
> .   .   .   .   .   .
>
> Nor, to please your sense bring forth
> Bruisèd nard, or what's more worth . . .'

CCXL

Page 213—'Roses, their sharp spines being gone.' From *The Two Noble Kinsmen*. On the title-page of the first edition of this play (1634) Shakespeare is claimed as part-author of it, along with Fletcher; and if internal evidence be worth anything, this bridal-song, with which the play opens, must go to Shakespeare's credit.   Such lines as—

> ' Daisies smell-less, yet most quaint '

or

> ' Oxlips in their cradles growing '

or

> ' Not an angel of the air
> Bird melodious, or bird fair '

have Shakespeare's note rather than Fletcher's.   The opening lines of the second stanza have generally been printed thus :

> ' Primrose, firstborn child of Ver,
> Merry springtime's harbinger,
> With her bells dim . . .'

and many have wondered how Shakespeare or Fletcher came to write of the ' bells ' of a primrose.   Mr. W. J. Linton proposed ' With harebell slim ' : although if we must read ' harebell ' or ' harebells,' ' dim ' would be a pretty and proper word for the colour of that flower.   The conjecture takes some little plausibility from the circumstance that elsewhere Shakespeare links primrose and harebell together :

> ' Thou shalt not lack
> The flower that 's like thy face, pale primrose, nor
> The azured harebell, like thy veins. . . .'
>
> *Cymbeline*, iv. 2.

I have always suspected, however, that there should be a semicolon after ' Ver,' and that ' merry springtime's harbinger, with her bells dim ' referred to a totally different flower—the snowdrop, to wit. And I now learn from Dr. Grosart, who has carefully examined the 1634, and only early edition, that the text actually gives a semicolon.   The snowdrop may very well come after the primrose in this song, which altogether ignores the process of the seasons.

CCXLI

Page 214—' Now hath Flora robb'd her bowers.'   From a Masque presented at Whitehall, on Twelfth Night, 1607, ' in honour of the Lord Hayes and his Bride, daughter and heir to the Honourable the Lord Dennye.'

CCXLII

Page 215—' What is it all that men possess . . .'   From Campion's *Third Book of Airs*, circ. 1617.

CCXLIII

Page 216—' Upon my lap my sovereign sits.'   From Martin Peerson's *Private Music*, 1620.

CCXLV

Page 219—'Come little babe, come silly soul.'   From '*The Arbour of Amorous Devices*, by N. B., Gent., 1593-4.'   The famous *Lady Anne Bothwell's Lament* ('Balow, my babe, lye still and sleipe!' *vide* Percy's *Reliques*) is almost certainly an imitation of this beautiful song.

CCXLVI

Page 221—'O waly waly up the bank.'   'Arthur Seat' is of course the hill by Edinburgh, near the foot of which is St. Anthony's Well.

There is some doubt about the date of this lament. Some believe it to be a portion of the ballad *Lord Jamie Douglas*, and therefore at least as recent as 1670. But Professor Aytoun and others believe that the verses *Waly Waly* were stolen for this ballad, like the famous brooms, ready-made; and that they belong to the sixteenth century.

A traditional west-country song, 'Deep in Love,' obtained by the Rev. S. Baring-Gould and published in his *Songs of the West* (Methuen: 1892), has two stanzas:

> 'I leaned my back against an oak,
> But first it bent and then it broke;
> Untrusty as I found that tree,
> So did my love prove false to me.
>
> I wish—I wish—but 'tis in vain,
> I wish I had my heart again!
> With silver chain and diamond locks
> I'd fasten it in a golden box.'

CCLI

Page 226—'Take, O take those lips away.'   This song occurs also in Fletcher's *The Bloody Brother* (first ed., 1639) with an inferior stanza added:

> 'Hide, O hide those hills of snow,
>   Which thy frozen bosom bears,
> On whose tops the pinks that grow
>   Are of those that April wears;
> But first set my poor heart free,
> Bound in those icy chains by thee.'

CCLII

Page 226—'Harden now thy tirèd heart . . .'   From Campion's *Second Book of Airs, containing Light Conceits of Lovers* (circ. 1613).

CCLIX

Page 231—'Whoever comes to shroud me; do not harm.'

Compare with this Donne's equally subtle and even more vivid piece, *The Relique*, beginning

> 'When my grave is broke up again
> Some second guest to entertain,
> (For graves have learn'd that womanhead,
> To be to more than one a bed)
>   And he, that digs it, spies
> A bracelet of bright hair about the bone,
>   Will he not let us alone,
> And think that there a loving couple lies,
> Who thought that this device might be some way
> To make their souls at the last busy day,
> Meet at this grave, and make a little stay?

See note on CCXXXII. for the loss that broke Donne's heart.

CCLX

Page 232—'How happy was I when I saw her lead.' The beauty of these stanzas as they stand is my only excuse for having torn them violently from their context in Spenser's lovely lament.

CCLXI

Page 234—'When thou from earth didst pass.' Here also I have but torn out the heart of a beautiful lament beginning

> 'Sad Damon being come
> To that for ever lamentable tomb . . .'

CCLXVI

Page 238—'Marina's gone, and now sit I.' The opening of a song in *Britannia's Pastorals*, book iii. l. 45. With 'So shuts the marigold . . .' compare Shakespeare's

> 'The marigold that goes to bed wi' the sun,
> And with him rises weeping.'
>
> *Winter's Tale*, iv. 3.

CCLXVIII

Page 240—'Glide soft, ye silver floods.' The friend that William Browne (Willy) here laments was William Ferrar, son of Nicholas Ferrar, a London merchant and adventurer; and brother of the famous Nicholas Ferrar of Little Gidding. He entered the Middle Temple in the spring of 1610; and died young, at sea.

'Let no bird sing.' It hardly needs pointing out to what splendid use Keats (an admirer, and, in a sense, an imitator of Browne) turned this line in his *Belle Dame sans Merci*.

CCLXIX

Page 242—'High-spirited friend.' From *Underwoods*. The name of the high-spirited friend, to whom Jonson addressed these high-spirited lines, is unknown.   It is just possible that 'this same' in stanza 2, should be 'this fame,' the long 'f' having crept in by mistake for 'f' in the early editions.

CCLXXIII

Page 246—'My prime of youth is but a frost of cares.' From *Reliquiae Wottonianae*, where the verses are said to have been written 'by Chidiock Tychborne, being young and then in the Tower, the night before his execution.'   Young Chidiock Tichborne, of Southampton, suffered in 1586 for his share in Babington's Conspiracy.   A beautiful letter to his wife, written just before his execution, is preserved.   I have given these lines to Tichborne, though verses supposed to have been written on such occasions are always open to suspicion.   It were worth a man's while, for instance, to count the poems written by Raleigh on the night before his death.   The truth probably is that they were written by outsiders and attributed, as appropriate, to the dead; having in fact about as much authenticity as the 'last dying speech and confession' hawked around after the death of any famous highwayman in the last century.   The lines here given were set to music in John Mundy's *Songs and Psalms*, 1594; Richard Alison's *Hour's Recreation*, 1606; and Michael Este's *Madrigals of three, four, and five Parts*, 1604.   A reply to them will be found in Hannah's *Courtly Poets*, p. 115.

CCLXXVII, CCLXXVIII

Page 249—'Fair summer droops . . .'   'Adieu, farewell earth's bliss.'   From Nashe's *Summer's Last Will and Testament*.   Cf. note on No. XXVIII.

CCLXXX

Page 252—'His golden locks hath time to silver turn'd.' From George Peele's *Polyhymnia*, 1590.   The reader may remember the beautiful application of this poem, or rather the first half of it, in Thackeray's *The Newcomes*.

CCLXXXIX

Page 257—'The Indian weed witheréd quite.'   Kindly sent to me by Dr. Grosart, from a MS. in Trinity College, Dublin. Wisdome was a Protestant fugitive in Mary's reign: afterwards Rector of Systed in Essex and of Settrington in Yorkshire.   He died in 1568.
Ralph Erskine's 'Tobacco Spiritualised,' beginning

'Tobacco is an Indian weed . . .'

is clearly but a copy of this old ditty of Wisdome's.   Erskine died in 1752.

CCXC

Page 258—'In going to my naked bed. . . .' From *The Paradise of Dainty Devices*, 1576, where Edwards is named as 'sometime Master of the singing-boys at the Chapel Royal.' He was dead some ten years before *The Paradise* appeared.

CCXCII

Page 261—'Say, crimson Rose and dainty Daffodil.' From *The Flower of Fidelitie*, 'displaying in a continuate historie the various adventures of Three Foreyn Princes. By John Reynolds.' Published in 1650.

CCXCIII

Page 263—'Alas! my love, you do me wrong.' These words of the famous song 'Greensleeves' were composed before 1580. I have included them partly for their own artless charm, partly for their connection with one of the most taking of English tunes.

CCXCIV

Page 264—'Though beauty be the mark of praise.' In this lovely 'elegy,' and in the succeeding verses by Lord Herbert of Cherbury, we have anticipations of the much discussed stanza used by Tennyson for his *In Memoriam*. Yet Tennyson (it is said) for a long while believed himself the inventor of this stanza.

CCXCVI

Page 266—'Ye buds of Brutus' land . . .' *i.e.* scions of England, held of (mythical) descent from Brutus. The verses come from *A Posie of Gilloflowers*, 'eche differing from other in colour and odour, yet all sweete. By Humfrey Gifford, Gent.,' 1580.

CCXCVII

Page 269—'O wearisome condition of humanity!' From the tragedy of *Mustapha*, first printed in 1609.

CCXCIX

Page 270—'The World's a bubble, and the life of Man.' For the evidence that Bacon was the author of these lines, cf. Hannah's *Poems by Raleigh, Wotton, and others*, p. 117, footnote (edition of 1891). They are paraphrased, at any rate, from the famous epigram of Posidippus, beginning:

> Παντοίην βιότοιο τάμοις τρίβων· εἰν ἀγορῇ μὲν
> κύδεα καὶ πινυταὶ πρήξιες, κ.τ.λ.

The epigram has been translated over and over again by the

Elizabethans: notably by Sir John Beaumont, whose translation closes:

> 'Who would not one of these two offers choose:
> Not to be born, or breath with speed to loose?'

Drummond closes:

> 'Who would not of these two offers try,—
> Not to be born, or, being born, to die?'

and Bishop King:

> 'At least with that Greek sage still make us cry
> Not to be born, or, being born, to die.'

Bacon's paraphrase has been overrated; but it was well worth writing, if it persuade a hesitating soul here and there that his lordship was not Shakespeare.

CCCII

Page 273—'Corpse, clad with carefulness.' 'Newe *Sonets*, and pretie *Pamphlets* written by Thomas Howell, Gentleman. Newely augmented, corrected and amended' (1567). Reproduced among the poems of Thomas Howell in Dr. Grosart's *Unique and Rare Books*, 1879.

CCCIV

Page 274—'How happy is he born and taught.' These lines were printed by Percy from the *Reliquiæ Wottonianæ*: believed to have been first printed in 1614. Ben Jonson admired and had them by heart, and in 1619 quoted them to Drummond as Wotton's. They are also said to be almost identical with a German poem of the same age (Hannah, p. 90, and *Notes and Queries*, vol. ix. p. 420). Wotton may have seen the original in one of his several embassies to Germany on behalf of Elizabeth of Bohemia.

CCCV

Page 275—'My mind to me a kingdom is.' Alluded to by Jonson in *Every Man out of his Humour* (first acted in 1599), Act i. scene 1. For Sir Edward Dyer and the authorship, see Hannah, pp. 149 and 243. Hannah's text is here taken.

CCCVI

Page 277—'It is not growing like a tree.' A strophe from the Ode *To the immortal memory and friendship of that noble pair, Sir Lucius Cary and Sir H. Morison*; which may have been written in 1629, the date of Sir Henry Morison's death, but was first published in the *Underwoods* in 1640. Sir Lucius Cary is of course the Lord Falkland who fell at Newbury. The conclusion of Clarendon's famous account of him reads like a commentary on Jonson's verse :—' In the morning before the battle, as always upon action, he was very cheerful, and put himself in the first rank of the Lord Byron's regiment, then advancing upon the enemy, who had lined the hedges on both sides with musketeers, from whence he was shot with a musket in the lower part of the belly, and in the instant falling from his horse, his body was not found till the next morning ; till when, there was some hope he might have been a prisoner ; though his nearest friends, who knew his temper, received small comfort from that imagination. Thus fell that incomparable young man, in the four-and-thirtieth year of his age, having so much dispatched the true business of life, that the eldest rarely attain to that immense knowledge, and the youngest enter not into the world with more innocency : whosoever leads such a life needs be the less anxious upon how short warning it is taken from him.'—*History of the Rebellion*, book vii. Cf. also Matthew Arnold's essay on him.

CCCVII

Page 277—' Wise men pity never want.' From one of the ' Divine and Moral Songs ' in Campion's *Two Books of Airs*, circ. 1613.

CCCVIII

Page 278—' The man of life upright.' From Campion and Rosseter's *A Book of Airs*, 1601. The same poem with variations occurs with the preceding numbers in the *Two Books of Airs*. Hannah gives the lines to Bacon.

CCCIX

Page 279—' The chief use then in Man of that he knows.' A stanza from *A Treatie of Humane Learning*. Lord Brooke was murdered in September 1628 by a serving-man in his London house in Holborn : the *Treatie* was not printed until five years later.

CCCX

Page 279—' All I care.' From a song in Robert Jones's *Ulti-mum Vale, or Third Book of Airs*, 1608. Mr. Bullen points out that the last line is from Seneca's *Thyestes* :

' qui, notus nimis omnibus,
Ignotus moritur sibi.'

CCCI

Page 279—' Come thou, who art the wine and wit.' The allusion in ' no Court for our Request,' is to the Court of Requests, established in the reign of Richard II. as a subsidiary Court of Equity for the hearing of poor men's suits, and abolished (with the Star Chamber) in 1641.

CCCXII, CCCXIII

Pages 281, 282—'Full fathom five thy father lies.' 'Call for the robin-redbreast and the wren.' Lamb's famous comparison of these two pieces must be quoted again. Speaking of the second he says, 'I never saw anything like the funeral dirge in this play (*The White Devil*) for the death of Marcello, except the ditty which reminds Ferdinand of his drowned father in *The Tempest*. As that is of the water, watery, so this is of the earth, earthy. Both have that intenseness of feeling, which seems to resolve itself into the element which it contemplates.' In a footnote he adds, 'Webster was parish clerk at St. Andrew's, Holborn. The anxious recurrence to church matters, sacrilege, tomb-stones, with the frequent introduction of dirges, in this and his other tragedies, may be traced to his professional sympathies.'

CCCXV

Page 283—'Urns and odours bring away!' From *The Two Noble Kinsmen*. Cf. note on CCXL.

CCCXVII

Page 284—'Mortality, behold and fear!' Mr. Henley (*Lyra Heroica*) aptly compares Shirley's succeeding numbers and Raleigh's great apostrophe in the *History of the World*: 'O Eloquent, Just, and Mighty Death! Whom none could advise, thou hast persuaded; what none hath dared, thou hast done; and whom all the World hath flattered, thou only hast cast out of the World and despised: thou hast drawn together all the far-stretched Greatness, all the Pride, Cruelty, and Ambition of Man, and covered it all over with these two narrow words, *Hic Jacet*.'

CCCXX

Page 287—'How near me came the hand of Death.' From *Hallelujah, or Britain's Second Remembrancer*, Hymn xxvii. 'For a Widower, or a Widow deprived of a loving Yoke-fellow.' There are six stanzas in the original.

I find on correcting the pages for press that Crashaw's noble epitaph, which should have followed this hymn of Wither's, has unaccountably slipped out of the text, and I here add it:

AN EPITAPH UPON HUSBAND AND WIFE,

Who died and were buried together.

'To those whom death again did wed
This grave's the second marriage-bed.
For though the hand of Fate could force
'Twixt soul and body a divorce,

It could not sever man and wife,
Because they both lived but one life.
Peace, good reader, do not weep;
Peace, the lovers are asleep.
They, sweet turtles, folded lie
In the last knot that love could tie.
Let them sleep, let them sleep on,
Till the stormy night be gone,
And the eternal morrow dawn;
Then the curtains will be drawn,
And they wake into a light
Whose day shall never die in night.'

CCCXXV

Page 293—'May! be thou never graced. . . .'   In the title
'M. S.' probably stands for 'Maritæ Suæ.'   Browne was twice
married.   His first wife is the subject of this epitaph.

CCCXXVI

Page 293—'Underneath this sable herse.'   These lines are generally given to Jonson; but the evidence that Browne wrote them,
as it is marshalled by Mr. Gordon Goodwin in the latest edition
of Browne's poems (*The Muses' Library*.   London: Lawrence
and Bullen, 1894), is certainly very strong.   Briefly, it comes to
this: (1) They were first printed in Osborn's *Traditional Memoirs
on the Reign of King James*, 1658, and next in the *Poems* of the
Countess's son, William, Earl of Pembroke, and Sir Benjamin Rud-
yerd in 1660; but in neither volume are they signed.   (2) Writing
about the same time, Aubrey, in his *Natural History of Wiltshire*,
gives the lines to Browne.   (3) They are signed 'William Browne'
in a middle seventeenth century MS. in the library of Trinity
College, Dublin.   (4) They do not appear in the 1640 edition of
Jonson, nor indeed in any edition, until in 1756 Peter Whalley
included them on the ground that they were 'universally assigned
to Jonson.'   (5) Browne seems to refer to this very epitaph in his
Elegy on Charles, Lord Herbert of Cardiff and Shurland (written,
too, in the same metre):

'And since my weak and saddest verse
Was worthy thought thy granddam's herse;
Accept of this!'

CCCXXVIII

Page 294—'The Lady *Mary Villiers* lies.'   Carew penned two
other epitaphs upon her little ladyship, of which one deserves to
be quoted:

'This little vault, this narrow room,
Of Love and Beauty is the tomb;
The dawning beam, that 'gan to clear
Our clouded sky, lies darken'd here,
For ever set us us; by Death
Sent to inflame the world beneath.

'Twas but a bud, yet did contain
More sweetness than shall spring again ;
A budding Star, that might have grown
Into a sun when it had blown.
This hopeful Beauty did create
New life in Love's declining state ;
But now his empire ends, and we
From fire and wounding darts are free ;
    His brand, his bow, let no man fear ;
    The flames, the arrows, all lie here.

With this and the following epitaphs compare Beaumont's

    ' 'Tis not a life ;
'Tis but a piece of childhood thrown away.'

CCCXXX

Page 295—'Here a pretty baby lies.' I cannot forbear from adding here in the notes another of Herrick's epitaphs upon children :

UPON A CHILD

' But born, and like a short delight,
I glided by my parents' sight.
That done, the harder fates denied
My longer stay, and so I died.
If, pitying my sad parents' tears,
You 'll spill a tear or two with theirs,
And with some flowers my grave bestrew,
Love and they 'll thank you for 't, Adieu.'

CCCXXXI

Page 296—'As I in hoary winter's night.' Ben Jonson (it is worth remarking) told Drummond of Hawthornden that he had been content to destroy many of his own writings to have written 'The Burning Babe.'

CCCXXXII

Page 299—' I sing the birth was born to-night.' With stanza 2, lines 4-6, compare Giles Fletcher's lines

' A Child He was, and had not learn'd to speak
That with His word the world before did make ;
His mother's arms Him bore, He was so weak
That with one hand the vaults of heav'n could shake
See, how small room my infant Lord doth take,
    Whom all the world is not enough to hold !
    Who of His years, or of His age hath told ?
Never such age so young, never a child so old.'

CCCXXXVIII

Page 304—' Yet if His Majesty, our sovereign lord.' From Mr. Bullen's *More Lyrics from the Elizabethan Song-books.* Mr.

Bullen discovered this fine poem—a fragment, apparently, but flawless in itself—among a collection of early MS. music in the library of Christ Church, Oxford (where he also found that 'odd little snatch,' printed as No. XXI.). He writes, 'The detailed description of the preparations made by a loyal subject for the coming of his "earthly king" is singularly impressive. Few could have dealt with common household objects—tables and chairs and candles and the rest—in so dignified a spirit.'

CCCXLI

Page 306—'Now winter nights enlarge.' From Campion's *Third Book of Airs*, circ. 1617.

CCCXLIII

Page 308—'Let not the sluggish sleep. From William Byrd's *Psalms, Songs, and Sonnets*, 1611.

CCCXLV

Page 310—'Never weather-beaten sail more willing bent to shore.' From *Divine and Moral Songs*, circ. 1613.

CCCLV

Page 320—'In the hour of my distress.' Barron Field, who reviewed Dr. Nott's edition of Herrick in the *Quarterly*, August 1810, gives an account of a visit he paid to Dean Prior in the summer of 1809, for the purpose of making some inquiries concerning the poet. He says, 'The person, however, who knows more of Herrick than all the rest of the neighbourhood, we found to be an old woman in the ninety-ninth year of her age, named Dorothy King. She repeated to us, with great exactness, five of his *Noble Numbers*, among which was the beautiful Litany. . . . These she had learnt from her mother, who was apprenticed to Herrick's successor in the vicarage. She called them her prayers, which, she said, she was in the habit of putting up in bed, whenever she could not sleep: and she therefore began the Litany at the second stanza—

'When I lie within my bed,' etc.

Another of her midnight orisons was the poem beginning

'Every night thou dost me fright
And keep mine eyes from sleeping,' etc.

She had no idea that these poems had ever been printed, and could not have read them if she had seen them.'

CCCLIX, CCCLX

Pages 324, 325—'Give me my scallop-shell of quiet.' 'Even such is Time, that takes in trust.' Of each of these poems it is asserted, probably upon inference, that Raleigh wrote them in the Tower on the night before his death. But, if Raleigh neither wrote them then nor at any time, that they should have been attributed to him as appropriate is evidence in favour of a character that has been judged so variously.

INDEX OF FIRST LINES

INDEX OF WRITERS